Advance praise for *Re*

'A thrilling, emotionally charged tou[illegible] structured and written. Halifax and Simpson at their best.'
Shane Brennan, creator of *NCIS LA*

'A riveting portrait of a woman who has no memory of the life she has left behind or the danger she is in. And when that woman is my beloved Jane Halifax, it is even more deeply disturbing. Roger has done it again.'
Rebecca Gibney, television's Jane Halifax

'A tense, edge-of-the-seat weave of complex characters and flawed relationships, Resurrection is an intricate and multi-layered mystery, expertly teased out by a master story-teller.'
Chris Nyst, Ned Kelly Award-winning writer of *Millen*

'Interrogating the mind of his greatest character, Roger Simpson delivers twists and thrills television never could provide an answer to: "who is Jane Halifax, f.p.?"'
Andy Muir, author of *Something for Nothing*

'How clever to turn Jane's smarts on herself as she stumbles through the labyrinth of post injury amnesia. Suddenly she's as much of a challenge to herself as that cold case she cannot forget.'
Caroline Baum, founding editor of *Good Reading*

'Forget serial killings. Here the crime is the theft of a mind. The story races along as you're left wondering if Jane Halifax is ever going to be herself again.'
Fenella Souter, award-winning feature writer

Praise for *Transgression*

'A nail-biter with graphic, shocking imagery and a fast pace that's no doubt a legacy of his work in film and television . . . Characters are deftly drawn and fleshed out, nuanced and humane.'
The Age

'An explosive read, packed with twists and turns you won't see coming . . . If you're looking for an addictive new crime series to get stuck into, look no further.'
Better Reading

'Taut and thrilling . . . Don't be beguiled and think this is just a TV spin-off. It's not. It's rip-roaring crime writing at its best. Emotional at its heart, thought-provoking and wise. You're in the tense grip of a master at work with this book.'
Tony Cavanaugh, author of *Blood River*

'A taut, well-written thriller with engaging characters, psychological complexity and a plot that will keep you turning pages right until the end.'
David Williamson, Australian playwright

ROGER SIMPSON

RESURRECTION

SIMON &
SCHUSTER

London · New York · Sydney · Toronto · New Delhi

RESURRECTION
First published in Australia in 2023 by
Simon & Schuster (Australia) Pty Limited
Suite 19A, Level 1, Building C, 450 Miller Street, Cammeray, NSW 2062

10 9 8 7 6 5 4 3 2 1

Sydney New York London Toronto New Delhi
Visit our website at www.simonandschuster.com.au

A catalogue record for this book is available from the National Library of Australia

ISBN: 9781761102530

Cover design: Luke Causby/Blue Cork
Cover images: Street scene, David Wall/Getty Images; Woman, Luke Causby/Blue Cork
Typeset by Midland Typesetters, Australia
Printed and bound in Australia by Griffin Press

The paper this book is printed on is certified against the Forest Stewardship Council® Standards. Griffin Press holds chain of custody certification SCS-COC-001185. FSC® promotes environmentally responsible, socially beneficial and economically viable management of the world's forests.

For my children,
Emma, Jol, Blake and Darcie,
and my grandchildren, Madeleine and Fraser.

PROLOGUE

Jane felt ill. She declined another glass of wine and asked instead for a weak black tea. As Peter went through to the kitchen to put on the jug, she found two Panadol in her handbag and washed them down with what was left of her sparkling water. Though the water was flat, it had enough fizz to release another wave of nausea and she wondered if she should simply excuse herself and leave. Instead, she went out to the terrace overlooking the pool to see if some fresh air would help.

Her car was parked across the street under a street light, advocating her escape. The wiser choice was to call for a cab and collect her car in the morning, but Jane didn't want to leave it in the street overnight with its precious cargo in the boot. They had placed the three heavy storage boxes in the car before they sat down to dinner. She was grateful Peter Debreceny had agreed to give her access to his personal files despite the ethical implications, though he had needed some persuading. As a prosecutor, it was improper to share his files with the other side, but the case was twenty years old and he knew Jane wouldn't misuse them. Her interest was personal not official, an opportunity to end a mystery that had dogged her for years. The Robert Millard case: a client she had failed to keep from going to jail, who had committed suicide after his guilty verdict; a rare and haunting failure that still kept Jane awake on those random nights when his ghost came to sit in silence at the foot of her bed, like her father had after she'd been punished as a child.

Jane drew deeply on the cool night air and convinced herself it was helping. It had been a passing giddiness and nothing more, a reaction to one of the exotic ingredients her host had added to his excellent, if overspiced, meal.

Peter arrived on the terrace with her tea and a glass of Laphroaig for himself. 'This is what you really need. Peat, smoke, salt-sea air and iodine. It's literally medicinal.'

Jane declined the scotch and scrutinised her companion. Had Peter been spiking her drinks? Of course not; they were old friends. That she'd thought he was resorting to a date-rape drug only confirmed she was having delusions. But the tea didn't help. She was feeling unsteady again. Maybe she should call that cab and take the risk the files would be safe. Or ask Peter to swap his car with hers so it could have the added security of his garage.

But as always with Jane, pride and stubbornness prevailed.

As Peter waved her car away from the kerb, she turned up the air-con and opened the windows, Google maps guiding her home. The journey would be over soon enough.

Not that the SUV behind her was helping, its headlights switched to high beam. Were they doing it to annoy her or was her queasiness affecting her patience? Jane tilted her rear-vision mirror and concentrated on the road ahead, but the pest was still behind her when she turned off Bridge Road and headed round Yarra Boulevard towards Toorak. So, they were heading in the same direction. No reason for a rational person to become paranoid over that.

Shivering from the cold, Jane flicked off the air-con and closed the windows and slowed to let them pass. Her shadower slowed as well so Jane sped up and so did they. Matching every variation in speed, they were now blatantly tailgating her. Jane's rational mind struggled for context. A young male, having fun at her expense? Someone she'd offended – had she cut them off at the lights? Or was it her expensive sports car that brought out the worst in the other driver? Road rage was so commonplace these days it was like trolling, anonymity giving people licence to do what they liked.

She planted her foot to burn him off on a sweeping right-hander. Under normal circumstances she would back her BMW 8 Series against his lumbering four-wheel drive any old day of the week, and under normal circumstances she would have been right. But this wasn't any old day – or any old night – of the week. Jane was sickening with something or had had an allergic reaction or her food was tainted or her alcohol spiked, or maybe it was blind panic. As the SUV nudged her right-rear fender, the BMW spun out of control, rolling over and over in an explosion of glass and metal and air bags and blood that ended with the car caught in a tangle of vegetation not ten metres from a river in which she would certainly have drowned.

The mocking sound of the four-wheel drive retreated into the night as Jane lay there, unable to move, the taste of blood metallic in her mouth. Her car's headlights appealed helplessly to the moon as the mournful wail of the car alarm called out in the hope some passing Samaritan might hear the cry and come to Jane's assistance before her life blood ebbed away.

The Samaritan would come and her life would be saved, but only in a manner of speaking. For when Jane awoke twenty days later she would remember nothing of dinner at Peter Debreceny's, or her name or address or date of birth, or her father's name, or her mother's face, or her grandmother's reassuring embrace by an open fire in winter. Even the image of herself in the mirror brought back nothing.

All she saw was a stranger with questioning eyes who reminded her of someone's little sister.

PART ONE

January, 2023

Two little girls squashed on toast,
That is the taste that we love the most.
Two little boys, squashed on bread,
They taste awful – but at least they're dead.

1.

I tentatively open my eyes – but only a little in case someone is watching – and stay in my state of pretended sleep. The strangers are still there across the room, drinking coffee with their backs towards me so I can't hear what they're saying. Talking about me like they always do. Don't they have lives of their own to live?

She's Chinese-Australian with big black eyes perpetually on the edge of tears. I call her Ming Zu and him Donis. He's younger than her, in his late forties I think, possibly the most beautiful man I have ever seen: high cheekbones, deep, soulful eyes, a wide smile like a sunburst with perfect teeth; exquisite, alluring, feminine. They're watchful, polite and attendant, slaves to my every whim. Except my freedom, on which they defer to 'the doctor'.

They call me Jane, which is all right with me. It's a perfectly nice and serviceable name. They probably have their reasons to avoid using my real one.

I have lost all sense of time. They say it's been three months since 'the accident' and that Zoe – whoever she is – sat by my bed every day until she had to go back to New York. Such a long way for someone to come. There has been another visitor, a reticent young woman with pale skin, a ring in her nose and bright blue hair. A volunteer, no doubt, organised by the hospital.

Everyone is trying to be so nice. Sickeningly nice. Smotheringly nice. I want to escape and go to a club with live music or a pub with no responsible alcohol policy. I want someone to pick me up and take me back to a dodgy motel and give me drugs until I get my old life back. I want to jump from an aeroplane with Javier Bardem and free fall until he pulls the ripcord and saves us both from crashing into the sea. But I won't of course, I'm too well brought up. Too obediently middle class.

'I want to go home,' I repeat like an empty mantra. I think it's what I'm expected to say. Not that I have any concept of where 'home' is, but I like the predictability of their reactions: silent tears from Ming Zu and an indulgent smile from Donis.

'Of course you do, Jane,' he says. 'It's what I want as well. And you're getting better all the time.' Such a nice, beautiful androgyne.

He has been bringing photo albums for me to look at, and of course I pretend to be interested. But why would I want to see photos of *his* life and family? Nothing to do with me. I like it best when he plays the cello, one of those modern electrified things. Classical, jazz, jazz-classical fusion, traditional Irish songs that bring a keening ache to the soul. He's a virtuoso, a man whose beautiful form becomes an extension of his instrument, a Jacqueline du Pré without her Barenboim muse, solitary and singularly inspired.

Every time they take me outside, there's a policewoman in the hallway, or sometimes a male. They don't announce themselves as cops, but I can detect one with my eyes shut; I know I've been around them all my life. (Am I a cop myself, injured in the line of duty? I wouldn't be surprised.) 'Hello,' I say. 'Here again today? And your colleague yesterday who likes to tell jokes, the one who loves her sport and can't talk about anything else.' They never answer my questions directly, which is a give-away right there. Cautious, cards close to their chests, Johnny Hoppers. Am I under police protection?

I can't align my thinking with the words that come out. It's like I'm at the dentist and my mouth has been anaesthetised. Everyone speaks in riddles. Every question feels like a test. Not that I'm giving them anything: not till I know what they want.

Oh, here comes the doctor now. This will be interesting. It's amazing how everyone defers to him. But not me. He's not as clever as he thinks he is. I think he's a paediatrician who's used to dealing with children.

'Good morning, Jane.' He smiles. 'And how are you today?'

Well, where do you start with a question like that, given the state of the world? 'Fine,' I say. It's all I'm giving. He's a doctor. He can figure it out.

He shines a light into my eyes and asks what day of the week it is. I give him a look as if to say, 'You don't know?' Some kind of Masonic ritual, I suspect. He knows there are cops in the hallway. Maybe they're here for him?

'What's this, Jane?' he says, holding up a stick.

'A stick,' I say, as if he's the dumb one.

'What's this on the end?'

'Decoration.'

'Yes, but what can it do?'

He runs it through my hair and makes me flinch. Such a personal invasion.

'I'll leave it with you. You might like to use it. To get out the knots.' He places the decorated stick on the bedside table.

As if I'll be doing that. There's no 'nots' in my hair. No 'yeses' either.

—

There is a big white room with blonde-wood floors. It has an enormous dining table with twelve black leather chairs and a state-of-the-art kitchen that would flatter a three-hat restaurant. There's a two-door stainless steel fridge, a two-door freezer and glass-fronted wine cabinets filled with wine, exotic beverages and cigars. There's one of those dishwashers that uses super-heated steam to do a full load in minutes, a top-of-the-range range (pardon the pun) like a chef would use – gas, despite the environment. There are wine racks all the way up to the ceiling, like a mini-cellar, and a selection of chef's knives that would make a serial killer blush.

I think I know most of the people at the table, though I couldn't tell you their names. The pretty woman with the smiling cheeks and self-effacing ways is a poisoner, the man beside her with the axe, a charming killer. Dark, handsome, with a habit of laughing at his jokes with a raucous self-congratulatory roar, he is someone who needs to be watched. The woman seated on his other side is trying to ignore the gash in her throat, but her food keeps tumbling out. She dabs at the spillage with her napkin as if it's perfectly normal, and maybe it is: no-one else seems to care. A child, no more than ten, with parchment skin and bloodless lips, is sucking on a lollipop pacifier made of glass. She needs to take some iron.

I can tell the men (and a solitary woman) at the other end of the table are cops: they keep trying to chat me up. Even the blonde with Jonah Cole . . . There – I do remember a name after all. Jonah Cole, the crazy cop with a heightened sense of smell. Gave a whole new meaning to sniffing out a crime scene. He once bought me the entire contents of a florist shop in an attempt to impress me. All it did was make me worry about his medication.

The most charismatic man in the room is called Robert. Well, that's what they call him, though I don't know his name myself. Sometimes he looks twenty years old, sometimes twice that age. It's how the light catches him I think, or how he catches the light. Either way, it's a trick. I think I've encountered him a number of times, unless he's just a cypher. People often are, in that twilight world between wake and sleep. It's hard to know who to trust.

Robert is tall and thin and slightly hunched with incipient scoliosis. His preferred dress is a black fedora, a green velvet waistcoat, tight-fitting jeans to accentuate his skinny legs and big, too-white sneakers like clown shoes. A heavy leather bag swings on his left shoulder though you can tell there's not much inside. Like most things with Robert, the bag's an affectation, more signature than accessory, part of his swagger and groove.

Robert is a fabulist. He can't lie straight in bed. A born storyteller whose imagination is unfettered by logic or probability, he would be infuriating if he wasn't so exquisitely entertaining. He doesn't tell lies, he tells whoppers – stories whose facts are so patently disconnected from the truth that the listener's not fooled for a moment. Fables so extravagant and unbelievable, the only suspense is in wondering how far he will go.

'I once guided a party of amateur American ethnologists down the Sepik River in search of a lost tribe of headhunters. We built a shrine on a raft made of tractor tyres in the hope it would give us protection, and slaughtered goats to pacify the gods and fed the entrails to the crocs. An heiress from Florida, who thought she was the love child of Dian Fossey and Louis

Leakey, dressed herself in a loincloth and wore a necklace of papier-mâché shrunken heads like a priestess. When we failed to find the headhunters, she staged her own abduction, thinking the party would abandon the journey until they found her and hopefully stumble upon the lost tribe in the process. But the others in the party thought it would invalidate their travel insurance and voted to continue the journey without her. When we returned to civilisation, they claimed the headhunters had kidnapped the heiress and that they had only just escaped themselves owing to "the guile and bravery of their guide". The whole adventure reinforced the myth that headhunters really did exist along the Sepik and led to the *National Geographic* sending photographers out on a futile expedition to try to verify the story.'

This was classic Robert. I knew he had never been down the Sepik. He'd never been out of Australia, let alone to New Guinea. Or ever worked as a travel guide. In fact, he thought the river was somewhere in East Africa. The entire story was based on something he'd read in a magazine and seeing *Gorillas in the Mist*.

I think the big white room with blonde-wood floors is Robert's home. He seems familiar with the environment and knows where everything is.

'Where's the corkscrew, Robert?' Jonah Cole asks.

'In the drawers over there – second one down.'

'Is that a pink oleander in the garden?' asks the poisoner. 'Would you like me to decorate the table?'

'That would be nice,' says Robert.

'Maybe the axe man can cut you some branches if you ask him nicely,' I say.

'I'd swing more than my axe for you,' the man roars, as if his charm and sexuality are irresistible.

Sometimes the room is empty and, with nobody there, strangely familiar. I seem to know it intimately, like a room I have examined in detail. I could have told Jonah where to find the corkscrew. And the oleander is hardly hidden: you can see it through the kitchen window. I think the owners are older than Robert, a man and a woman we've seen on TV. I don't know why I think this. I don't think they're alive anymore but I don't know how they died. Violently, perhaps, but it's only a vague impression – like most things are at the moment; shadowy and indistinct, like motifs in a piece of cello music, resonant of something just out of reach.

There's a fuzz in my head like cotton wool, keeping my thoughts at bay. The doctor says this is normal, but how would he know if every case is different? Doctor Two-Bob Each Way, Doctor Spin the Wheel and Bet on Red, Doctor Don't Ask Me – I'm a Neurosurgeon.

I will have to figure it out for myself.

2.

I am not in the hospital anymore. I know I'm not in an aftercare facility, but probably should be. As far as I can ascertain, I am the recipient of Ming Zu's charity. How can I not be grateful for that?

I'm a guest in her house, but the guest room is starting to pall. I don't want to be here anymore, in a room so bland it probably came first in the Beige to Invisible Challenge in some homemaking magazine. Thank God she keeps the curtains drawn and the lighting dimmed. It's not that I'm being held captive or restrained in any way, though my ability to move around is limited. My physical injuries still need attention. The wound in my head is sensitive, especially where my hair was shaved.

'Good morning, Jane.'

'Good morning, Nadia.'

It always makes her smile. Like I'm making a major breakthrough by remembering her name. Well, it's not very difficult. It's written right there on her name tag. Nadia visits me frequently and makes me repeat her name every time. Is it because she's trying to reinforce it or because she hopes I might remember her in my will?

'So, what did Nadia get you to do yesterday?' she asks as if she's talking about someone else.

‘I don’t know,’ I say.

‘Don’t you remember? Will Nadia give you a clue?’ She holds up a big blue rubber band.

I know I’ve seen it before, but I still don’t know what it’s for.

She loops it over the bedhead and puts the other end around my hand. ‘Now push.’

I do as she says and stretch it out. It’s not so hard to do.

‘Now, Nadia wants you to release it. Slowly. That’s good. Now do it again.’

In and out I push on the blue rubber band until Nadia counts to fifty. Then she loops it on the other side of the bedhead and does the same with my other arm. It is a complete and utter waste of time. It doesn’t pump up anything or make electricity or do anything useful at all.

‘Have you been doing this when Nadia’s not here?’ she asks, although I’m sure she knows the answer.

‘No,’ I answer, leaving out, *Why on earth would I want to do that?*

‘Nadia knows it’s hard for you to exercise while you’re still in bed, but it’s very important to keep the muscles from wasting.’

Wasting? This is wasting; wasting energy and wasting time – and a total waste of big rubber bands. Though God only knows what else you could do with them. Put them around great big bundles of letters?

Nadia helps me out of the bed to the chair across the room. This time the rubber band gets double-looped around the chair leg and my ankle. Another fifty ‘outs’ and ‘ins’ and the same with the other leg. And still nothing inflated nor a single watt produced.

I know I've been in an accident and that Nadia is trying to help me. But my routine seems to be designed around everyone else's needs, not mine. Am I here to justify their existence?

'If you'd like to get out of your nightie, Nadia will take you outside. It's a lovely day.'

Well, maybe it is, but I'm not going anywhere naked – in that wheelchair or otherwise.

'Will Nadia help you dress?'

Now she's reading my thoughts. That must be wrong. Against the Geneva Convention or something.

'Where are your things? Oh, look – Nadia's found your underwear under your tracksuit.'

Well, of course Nadia did. Because I put them there. Though, now that I think about it, it seems such a prudish thing to have done. I didn't used to be this puritanical. Not in the presence of women anyway. Or in the presence of men, for that matter. I don't remember being this sensitive about my body. It's not in bad shape. I've looked after myself. Taken pride in my appearance. I don't think I've ever been troubled by nakedness or intimacy, so why am I worrying now and hiding my underwear from prying eyes? Did the bump on my head cause this?

Nadia helps me dress and I can't stop blushing. I hate myself for that. Whoever 'Jane' is must have been such a person. If only they'd use my proper name.

Am I being reprogrammed with niceness and big rubber bands? I know they've been into my head. What did they do in there, I wonder? Take bits out or shift bits around? Or swap bits with someone else? I know the mirrors in this house aren't mirrors at all but some kind of projection of someone else looking back. Which should be alarming but somehow it isn't, because they're not fooling me for a second. I still have my faculties and the upper hand. I can see through everything they do. And I know I have to keep thinking like this – if I don't, I will fall apart.

'Courage, Jane,' I say to myself. 'Or whoever it is you are.'

It is nice being out in the garden. Nadia enjoys it too, pushing me around in a wheelchair as if I've lost the use of my legs. Which I know isn't true because I've tried and they're strong. It's my balance that lets me down.

'Tell Nadia if you get cold,' says Nadia.

'Yes, Nadia,' I say, playing the part of 'Jane' to keep everyone else from worrying. It's such a responsibility. Is that why they call us patients? Because it's the virtue we have to have as we carry the world and everyone around us until we manage to get back to where we were? Or beyond, to where we are going? Or into the next existence or parallel realm? Is this place with wheelchairs and big rubber bands called Limbo? Am I finally in that spiritual world I have rejected all my humanist life? Some in-between, separating this life and the next?

The walls of the garden are so high it feels like a prison, but I know my prison is all in my head. How I know this, I'm not sure. But for some reason my world seems familiar, like I know the state I'm in because I've seen it before, if not in myself then in others. This knowledge is a clue, I keep thinking, a lifeline I mustn't let slip, a thin vein so delicate it could snap in an instant if I weigh it with too much expectation.

And if it breaks then I know I'll be lost, adrift in unfathomable dark, my fragile grasp on sanity severed forever, gone and irretrievable. It's a bleak and terrifying prospect. It's a dangerous game, this game of life, this balancing act on the edge of annihilation. But like a pilgrim, I know I have been here before and that I had better not screw it up.

Today's the day we go to the spaceship. Ming Zu takes me there every week. I would rather go to the movies. She calls it the hospital but I think that's her little joke. All those blue uniforms and shiny surfaces and coloured lines to follow as you move from one sector to the next. It certainly feels like a spaceship to me.

The big machine is like an airlock as it whirs and clunks around me. Sometimes I worry it might spit me out, casting me into the void. The crew always tell me how important it is to keep still and I imagine someone's finger hovering over a big red button marked 'eject' in case I inadvertently twitch. I exist in a world where the margins are thin and oblivion accompanies the slightest mistake.

There's another machine that slices my brain into a selection of colourful images. I wonder how many times they can do this without turning everything to mush. Afterall, a ham at the butcher's only gets to go through the meat slicer once. Why should my brain be any different? There's a lot to hang on to in there, and I need to keep it intact. I am struggling to remember a whole lot of things and shuffling the cards isn't helping.

Doctor Two-Bob considers the results and tries to explain them, but he's too hung-up on the pretty colours. It's just an inkblot test as far as I can see and who puts their trust in those anymore? This spaceship is time-travelling backwards . . . Wouldn't that be nice? I know I'm struggling to remember things, like the accident that seems so important. And people's names, like 'Zoe', and whatever it is Donis's photo albums are expected to trigger.

'Describe yourself to me,' asks Two-Bob. 'As if you were telling a stranger how to recognise you if you were arranging to meet.'

Well, that one came from nowhere. At least he's asking me something new. 'I'd send a photograph.'

'But if you didn't have one.'

Well, that's preposterous, but I don't have the energy to go into that. 'Female.'

'Yes.'

'Fifty. Something.'

'Yes.'

'Dark hair.'

'. . . Go on.' He didn't seem to like that answer.

'Brown eyes.' I can feel an unseen hand moving closer to the big red button.

He gets up and fetches something from across the room. 'See if this helps.'

A bright light reflects down from the ceiling and burns into my eyes. Two-Bob adjusts the object so it shows a face looking back at me.

'Is this an iPad?' I ask.

'No. A mirror.'

Now I know he's lying. I thought he was here to help.

'So, tell me again. To help the stranger. Female, fifty-something . . .'

'Dark hair and brown eyes.' I finish it for him although I thought it was me who was struggling to remember.

'Is that what you see in the mirror, Jane?'

'No.'

'Then who do you see?'

'Someone else.'

'And how can that be?'

Now he's making me cry, which he always does when his tricks become too clever.

'How do you know it isn't you?' he continues, feigning a bedside manner.

'Because this person isn't crying and I am. Plus she's blonde with blue eyes and I'm not.'

Two-Bob takes the mirror and puts it aside while I brace for the inevitable. But the eject button doesn't engage, thank God. The crew must be on a break.

3.

On the way back to the film set where Ming Zu pretends to live, we stop at an ice-cream truck by the river. She unfolds a wheelchair from the boot of her car and helps me into it. I don't complain. If I didn't qualify as disabled before, I have earned the label now. We sit in the sun and compare flavours. My chocolate chip and her apricot blancmange. She offers me a taste but I politely decline. It looks like 'brain orange' to me.

Ming Zu watches as I smile at the cyclists gliding by on the pathway. They have clearly got their lives together even if the rest of us haven't.

'You know you did that every day? Rode your bike along here.'

At first I think she's talking to someone else.

'When you get better, we should try it again.'

'We? Do you ride bikes as well?'

'Well, no,' she confesses, 'but I know I should. It's a great way to keep in shape.'

What shape is that? I wonder. Is she about to turn into a wolf? There's something lupine about Ming Zu. I bet she loves those vampire books where people shapeshift all the time. Is that what's happening to me?

I wish there was someone I could trust, someone who could tell me the truth or, in the absence of that, simply leave me alone. That would be nice. Then I could figure things out for myself. I seem controlled by other people's agendas: Doctor Two-Bob and his silly games and his uniformed crew with their big red button; Nadia with her blue rubber bands; and Ming Zu, deciding what ice cream I want and talking about going cycling. Did I ask for any of that?

There must be a way to reboot the brain, to turn it off and on again. To wind everything back to zero and open the stopcock so the past flows back when it's ready. Like everything in life, it's finding the key, the metaphor that's right for you. There are no answers to be found in the literal – in the black and white or the right and wrong. If it was as easy as that, then you'd do what you're told and put your faith in a mirror.

Ah, this is better. I am back with my people again. The big white room is warm and cosy despite the rain outside. It's another noisy dinner party with an overabundance of booze. Excess is in the air tonight, a licence to do what you like.

The couple who own the place are conjuring up a feast. Husband and wife, professional chefs – I've seen them on TV. You can tell when they place the plates in front of you that they have given you everything they have. Not just the taste, which is beyond sublime, but their hearts and souls as well. Their meal is a gift of love.

Robert holds court, telling fanciful tales while slipping chocolates to his little sister. She's made a bed for herself under the table but I'm the only one who seems to notice.

The cops and crooks still sit apart as a mark of mutual disrespect. The game depends on them and us and to mingle would blur the lines. I alone seem to slip between them, as if I'm the only one they trust.

'Tell the inspector that nobody likes him. And to stick his badge up his arse.'

'Tell Leftie to come and do it himself. He's been up more arseholes than me.'

The party is out of control with everyone talking at once. I try to join in but feel like an observer rather than an invited guest. Am I a spy? A professional go-between, some kind of double agent? I hold my hand over the candle but can't feel the heat. I laugh at everyone's jokes as loud as I can, but nobody laughs at mine. No matter how much I eat, my plate remains full and my lipstick leaves no trace on my glass. Do I even exist anymore? Am I only a memory, and if so, is that memory mine or somebody else's? And why am I even thinking like this, so obsessed with the mind's machinations, of thoughts and demons and fragile dreams and life at its most precarious?

I look at the fireplace and search for an answer in the dying embers, but there is only one thought in my mind: if a backdraft should come down that chimney right now, it would surely take me away.

Somebody's holding my hand. It's Donis. I must have fallen asleep.

'Hello, Jane,' he says with his perfect smile.

I wish he wouldn't call me that. They all seem to miss her so much. She must have been a special person.

'I've found some photos of the time we had at Margaret River when the orchestra played in the vineyard. Do you remember you were worried about getting away because your court case was running late?' He lays out a range of photos. I have never seen them before. I recognise him and his orchestra among the vines, but I can't see myself when he points me out, even when I put on my glasses. Of course, I go along with it all, not wanting to make a fuss. He shows me someone coming out of the ocean at Cottesloe and I can see why he likes to think it's me. Whoever it is looks great in a bathing suit, but she's got somebody else's head.

'Would you like to go back there, Jane?' he asks. 'You loved the warmth of the Indian Ocean.'

'But isn't it bad for shark attacks?'

'Jane – that's fantastic,' he says, jumping up. 'You remember?'

'Well, I remember reading it somewhere, Donis, but you're enjoying this more than you should.'

'You were there when one happened. We were walking the beach after breakfast. A swimmer, a man in his sixties. It's all coming back. Your memory is better than mine. As they dragged him ashore, you went down to help, because of your medical knowledge. Maybe I can find the newspaper article. I think you got a mention.'

There I am, caught out again for playing along as Jane. I blame myself and nobody else. When is this going to end? I want to tell him I'm not Jane or the person in the photos, but it shouldn't be this hard. There's too many of them lined up against me and not nearly enough of me. A patient needs an advocate to protect them from such a relentless attack. They should go hire a private detective, find Jane and leave me the fuck alone!

Sorry. I don't need to talk like that.

As Donis gathers up his photos, he spills some onto the bed. I help him to put them back in his folder. And there it is, as large as life. A photograph of me. There are four people in the photo. Donis and the woman in the bathing suit, though in the photo she's wearing a dress. And another man, who I have never seen before, standing with his arm around me.

Donis can see my reaction. He takes the photo and hands it back. 'Do you know the people in this photograph, Jane?' He sounds almost afraid to ask.

'Two of them, yes.'

'And who are the ones you know?'

'You and me.'

I can see Donis is barely breathing. 'Can you point them out?'

'That's you,' I say pointing at him, though I know the big test's to come.

'And you, Jane? Which one is you?'

'There,' I say, pointing at me. I so want to please him and please myself too, but I'm not going to lie to make him happy.

Donis looks at me with his soulful eyes. 'That's Virginia,' he says. 'That's Richard and Virginia at Richard's sixtieth. And that's you and me standing beside them.'

I might have known he'd say something like that. This fight for my brain is relentless. If I had only selected the Jane option, the one he wanted, and gone along with it all, then maybe they'd leave me alone.

Perhaps it is something I should seriously consider if I want to get out of this place.

4.

What happens next is utterly predictable. Donis tells Ming Zu and Ming Zu phones Doctor Two-Bob and here I am back at the spaceship. Donis's folder of photos sits on the doctor's desk; what a couple of snitches they are. Doctor Two-Bob checks my blood pressure and taps my knees with his little hammer. He's no better than any GP. It's like checking the health of a house by reading the water meter. A specialist should be more thorough than that.

'So, we've solved one of our little mysteries. Your memory of yourself has been confused with that of your friend, Virginia. Is she someone you particularly admire?'

No more than anyone else, I think, not feeling the need to explain.

'It's not something I've encountered before, but as I've said . . .'

'. . . every case is different,' I finish for him. If he doesn't have anything new to say, why say it at all?

'Exactly. Memory returns in its own way when it's ready. With many deviations along the way. There's no logic involved. When the mind goes blank, people panic to fill the gaps and your vivid memory of your friend became confused with your image of yourself. Which is why the mirror confused you. It must have been very distressing.'

There he goes again, reinforcing his conclusions at my expense. No wonder I keep my mouth shut.

'I think you've been trying too hard, Jane. Trying to force things along. I know Elizabeth and Tim want to take you back to your apartment.'

'Who?'

'Sorry. You call them Ming Zu and Donis.'

I call them that because that's who they are. Though admittedly Donis is a nickname for Adonis. But if everyone persists in calling me Jane, then aren't I free to return the favour?

'You need to tell me what you're thinking, Jane.'

'Why?'

'Because if you don't tell me, I have no way to know.'

Uh oh. He's going for his cardboard box of tricks again.

'What's this, Jane?' he says, holding up a toothbrush.

'A toothbrush.'

'Can you show me how to use it?'

Against my better judgement, I humour him and rub it against my teeth.

'Very good, Jane. Very good.' He takes it from me, puts it back in the box and takes out a pair of scissors. 'And what's this?'

Doesn't he mean 'what are these?'? But I'm not here to correct his grammar. Or cut my hair, if that's what he wants. I'll be shaving my armpits next.

'Tell me what you're thinking.'

'I'm thinking you want me to shave my armpits.'

Is it my fault he looks confused? A neurosurgeon should be cleverer than this by definition. Don't ask the question if you don't want to hear the answer.

'How would you feel if Elizabeth . . . Ming Zu . . . arranged for Virginia to visit?'

'No.' Doesn't he realise how terrifying that prospect might be? What if he's right and I've confused her for me? Or if he's wrong and she's nothing like I imagine? And if I am using her as my reference point, what happens if that's taken away?

'Would you look in the mirror again for me, please?'

He has got to be fucking joking. 'No.'

'Well, when you're ready, Jane. There's no need to push things along. But I think we're making progress at last. I think we're doing fine.'

Which is where every session ends with Doctor Two-Bob. Where he feels better and gives me a smile and checks his watch for the next appointment. I am glad he is doing so well because I am most definitely not.

Ah, peace at last. The house is mine. Everyone has gone to bed. Ming Zu and her husband who smiles but never speaks; their two children, the boy with his head in his iPad and the girl who goes to tennis lessons twice a week. 'She'll play in the Australian Open one day,' says Ming Zu. 'Her coach thinks she's a natural.'

With the walker to help my balance, I can go anywhere I like and I start by looking for the bathroom. Where have they hidden it tonight? Yesterday, I found it in a cupboard under the stairs. Not only had they gone to the trouble of moving it from the other end of the hallway, they had removed the bath and shower as well.

This house is like a Chinese puzzle, though I'd never say that to Ming Zu. Sometimes the kitchen's to the left, sometimes it's to the right. Why they want to mess with my sense of direction, I don't know. It seems counter-intuitive to my recovery. Now the kitchen is back where it was last week, looking out into the garden.

It's a disappointing room. No top-of-the-range range and double-door fridges. No wine racks all the way to the ceiling. No blonde-wood floors, no table for twelve, no laughter and gaiety either. This is a kitchen for a nuclear family of ghosts who are never seen. Ming Zu insists on keeping them quiet. I would prefer some noise myself, if only to prove they were here.

I run some water from the tap into my hand and get a wet sleeve for my trouble. There's a cup by the sink, but all that does is send the water over the wall. The pressure is so strong it is clearly intended to put out a fire and the taps are designed so the water goes straight down the drain. I pull up my sleeve and cup my hand to drink from the raging tap, which is now running hot. Everything is lined up against me. What this kitchen needs is a bubbler.

Across the garden, there's an open door beside the pool house and I see they've now put the toilet out there. Don't they know I can't manage the walker on the lawn? It won't be my fault if I pee on the floor.

There's a mirror on the wall nearby. Am I game to take a look? It hasn't been a good experience. I meet myself halfway and take the walker across the room to examine what's under my bandages while carefully avoiding my face. The scars are healing but still purple. I seem to know the significance of this, though I am sure I haven't been told. Doctor Two-Bob never discusses this stuff; I think he thinks my weals are for his eyes only. The main scar begins in front of my ear and extends up through the temple like a question mark ending in the middle of my hairline. I can count where twenty-two sutures and skin clips have been. I can only guess what has gone on in there. Nothing good, I suspect.

I turn away from the mirror in case someone else is watching me back and try to conjure up this 'Virginia' person who I'm told is a very close friend. Well, not so close that she didn't borrow my identity when I needed it most. Ming Zu, who calls herself Elizabeth, thinks the three of us go out for dinner together with someone else called Jasmine. At least every couple of months, she says, so we don't lose touch with each other. Well, it's easy for her to say; she hasn't lost touch with herself.

Is that what's happened to me? I've lost touch? My life is inhabited by strangers who somehow feel familiar. Is that because I have been in this state for so long? That I know them because I am getting to know them, not because I knew them before? Maybe there's no history between us apart from what they tell me. Am I expected to take them on trust?

So they think the accident may have been deliberate, but how would they know? Were they there? Was anyone else? They agree there were no witnesses, apart from the other driver, so why do they have to be so melodramatic? Who would want to run me off the road and do me harm? I don't have any enemies – at least none that I can remember. Isn't it enough that I'm struggling to regain my memory without elaborate conspiracy theories to make the path to recovery more precarious than it needs to be?

But why am I thinking of this in a kitchen instead of a favourite recipe? That's what I'll do. That's the best remedy. I'll bake a cake. Out come the eggs and the flour, the sugar and butter. You never forget something you've done since you were a child. It's like riding a bike. You can simply surrender yourself to the process. This goes with that and that goes with this. Or is it the other way round? Eggs with the butter and milk, or eggs with the flour and sugar? Just start again: you'll find your rhythm. Thank God Ming Zu keeps a full larder. But where does she keep the chocolate?

I am making a mess but that doesn't matter; I have never been a tidy cook. And the deal we have in our household is that the one who cooks never cleans up. That's for the other person to do . . .

Household? Other person? What other person is that? I know Donis would like to think it's him. And he's got photos to back it up.

Is it my suspicion that's holding me back? A stubbornness that prevents me from accepting being told who I am? A conviction that it is something only I can discover? When I'm ready, in my own good time.

What a mess I've made. There's flour all over the place and not even the beginnings of a cake. And what's the point? I can't use the oven anyway. I don't even know how to turn it on.

My tears splash onto the flour on the bench, a pattern in the snow. I don't hear myself sob, but the tears fall like rain. I have read somewhere that six minutes is normal for a woman to cry. (Only two minutes for a man.) Should I set a timer and go for the record?

I can't remember this accident they talk about. Or what my life was like before that. I can't remember cycling along the river or listening to an orchestra in a vineyard in Western Australia.

I can't remember a shark attack. I can't remember any birthdays or where I go for Christmas. I can't remember those dinners with Virginia, Jasmine and Ming Zu when she is Elizabeth, if that's who she is. I also can't remember the last time I cried, but I am crying now as if I need to empty a deep dark well. Maybe this purging will clear my head. I am trying to sign my name in the flour, but the tears keep distorting the signature so I can't read what it says. Talk about self-sabotage. I think I'm an expert at that.

I have to find a toilet, quickly. I'll take the chance it's still at the end of the hall.

Shit. I think I have woken them up. Come on, walker, don't let me down.

I stay in the dark as quiet as a mouse and hear Ming Zu calling out.

'Is that you, Jane? Are you in there? Is everything all right?'

I wonder if she's been to the kitchen. That would have given her a clue. God. Now she's knocking on the door. Doesn't she know toilets are sacrosanct, a refuge, like a church?

She opens the door and turns on the light. Thank God I am sitting with my back towards her. Oh, look – the bath and the shower are back.

'Jane. What happened? You're covered in powder. And why are you sitting like that?'

At least I know she hasn't been to the kitchen.

'What happened?'

Overloaded again with too many questions. Where do I start? I needed a pee, I failed to bake a cake and the design of this toilet is terrible. While it's good to be able to rest your arms on the cistern, the seat is not designed for facing this way round.

So, full marks for originality, but none for execution. Of course, I tell her none of this. It would only lead to more questions.

She helps me back to my bedroom and finds a nightie without a wet sleeve and bathes my face with a flannel. 'You've been crying, Jane. That's really good. I was worried you were holding back.'

That's wise, I think. That's insightful. Does she get me after all? Maybe now she'll give me a break and stop hiding the toilet.

5.

I knew there would be a breakthrough, that I'd find a way out of the maze. That if I could remember one thing clearly, then the rest might reasonably follow. I started by thinking of my memory like a box of index cards, a puzzle to be unlocked after I manage to decipher the first one. It's only a theory and there's no guarantee that the cards that follow would line up in any meaningful sequence. But I'm getting ahead of myself . . .

I never thought I could derive so much pleasure from a TV cooking show but *Top Cook* is one of those programs. It helps that the hosts have sexual chemistry, that each episode is a kind of seduction. Although they are husband and wife, it's like they are eloping each week. The format follows the usual weekly elimination but the contestants play second fiddle to the loving couple. The whole thing is intoxicating. Food as aphrodisiac. You can't taste it but you can't deny the thrill.

Skyla and Herman are Dutch. They don't use their surname in the show. You only glimpse it in the closing titles under their producer credits: Van Meulenbelt or some name like that. But the *Top Cook* brand is international. Cookbooks and product endorsements, *Top Cook US* and *Top Cook UK*; there are formats around the world. He, apparently, is the business brains and she the genius chef. But they compete for each other's title as seriously as the show's contestants. Skyla is determined to show her talents aren't limited to the kitchen and Herman is just as determined to show their branding means nothing if he can't put something inspired on the plate. They are so competitive and obsessed with each other that you can't take your eyes away. There are tabloid rumours linking Herman romantically with a number of prominent actresses and models, and gossip that suggests Skyla is more than capable of fighting fire with fire, but all that does is increase the temperature of the show. Insiders say the whole thing is stage-managed, that they're quiet and domestic at home. If it's a deliberate ploy for ratings, it's an inspired one, despite the moral implications. It's like we're waiting for their jealousies to explode on screen, but they never do. Not yet.

Last night's show was a cracker. The contestants had been whittled down to the last four and Skyla and Herman took two of them each and staged a team cook-off. The contestants then had to score all six cooks in a secret ballot. If either Skyla or Herman came last, they would give $100,000 to a charity nominated by the winner. The money was never at risk. Skyla came first and Herman third, with a tie between fifth and sixth. Because of the tie, both contestants survived until the following week – when Skyla and Herman would have the vote and where the bottom two would go home. The concept was inspired. Instead of two lame eliminations, the show had two semifinals then straight to the grand finale. And Skyla and Herman seemed more in love than ever.

When I told Ming Zu about it and suggested she try and watch it on catch-up, she couldn't find it in the TV guide. After a little research, she found it on YouTube. The program had been out of production for twenty years.

I've been asked to talk to an eight-year-old girl who is obviously quite distressed. She's very distracted and plays with the tassels on her top and won't look at me directly. She dodges my questions and makes it clear she doesn't want to be here. Things improve when I get some paper and crayons though the first colour she chooses is black. I ask her if she'd like to draw a picture and she draws a primitive house like a preschooler might, with a door in the centre and windows up high on either side. When I ask if she'd like to colour it in, she scribbles all over it in red.

On a fresh sheet of paper she draws a toaster and two pieces of bread on a plate. On each piece of bread (or is it meant to be toast?) she draws a face, little-girl faces with plaits and over-bright eyes, though it's hard to tell if the eyes are smiling or startled.

I am struggling to work out my relationship with the little girl and I can't remember her name. I know I am not her teacher. I think I might be a family friend. I keep looking at my watch as if I've been given a deadline, that I only have a limited amount of time to make an assessment. And once that word comes into my head, my focus changes from her to me. *Assessment.* Such a formal term. Does it hold a clue as to who I am? Assessment, appraisal, evaluation, judgement. Words implying an intimate process, but somehow one step removed. Dispassionate, calculating, like a scientist.

I'm not going to help her feeling like this. I force myself back to the task at hand and ask her to tell me about what she's drawn.

She tells me it's about two little girls – which is 'good' she says, because 'at least they're not little boys'.

My watch consumes the soundless digital seconds and I know if I can't make a breakthrough by the time the hour is up, I may never have the chance again. The pressure is becoming unbearable and I'm losing sight of why I am here. *Focus on the little girl*, I tell myself, *she's in far more trouble than you.*

But is she? At least she knows who she is. At least she knows her name. At least she can concentrate long enough to do some drawings instead of being obsessed with a watch eating time like acid. And what do I think will happen when the hour is up? That I'll go 'poof' and cease to exist?

Two little girls, squashed on toast,
That is the taste we love the most . . .

Where have I heard that before?

Time is racing now, time I haven't got to waste.

I am back in the big white room but, like my session with the little girl, I seem one step removed. I am looking at some sort of video recording, vision that has no sound. There's a wooden rifle on the floor but it is not a toy: the proportions are too precise. There are two dummies as well – one female, one male – and some detectives with spiral-bound notebooks and serious faces. Robert is there, talking animatedly, adjusting the positions of the rifle and dummies on the floor. He enters and leaves the room repeatedly as if to make sure he's got things right. The recording is amateur, like it's being done by a policeman with no sense of filming, with the light behind him. These days, cameras are more forgiving. And spiral-bound notebooks? Antediluvian. Am I getting a sense of time at last? The detectives' suits seem to place them in the 1990s or 2000s though cops are hardly harbingers of fashion. (Did I make a little joke to myself just then? Well, that would be a first.)

I am watching a video of a police reconstruction and the remarkable thing about that is that I know what a police reconstruction is. The argument is building that I'm a cop – though not one directly involved in this case or I would be with them there in the room. It's a flash of recognition that fades as soon as it comes, like my brain is playing games, toying with me and mocking my theory about the index cards. I'm in serious danger of overthinking things. It would be nice to give myself a break.

Now I'm in a room with Robert, trying to calm him down. He says he's made a terrible mistake, that he's confessed to things he didn't do. He wants me to help him put things right and I know I'm his only chance. The weight of that responsibility oppresses me. Part of me doesn't want to remember. It pushes down like a serious illness and I know, without any evidence or detail, that I failed him, that I let him down. That I couldn't reverse his lies and – worse than that – had no insight as to why he told them.

You never remember the triumphs in life, only the things you regret. Unlike success, your failures are loyal and never desert you. It's good to know you can count on something.

Some cop. I couldn't find a stowaway on a dinghy.

I'm at the top of a mountain, skiing on powder snow. I haven't done that for years. The slope is steep and I'm weighing the danger of causing an avalanche. Good sense tells me to stick to the trail, but the shortcut seems more exciting. I haven't got any of the right equipment. They didn't have transceivers and airbags back then. At least I know it's not a recent memory.

I launch myself off down the slope, not daring to glance behind, keeping my knees soft and my focus on an escape route away from the valley. I wish I wasn't a thrill seeker. It seems so immature. Do I only know I'm alive when I'm scaring myself to death?

The avalanche, when it comes, is small and I ski off to the side as planned. I have to climb all the way back up the slope to rejoin the trail, but convince myself it was worth the experience. I'm glad no-one was here to see my foolishness but wonder why I was skiing alone. My mountain craft is too good for that. Am I there for another reason? Did my companion get injured and I was going for help when I got distracted by the powder? Or is it just another anxiety dream I have lived with all my life?

Finding the metaphor that matches the moment. What was I skiing away from? Was I skiing away from Robert? Is this what recovering memory means – scraping out all the muck at the bottom of the well before you can fill it again?

Eric Ringer always said I think too much (there, that's another cop whose name I remember) and maybe I do. But this time I'm trying to think my way back to health.

Two little girls squashed on toast,
That is the taste that we love the most.
Two little boys, squashed on bread,
They taste awful – but at least they're dead.

Finally, an index card makes sense.

It was Robert who wrote that poem – he wrote it for his little sister.

'Well, that's reassuring. He's still watching the house.'

Ming Zu has returned from the school drop-off and is cheerfully talking, as some people do, as if I was privy to her thoughts. I hate it when conversations are so cryptic that it obliges the listener to ask for clarification.

'Who's watching the house?' I ask. 'And why is it reassuring?'

'He's a policeman, we think, not that he'll say. No doubt undercover. My husband talked to him the other day and he said he was interested in buying that house that's for sale along the road and was checking it out to see how it caught the morning sun. Likely story. Sitting in his car at various places up and down the street, eating his takeaways and checking his screen and trying to look inconspicuous.' Ming Zu gives a chuckle. No-one's fooling her. 'But it's good to know he's out there, keeping an eye on you, like the police did at the hospital after the accident. In case someone wants a second go.'

Well, Ming Zu might find it reassuring but I most certainly don't. Number one: Undercover cops, by definition, do not attract attention. Or if they do, they come up with a better reason for sitting in their car for several days. Number two: If cops are providing protection, they would inevitably work in twos and on rotation, not randomly and not on their own. Number three: If they are 'keeping an eye on me', then why wouldn't they say and actually ask from time to time if everything was okay? Ming Zu may well be a talented lawyer in that particularly rarefied field of commercial insurance, but she has zilch understanding of police surveillance and protection. Number four: How can some stranger's presence 'up and down the street' be in any way 'reassuring'. And number five: 'In case someone wants a second go?' Really? To finish off what he failed to do when he ran me off the road? Is she seriously suggesting that?

I am grateful to Ming Zu for providing me refuge and to her law firm for permitting her to work from home. And I am grateful for her family's consideration in allowing me the run of an entire wing of their sprawling mansion and to her boisterous teenagers for not making a peep and for her husband's cheery silence. But Ming Zu's theories I can do without.

There is no evidence that someone tried to run me off the road any more than there is anything to suggest the man in the street is a cop.

Which kind of begs the question: Who is he?

PART TWO

February 2023

People are exploding,
You see it all the time.
They try to patch the problem up,
With medicines and twine.
But the answer is quite simple,
There are no in-betweens.
You either keep a secret or
Get blown to smithereens.

6.

I am beginning to put things together but they don't make total sense. Why do I recall a two-decades-old television cooking program by a husband-and-wife team who both met violent deaths, their twenty-year-old son who tells outrageously tall tales and his eight-year-old sister who likes to eat chocolates under the dining table? And why are the parents called Skyla and Herman Van Meulenbelt while their son is known as Robert Millard? And what is the little girl's name? Why do I recollect their big white kitchen so well – and the video of a police reconstruction?

This is the closest I have come to recalling anything from my past since the accident, apart from the names of two detectives. I am still intensely embarrassed that I mistook myself for a supposedly close friend, who I am still too mortified to meet in person. I remain deeply suspicious of everything in general and extremely wary of mirrors in particular. I would like nothing more than to discuss the beginnings of my returning memory with Ming Zu or Donis, but I know they'd go straight to the doctor. Not that he's not entitled to know, but I know he won't be satisfied and will only press me for more. I have to do this cautiously for, however clear these things might be in my head, the way I express them is often incoherent.

I still don't trust what people tell me. Or what they show me either. Please, no more photographs. I know I've been in a serious accident that I can't recall. I know I've had surgery on my brain and how critical that can be. Especially when it comes to memory. I have been told my name and who I am, but none of it rings true. Surely, I have to feel it first? Otherwise, I'm just playing a role. Which I know would please everyone around me. Everyone, that is, but me.

Until I get my sense of balance back, I remain utterly dependent on a stick or a walker or a wheelchair. I can't feed myself, clothe myself or find a toilet without a plan of the house. But I do remember Robert Millard and a false confession he made about murdering his parents. And the doggerel he wrote for his little sister. And if I can only put it all together in the right time and place, who knows what it might release? Maybe I'll take the risk and tell the doctor. After all, today's the day we go to the spaceship.

'How long have we been doing this?' I ask Ming Zu as she helps me dress.

'We've been going for two months.'

I wobble across to the wheelchair and Ming Zu gives a silent gasp. 'Do you realise what you did then, Jane? You walked without your stick. Is your balance coming back?'

'I think it is,' I say with delight and move around the room unaided. No dizziness, no sense I'm going to fall. It feels like a major breakthrough.

'Do you want to walk to the car? Here, hold my arm.'

Such a small victory, but I want to cry.

When we get to the hospital, I use one of their wheelchairs as I usually do, but short of Two-Bob's consulting room, I get out of the chair, walk a few paces and knock on the door.

Ming Zu watches like she's at a prize-giving for one of her children.

Two-Bob opens the door. The look on his face is everything I hoped. He's almost as excited as me.

'Doctor Halifax, I presume.'

Well, that may be going too far.

He gestures towards a chair and watches as I carefully walk across the room.

'And she made a cup of tea this morning, all by herself. Boiled the jug, added the water, took out the teabag.'

I think walking unaided is more of an achievement but I let Ming Zu have her moment.

'That's a second task completed,' says the doctor.

He can tell I don't understand what he means.

'We look for two markers: the completion of two basic tasks. The first one was using a toothbrush. And now you've made a cup of tea.'

I would have preferred a bigger reaction to walking without the aid of a walking stick, but who am I to rate my progress? Will he be as impressed about Robert Millard?

And so I explain, in my own stumbling way, my thoughts racing ahead of my words, how I am beginning to remember something from my past. Twenty years ago, admittedly, but more momentous, I would argue, than using a toothbrush or making a cup of tea.

'That's very good, Jane. And what else can you tell me?'

There we go, just as I predicted. Not content with what I've told him, he wants to press me for more. Can't he acknowledge what I've achieved, if only for a moment?

'Have you discussed this with Tim or Elizabeth? Maybe one of them could look through your files.'

I surrender. He has worn me down. I will no longer offer resistance to being Jane Halifax, forensic psychiatrist – whatever that is. Just show me where to sign and send me home.

'Think of memory like a box of index cards: unlock the first and the rest may follow.'

And now he's stealing my theory.

'I think I've explained this before. It might not just be the physical trauma of the accident and the former brain swelling we have to cope with. There could be psychological barriers to recalling your memory that may need to be negotiated.'

Maybe the index cards were his idea. Maybe he explained them while I was semi-comatose. Maybe I don't have an original thought in my head and only know what's been suggested. But doesn't that make my situation even more precarious? Isn't this what I fear most of all? What if, instead of Jane Halifax, he suggests I'm Lady Di?

I start to laugh uncontrollably. The preposterousness of the proposition is liberating. And laughter, as they say, is very good medicine.

Doctor Two-Bob and Ming Zu sit there, bemused, as I laugh away at something unsaid, which is surely the first sign of madness. Be wary of the voices in your head. They are invariably your own.

'I think it could be time, Jane, to go to your apartment.' Now he speaks to Ming Zu. 'But we need to be careful. The experience could be overwhelming.'

I hate it when they do this, as if I have suddenly become an object. A specimen to be dissected between them, as if I'm no longer in the room.

'Overwhelming?' I ask. It seems like a very big word.

'Or it could be completely normal. As if you have never left.'

See what I mean? Doctor Two-Bob Each Way, Doctor Nobody Knows, Doctor-It's-Impossible-To-Make-Predictions-When-We-Are-Dealing-With-The-Brain.

'I'll let Tim know,' says Ming Zu. 'He has the keys.'

Oh, has he indeed? Did I agree to that? I can't remember it being discussed. He's probably using the opportunity to replace my photographs with his.

I remember when my paternal grandmother got dementia when I was a child. I thought it was terrible then. How I projected how she must have felt when she couldn't find her way home or distinguish the neighbour's place from hers, or remember how many brothers and sisters she had and that Grandpa had died the year before. Even as a child, I could understand the dread of her condition. But her face never betrayed the horror of what she was feeling. It was as if she were trying to fake it and pretend that everything was all right. I hope it's not hereditary. I hope it's not happening to me.

But is that another memory? Another look beyond the veil? If I could only remember the recent past as well as things back then.

I am allowed to be terrified. In fact, I would argue that, under the circumstances in which I find myself, terror is perfectly normal.

Since I have no memory of where I live, the prospect of going there is not something I look forward to. I know it is going to be confronting: more so, because I will be experiencing it under the judgemental gaze of my two erstwhile companions who will, whatever my reaction, glance knowingly at each other with a mixture of disappointment and weary resignation. Don't they know how patronising that feels? Don't they know how terrifying this experience will be for me? Why can't they take me to the door and let me endure it alone?

Except I've got that enemy out there, lurking in the shadows. He's not outside the house anymore, but it doesn't mean he's gone away. What if he's following me still and I just can't see him? What if he's getting cleverer? Do I have the resources to worry about that as well?

Ming Zu has driven me past the building before but since I didn't recognise it, I elected not to go in. It's one of those places that are everywhere in Southbank and along St Kilda Road, well-constructed and lavishly appointed – but would I live in a place like that?

My heart is pounding as Ming Zu's Lexus turns down the ramp to the carpark, the building swallowing us whole as I sit beside her with Donis in the back. With the passcard in hand, he leads us to the lift as I hang on to the arms of my wheelchair for dear life, not because I am fearful of falling out but because I am fearful of being overwhelmed. Did Two-Bob have to use that word?

We emerge from the lift on the seventh floor and Donis opens the door to apartment three. Now, as well as a rising heart rate, I am struggling to breathe. I try and concentrate on belly breathing but I know I am falling apart. If I could run, I would, as fast as my legs and new-found equilibrium would take me.

7.

I enter the apartment with the trepidation of an intruder. I want a rush of recognition, the bliss of the familiar, I want to be overwhelmed with the evidence of my existence. It is a pleasant, even welcoming, room, but I have never been here before.

'How long have I lived here?' I ask, being careful to give nothing away.

'Almost two years,' Donis answers, finding reassurance in my question and the implication I know where I am.

'It's a beautiful room, isn't it?' Ming Zu observes. 'Your aerie in the sky.'

Yes, it is a beautiful room and I can hear myself making such an observation. But this apartment isn't mine.

I get out of the wheelchair, steady myself until I find my balance, and move about the room. I try to take it in as a whole. I try to focus on the detail. I examine a bowl. I study a painting. I run my hand against the fabric of the couch in the hope the upholstery will feel familiar. I look at the rug on the floor and hate it. It doesn't go with anything else.

'Come through to your study, Jane,' says Tim, 'and see if there's anything you remember.'

Yes, keep calling me *Jane* and call it *my study* and you'll get your way in the end.

It is another pleasant room, lined with books and landscape photographs. Photographs I have never seen before; you'd imagine I would remember one of them.

Donis sits me down at the desk but I don't want to be watched.

'Do you mind if I do this alone. Please?'

'But of course,' he says with an indulgent smile.

A smile of affection would have been more reassuring.

I start with the files on the desk, many of them legal documents and police reports. There are a lot of names but none of them familiar. And none of them Robert Millard. I get up and look through the older files on the shelf. I look for anything dated twenty years ago, but they are all more recent than that. I find a diary and flip through the pages. The name 'Luna' seems familiar but I can't put a face to the person. I repeat the name in my head and run my finger over the words. But if you look at anything long enough, you start believing you've heard it before.

I find my way back to the lounge room. I can see the others are waiting for my report. 'Where's the bedroom?'

Donis and Ming Zu exchange glances. I am sure they don't think I notice, but I know a conspiracy when I see one.

'Through here. Don't you remember?' says Donis superfluously.

If I remembered, would I need to ask? He goes to lead me through but again I assert my independence.

'I'll be all right.'

The bedroom is enormous with a walk-in dressing room and marble ensuite. Whoever lives here has a lot of clothes. Expensive clothes, many of them recently purchased, a woman who likes to update her wardrobe on a regular basis, a woman with far too many shoes and drawers of underwear that, to be brutally frank, suggests a much younger woman than the clothing on the hangers. Does she buy her underwear for herself or someone else? There are men's clothes in the dressing room as well. If anything convinces me this is not my place, it is that. I might not remember where I live but I know that I live alone.

I hold one of the dresses against me and, avoiding my face, look at myself in the mirror. The dress seems drab and disappointing. This is a woman who thinks she needs to appear professional at all times. I try on a pair of jeans but they are too big around the waist. I pull on a jumper but it swamps me and I'm certain is not my style. In the ensuite, I check the toiletries, none of them brands I know. (Though, to be fair, could I name any others?) Then the big test. Her lipstick. A dark, purply red. I spread it across my lips. It is not a colour I would choose in a hundred years: her taste is so conservative. I find a tissue and wipe it off.

When I join the others in the lounge room, I can tell they think the worst. Do they think I'm doing this deliberately? That I'm being impudent by choice?

Donis suggests we have a gin and tonic. It seems such a liberty to take in someone else's apartment, but I keep my mouth buttoned shut. I sense that Donis needs a drink more than anyone. Ming Zu worries I shouldn't be drinking so soon after the accident, but Donis insists we will only have one and convinces her it might even help. I suppose endless suggestion and nagging hasn't broken my will, so let's try alcohol and go for broke.

The taste at least is familiar. Just enough bitterness in the tonic to balance the gin and the right amount of lime and ice. But if this is my apartment, where did the fresh limes come from if I haven't been here for months? I so want to ask the question but don't want to deal with the blowback.

'So, it's not your apartment, Jane?' Donis asks with an edge of impatience.

'Sorry.'

'Can we at least agree it *is* your apartment and the problem is you don't remember?'

Even Ming Zu seems shocked by that. The beautiful man is becoming a bully.

'The doctor warned it was a risk coming here, so soon after Jane's recovery. We need to be gentle, Tim.' At least she understands.

Donis finishes his drink and pours himself another. 'She needs our guidance. This pussyfooting isn't helping anyone. Least of all Jane.'

'Oh, shock therapy now,' I say with a grin. I am not going to sit here in silence.

'Do you want my assessment, Jane, for what it's worth?'

From a cello player? Probably not, but I get the feeling I'm about to hear it.

'You've been in a terrible accident. We all thought you were going to die. But thank God you didn't and you're here with us and well on the road to recovery. But . . .'

Come on, pretty boy. Cut to the chase.

'You're giving in to paranoia. Not that I'm saying your paranoia isn't real, but a little belief in your friends might help. Do you really think we're against you?'

'Tim, I don't think we're qualified,' interrupts Ming Zu.

But Donis is not to be stopped. 'Can't you take some things on trust? You are at last beginning to remember and I am sure we can hasten the process. This is too much for you to face on your own. You need us – even if you think you don't.'

'Where did the fresh limes come from?'

'What . . . ?'

There, that's set him back on his heels. 'If this is my apartment,' I continue, 'and I haven't been here for months, how are there fresh limes in the fruit bowl?'

'Because I put them there. I live here as well.'

The words wind me like a blow to the solar plexus. My unsteadiness returns and Ming Zu helps me to a chair and fetches a glass of water. It's distressing enough that I can't remember where I live; even more disturbing that I confused my physical appearance with that of a friend. But is Donis now suggesting that he and I actually live together?

'Are we flatmates?' I ask, regretting the words as soon as I say them. I can see how hurtful and cutting they are.

'I need to go for a walk,' says Donis and heads for the door.

Nothing is said for a long time. Ming Zu waits, fighting back her tears, patient until I'm ready to speak.

When something takes your memory away, the void is all you've got. And as illogical as it sounds, the emptiness feels precious, as if it's something that needs to be guarded and conserved. It feels like a sacred place only the owner should control. While it craves to be filled, you know it's vulnerable to suggestion. I have tried to hang onto this thought and maintain the courage to wait until recall – my recall – returns unaided. But if memory won't return by itself, is it so wrong to rely on others for help?

'Is this my apartment?' I ask quietly.

'Yes, Jane, it is.'

'And you're Elizabeth?'

'Yes. One of your closest friends.'

'So, you wouldn't lie to me?'

'No, I wouldn't.'

'Do I live here with Donis? With Tim?'

'Yes. Well, some of the time. He's kept his apartment as well. As you always say, you both like your independence.'

'Are we in some kind of relationship?'

'Yes.'

'An intimate relationship?'

'More or less. You're a private person, Jane. It's not something you discuss. But you've been going out together for two years.'

'How did we meet?'

'You've known Tim forever. Wasn't he Ben's best friend?'

'Ben?'

'Your former partner. Zoe's father.'

'Oh, yes. And what happened to him again?'

'He was shot. As he sat beside you in your car. I'm glad you don't remember that.' Elizabeth is crying freely now, but they seem to be tears of relief, not pity.

Is it because I'm listening at last?

Tim returns from his walk and apologises. He knows he was out of line, but I thank him for what he said. It has given me a lot to think about.

I remember the doctor saying that as well as memory loss there could be psychological barriers that need to be negotiated. Is one of those barriers the death of my former partner? Have

I even processed that properly? And if loss of memory is a form of self-protection, am I ready for it to return?

I need to read about forensic psychiatry and see if that helps. Working with the police does seem familiar and it would explain those dinner parties in the big white room. It may even explain Robert Millard.

Tim wants to take me to see someone called Peter Debreceny. Apparently, that's where I was on the night of the accident. Tim was away on tour with the orchestra and I went to Peter's alone. Peter's a Crown prosecutor and from what I had said to Tim beforehand, I needed to see him for something to do with work.

Is it worth the risk? Is the new, trusting Jane ready to jump off the cliff? What's the worst that can happen? *No, don't ask yourself that. Not with your overactive imagination. Not with an enemy out there in the shadows.*

8.

It takes another week to line up everything and get Doctor Zhou's permission. (I don't call him Doctor Two-Bob anymore: it's part of my new resolve.) Tim is still affected by my inability to relate to him personally. I am polite, of course, but intimacy is not something you can fake. His hugs still feel intrusive, like a stranger's, which may be worse for him than me. I'm sure he feels he is being cancelled, but all my friends feel that. Nothing of my recent past has any reality and not much before that either. If suspicion was holding me back before, am I now allowing people to guide me? The doctor thinks my shift in attitude could hasten my recovery. It's a leap of faith but a risk I'm prepared to take.

As Tim parks his car across the road from Peter's house in Richmond, I search for any detail I might have seen before: the broad expanse of the well-lit road; the house with its high defensive walls; the big brass numbers on the gate and its integrated security system. But it is just another house in another street. The lack of a familiar reference is disturbing. Memory is something you take for granted until it isn't there. How long must I continue to drift in uncharted seas?

Peter Debreceny greets us with apprehension. He's been warned I may not remember who he is. He searches my face for some evidence of recognition and I try to be reassuring. But he can't pretend his shock away.

Tim thanks Peter for having me back and helping me 'retrace my steps'. It's not a question of *if* my memory is returning, he explains, but *when*, though he says it with hope rather than conviction. Everyone is looking for triggers and I look around the room myself. One simple moment of recognition might be all it will take and the past will come flooding back.

Someone – Elizabeth, I imagine – suggested Peter prepare the same meal he did the last time I was here and it has an unexpected result: I recall it in every detail. Overspiced red chicken curry and homemade naan, an elaborate range of condiments and wine in crystal glasses. But as exciting as it is, the food is all I remember.

As we sit down to dinner, Peter needs to make a confession. 'I blamed myself then and I blame myself now. I should never have let you drive.'

'I wouldn't be too harsh on yourself. Jane's blood test was within the limit,' says Tim.

'But she wasn't feeling well.'

'We know that's not what caused the accident.'

The men are talking in code and it isn't helping. 'Can we start at the beginning?' I ask. 'Why did I want to see you?'

I can see Peter was prepared for some gaps in my memory, but nothing as comprehensive as this.

'You wanted to see my files on the Millard case. Don't you remember? I was concerned about the ethical implications, given we appeared on opposite sides. But the case was twenty years ago and I trusted you not to misuse them.'

Tim watches on protectively, as a good companion should. But there's a competitiveness between the two men I find distracting. Is Peter a rival for my affections?

'You're going too quickly, Peter. What do you mean, opposite sides?'

'Well, I was assisting with the prosecution and you were an expert witness for the defence.'

'Expert witness?'

'You gave evidence as to why you thought the accused – Robert Millard – had made a false confession.'

'A false confession? About what?'

'About killing his parents.'

'Skyla and Herman?'

'Yes.'

'So why did I want your files? After all this time?'

'Because Millard was found guilty and killed himself in jail. And I got the impression, well, that you may have felt responsible.'

The Millard case. It was coming back. TV celebrity chefs murdered in a double shooting, thought to be a murder–suicide. Until a sensational confession by their adult son that he had killed them both. A confession I didn't believe.

'And your files,' I ask, 'where are they now?'

'Well, that's a story in itself. After some haggling, I managed to recover them from the police. They opposed it at first. The Accident Investigation Unit had impounded them as possible evidence. But I convinced them the files belonged to the DPP and should be returned.'

'How did you explain the files being in my car?'

'I said you were writing a book about your previous cases and that you had borrowed them to check some dates. But I never really knew why you wanted them.'

'I don't understand. What would I learn from your files that I couldn't learn from my own?'

'I wondered that as well.'

'And I gave you no explanation?'

'No.'

'And you didn't ask for one?'

'You wanted my help and I was happy to give it. As a friend.'

'Is any of this helping?' asks Tim hopefully.

'Well, I am starting to remember something,' I concede.

'Then let's hope the rest will follow.'

I find it hard to share Tim's optimism and suspect his motives. I sense he wants to move all the way from a cold case from twenty years ago to the warm embrace of our relationship. Pass Go and collect $200.

'Can I ask you for your files again, Peter? I promise to take more care of them this time round.'

The men laugh at my joke and top up their glasses. I decide to sit on mine. I have a passing impression that what I drank with this meal the last time I was here was tainted in some way. But it's only a fleeting notion.

As we drive away, I don't want to talk, though Tim seems to need to. But he doesn't want to talk about the progress I've made with Peter tonight and recalling Robert Millard, he wants to talk about 'us'.

'We could go back to the apartment if you like?'

'No, thanks.'

'Spend some time there without Elizabeth. See if it feels more familiar on a second visit.'

'No. I need to go to bed.'

'A nightcap gin and tonic. There's still some limes in the bowl.'

I say nothing. I feel I'm on a first date and being pressured. I know my inability to recall our relationship must be personally affronting, but if he can't give me some space, he will push me further away. I would like to feel some human rapport, but I feel closer to Elizabeth than Tim. He's a very nice man, a beautiful man, but I like him better when he's playing the cello, when he touches me with his music.

'Let's go back to Elizabeth's,' I say. 'Maybe you could play for me again.'

He swings his car onto the service road that leads to the rowing clubs on the Yarra. He finds a deserted parking space that looks across the river towards the city, turns off the engine, kills the lights and puts his arm around me. I feel as if I'm being abducted.

'Please don't.' Now I am cringing at my behaviour, though the discomfort should be his, not mine.

He takes his arm away. 'I'm sorry.'

'Tim, this is probably worse for you. For me, it's like we're only meeting now. If we're to have a future, you can't assume any history. There's no way to put this nicely, but I don't remember where we met or who you are. Or anyone else for that matter, including Zoe, who I have known for twenty years. Can you imagine how that feels?'

'I'm sorry.'

'The only way this is going to work is if we treat each moment for what it is. Without expectations or assumptions.

I have no shared past with you that I remember. Can you understand that?'

'I'm sorry.'

'And stop saying you're sorry.'

'I wish I could help you.'

'I will feel normal again one day. And we will get our old life back. Maybe. But right now, I want you to take me to Elizabeth's and play your cello until I fall asleep. Can you do that for me?'

He looks at me with his beautiful eyes and smiles his understanding. As he starts the car, I can sense his connection to me though I can't find my feelings for him. And, worse, I wonder if I can be bothered. Be bothered with friends, with other people's needs, with the burden of being intimate – with Tim or anyone else.

The accident has shattered me, the small fragments of what I remember my only comfort.

Robert Millard holds out his hand, and he seems my only way back.

9.

The police had been wanting to speak to me ever since the accident. Doctor Zhou had informed them that I had no memory of what happened but, being police officers, they needed to confirm that for themselves. The doctor organises a room at the hospital where the interview can take place and makes sure I understand that I could end it at any time. On the one hand, given the state of my recovery, it seems premature to be talking to the police at all. Yet on the other, the good doctor thinks the process could be helpful and that their formal questioning might help unblock some of the events of that night. Still Doctor Two-Bob.

Arrangements are made to hold the interview after my monthly appointment and as we gather around a conference table, the detectives make their introductions. Senior Sergeant Tony Poulos does his best to keep things informal, but with Detective Nena Abbas writing down everything I say, it's clear they aren't here for a chat.

'So, what do you remember about the accident?' Poulos begins.

'Nothing. I only know what I've been told.'

'What was the last clear memory you have – before the accident?'

'Probably a double murder.'

'I'm sorry . . .'

'My last clear memory, sergeant, is of an event that happened twenty years ago.'

'In which you were involved as a forensic psychiatrist?'

'I've been told that's the role I played.'

'I don't understand.'

'I remember the case. But I'm only learning now what an f.p. does. I don't remember being that person.'

'Tell me about the murders?'

'They were celebrity chefs. On television . . .'

'Skyla and Herman. The *Top Cook* show?' Abbas says, looking up from her notepad.

'That's the one.'

Poulos gives her a look. It isn't her role to prompt me.

'It was big news when I was a kid,' Abbas explains.

'And why do you think it's that particular case you're remembering?' Poulos asks.

'I have no idea.'

'Well, it must have been on your mind for some reason.'

'I'm sure you're right, sergeant.'

'But you can't explain why?'

'Unfortunately.'

'Had something happened recently? To make you revisit these murders?'

'Probably.'

'But you can't remember what that may have been?'

'No.'

'The accident itself. Do you have any recall?'

'No.'

'Or where you were that night?'

'No. Though I have recently restaged the evening.'

'Why was that?'

'Friends thought it might help me remember.'

'And did it?'

'I remembered the meal.'

'If this had been a routine car accident, you know we wouldn't be here?'

'No. I don't know that, having never been in a serious accident. That I remember.'

'You answer your questions in a particular way, Doctor Halifax. Like you're in court.'

'Must be habit.'

'There's no need to be defensive.'

'I am not being defensive, sergeant. I genuinely don't remember. Of course, I want to help you. Why would I not? Perhaps if you told me what you know about the accident.'

Poulos hesitates. Cops like asking questions, not answering them. Unless it's to their advantage. 'We know the other car involved but are yet to establish who the driver was. It was stolen in Ringwood about an hour before the incident and found abandoned and burned out afterwards.'

Stolen and burned out. Like criminals would do.

The detectives are watching me closely for my reaction.

'Are you suggesting the accident might not have been an accident at all?' I ask.

'It's possible. Do you remember receiving any threats or warnings?'

'No.'

'Or working on a case where people may have wished you harm?'

'No. I don't remember anything.'

'Can I ask you about Paul Bathgate?' asks Poulos.

'Who?'

'The name doesn't mean anything to you?'

'Sorry.'

'You took out a PSIO against him six months ago.'

A Personal Safety Intervention Order. That sounds serious.

Events were a blur but my occupation at least is beginning to force its way back. I had jokingly accused Tim of resorting to shock therapy, but this interview is achieving just that. I am the forensic psychiatrist they tell me I am. I am trained in matters of the human mind. I understand that physical injury to the brain may be one reason why people don't remember events but that psychological trauma can be another, that people block out things sometimes for self-protection. Is that what is happening to me?

I suddenly feel a oneness with Doctor Zhou. That his honorific of 'Doctor Halifax', which I had treated as his little joke, may in fact be deserved. The medical world is beginning to feel familiar and the world of the police as well. As is the legal world of Peter Debreceny. Has my resistance been deliberate, an avoidance of some terrible truth? Did I know someone was trying to kill me? Who wouldn't want to misremember that?

'Is that something you recall?'

'Maybe there's been a mistake . . .'

Abbas pushes a court-certified document across the table. 'Paul Bathgate: Respondent. Jane Halifax: Protected Person.' It didn't leave much room for error.

'I am sorry, sergeant, I have no idea who he is.'

'You assessed Bathgate regarding a forthcoming trial and he was apparently unhappy with your conclusions. He kept sending you emails and phoning you at home and there was evidence he was stalking you as well.'

'Have you talked to him?'

'Yes, of course. And warned him we would come down hard if he breached the PSIO. But he has an alibi for the night of the accident.'

'I wish I could help you, sergeant. I wish I could help myself. Can I ask you a question?'

'Yes, of course,' says Poulos.

'When I was in hospital after the accident, I had the feeling I was under police protection. Was I?'

'As a precaution, yes, you were.'

'But not anymore?'

'We're still keeping an eye on you. Until we have a better idea of what happened.'

'Well, that's a relief,' I say. 'The people I'm staying with thought there was a policeman watching the house.'

The detectives shuffle a glance at each other.

'When I say we're keeping an eye on you,' says Poulos, 'there's no single person who'd be doing that. If someone's hanging around outside, it won't be one of us. But we'll look into it, doctor. And increase our surveillance. Thanks for letting us know.'

The detectives stand and give me their cards.

'We'll continue this when you're feeling better,' Poulos says. 'Please phone if you remember anything else.'

After the interview, Doctor Zhou asks how I'm feeling.

'Worried. But maybe in a good way. I think I may have turned a corner. Like I want to go back to the apartment and give it a second shot. To embrace the idea of Jane Halifax f.p. instead of not wanting to face it.'

'Don't take on too much too quickly.'

'Why do you think I wanted to see myself as my friend Virginia?'

'I'm a surgeon. It's not my area. I slice up brains, take things out. I don't pretend to understand the mind. You'll come up with a better answer than me. Why do *you* think you made that confusion?'

'Because I don't want to be who I am? Because I think I might be in danger.'

'You mustn't be on your own at the moment, Jane. Things are still very raw.'

'You don't need to worry about self-harm,' I assure him.

'No. But I think the place you are in right now must be terribly lonely.'

Lonely. Desolate would be a better description, though not as desolate as before. I think I can see a path at last, a way out through the fog. A preparedness to embrace things rather than resist them, a readiness to accept the evidence around me.

There's a certain comfort in playing with the ghosts and spectres of my dreams, but I need to live in the real world, even one in which people wish me harm. For bad though it is to have enemies, it is far worse to have them and not know who they are.

10.

I am in the car with Tim, though my name for him suits him better. He's not as youthful as Adonis might imply, but there is something mesmeric about his slender body and flawless skin. I have this sense I have seen him naked – though not in a sexual setting – and I wonder why this might be.

I have agreed to go back to the apartment and he's on his best behaviour, attentive to my needs and unhurried about his. Who wouldn't want a man like that in their life? Except I don't want a carer, I want a companion. Is it my resentment about being dependent that's stopping me from letting him in? Am I the classic wounded patient pushing away those I depend on the most?

As Tim puts flowers in a vase and unpacks the food he's bought for lunch, I try to get reacquainted with my apartment. I am trying to accept that this is where I live but it would be nice to find some proof.

I head through to the study and sit down at the desk. I open a notebook and read the words but nothing seems familiar. I copy a sentence onto a sheet of paper but my handwriting is scratchy and uncertain; probably the result of the accident. I open the diary and go through the entries and stop again at

'Luna'. There's no contact number or anything to explain why the name is there.

I look along the files on the shelf above the desk and stop at the only name that registers: Bathgate. I take down the file and open it with trepidation – there it is, in black and white: *Psychological Assessment of Paul Raymond Bathgate* by Jane Halifax, RANZCP.

My eyes race through the document in the hope that the flood gates will open, that this detailed account of someone's psychological profile will be instantly familiar, that the past will become the present and that my memory will be whole again.

I cannot recall a single word.

The report states that Bathgate was facing domestic violence charges brought by Laura Jean Semple, which he was seeking to have dismissed under the Mental Health Act. His defence claimed he was suffering from bipolar II or, in the alternative, attention deficit or borderline personality disorders. Historically, there had been a number of women involved, all of whom thought they were in an exclusive relationship with the accused. None of them had suffered physical violence but their torment at Bathgate's hands had been relentless. Constantly accused of infidelity and betrayal, Bathgate harassed them with an avalanche of texts and emails, many of them sexually explicit. He controlled them with tantrums and threats to kill himself. He shouted and cried and broke furniture. He would rage at perceived slights, demand to know their movements and had trackers placed in their cars and mobiles so he could find them at any time. He stalked them, intimidated them, broke protection orders on multiple occasions and isolated them from family and friends. His was a textbook case of coercive control, but he wasn't suffering from manic depression or any other mental disorder. Bathgate was an alcoholic. Charming, energetic and outgoing one moment, he could turn into a slavering monster at the flick of a switch. A former Australian Rules Football star, he had recently lost his job as a commentator and his drinking was no longer a secret. But bipolar II he was not, as the assessment made crystal clear.

I close the file, my anxieties running ahead in panic mode. Is this the person who had been lurking outside Elizabeth's house, who her husband had talked to, who had pretended to be interested in buying the house along the road? Is this the reason for the police surveillance following the accident, the person the police had confirmed was not one of theirs? Is this my enemy I can't recall?

It was less distressing when I thought everyone was conspiring against me, when I thought I looked like Virginia. But now I have no point of reference, no relationships, no anchors to tether my sanity. I have lost my past and my present has no context. I am surrounded by evidence of a life I have no memory of having lived. My dread is impossible to describe. I felt more protected when I had delusions. Maybe that's what delusions are for.

As we sit down to lunch I can't explain any of this to Tim. He'd think I should be committed.

'How did you go?' he asks.

'I'm trying, Tim. Still trying.'

'Is this room any more familiar?'

'Apart from that dreadful rug on the floor, it looks like lots of rooms. Pleasant and unremarkable.'

Tim looks at me with a twisted grin. 'Yeah, well, the rug is actually mine.'

'What's it doing here?' It helps it's not mine. I was beginning to doubt my taste.'

'With all this rain we've been having, the roof of my apartment sprang a leak. Until I get it fixed, I've got this bucket in the middle of the floor, so I brought it here where it wouldn't be damaged.' He waited for a moment then made another confession. 'I rather like it.'

'Tim. I'm sorry, it's awful. And that's not something you often say about a rug. Did it look any good at your place?'

'Well, I thought it did. Anything else?' he says, eager to move on.

'I don't fit the clothes in the bedroom, but I realise I've lost a lot of weight. And I've never suited dark lipsticks, so I'm not sure what possessed me to buy that one on the dresser.'

Tim looks at me as if I am being difficult.

'I would just like to bond with something,' I say. 'A favourite piece of art. A chair I've sat in before.'

'But you have. In all of them.'

'A chair I *remember* sitting in.'

Even an enemy I remember would be less terrifying than this.

We hardly say a word as Tim drives me back to Elizabeth's. The distance between us has become a chasm. I have brought the notebook from the apartment and sit in Elizabeth's garden, trying again to replicate my handwriting. But the task seems hopeless, a disquieting reminder of how far my recovery has to go.

Elizabeth comes out from the house to inform me I have a visitor. 'It's that nice young woman from the hospital. The one with the blue hair.'

'I don't think I'm up to it,' I say, determined to struggle on with my self-imposed challenge.

But Elizabeth thinks a break might be helpful. 'I'll go get her and make some tea. She doesn't have to stay for long.'

Aware of my condition, the young woman approaches me with caution. She is in her late twenties, I think, and is carrying a bunch of flowers. It is impossible not to look at the ring through her nose. If one wanted to increase the chances of bacterial infection, one could not choose a better site. The whiteness of her skin and the blue of her hair makes me think of the North Melbourne Shinboners. Is that Aussie Rules team another memory fragment to add to Jonah Cole and Eric Ringer?

'How are you, Doctor Halifax? I'm grateful for your time.' Which seems less what a hospital visitor might say than someone who wants a favour.

'You will have to forgive me,' I say. 'But I have no idea who you are.'

'That's all right,' she answers. 'I know about the accident. It must have been awful. Did you think you were going to die?'

'No. But others did. You came to see me at the hospital?'

'Yes.'

'So how did you know to come here?'

'I told them I had these flowers to deliver and they gave me this address.' She hands me the arrangement of native flowers and foliage wrapped in greaseproof paper. They look as if they've been stolen from somebody's garden.

'That's very thoughtful,' I say, 'but I'm not sure the hospital should have given you that information.' Which sounds like something a cop might say. Or a lawyer. Or someone who works with cops or lawyers, like a forensic psychiatrist. 'Can you tell me your name?'

'I'm sorry. I thought you knew. I'm Luna.'

The name in the diary, the hospital visitor I thought was a dream.

Elizabeth arrives with the tea but I suggest we take it inside. I need time to think, time to force myself to remember.

As we settle in the lounge, Luna pours the tea. My pulse is racing.

'You'll have to start at the beginning, Luna. And remind me how we met.'

'Through a mutual friend. A neighbour of yours when you lived in Brighton, Jim Vecera – do you remember?'

'Not really,' I confess, 'but go on.'

'Well, he gave me your mobile number and you agreed to meet for coffee. And then to help me find my father. My real father, that is, as opposed to the one I grew up believing was mine.'

'And how was I going to do that?'

'By going back through your files and seeing what you could find.'

'My files on what?'

'On my brother's case. You were involved in his trial.'

'And forgive me, Luna, but what's your brother's name?' I ask, sensing what she is going to say even before she says it.

'Well, it's not his real name of course, but you would have known him as Robert Millard.'

Robert Millard, the only person in the empty sea of my past that has any semblance of having existed, along with his parents, Skyla and Herman, their cooking show, their house with the big white room, and Robert's little sister, who I now know as Luna, all grown up and seated before me. Is my memory loss linked to the physical trauma of the accident or to something more psychologically profound? Is the accident – which I have discovered from the police was probably not an accident at all – the barrier I'm unable to penetrate? Or is it the realisation that somebody wants me dead?

'Luna, I want you to tell me about the meetings we had. All of them. When and where they occurred, and what happened, down to the smallest detail.'

And so she recounts everything that happened. Our first meeting at a coffee bar on South Bank. Our second at 'my office at the university after I had been through my files'. (It would take a while for me to make any sense of that). And a third scheduled meeting that never happened, the one in my diary, two days after the accident.

Luna had come to me because she was convinced that Herman wasn't her real father, that she was the result of a liaison Skyla had had with someone else. My files were silent on the matter and I had asked Peter Debreceny if I could look at his to see if the prosecution had uncovered anything on the matter. It was never directly relevant to Robert's trial, so had never been discussed in court, but Luna was insistent that Robert knew the truth and she wanted to discover if he had said anything about it when he was interviewed by the police.

That I remembered nothing of my meetings with Luna was unsurprising, but Robert's trial was coming back. The violent double murder, the false confession, the guilty verdict against the evidence and his tragic suicide in prison.

Whether the theory of the index cards is mine or Doctor Zhou's is immaterial. I am recalling more and more of Robert Millard's case. And I am invested in it completely.

PART THREE

February 2003

Tiger was a naughty dog and Minx a naughty cat,
Only goldfish can be trusted to stay where they are at.
But others go a-roaming, it's in their natures, see,
To be naughty every moment – just like you and me.

11.

The Melbourne CBD was in gridlock and there was no way I was going to make my 5 pm appointment. The rally hadn't yet departed from the State Library to head along Swanston Street to Federation Square and already the side streets were crammed with demonstrators waiting to join the march. The organisers had cleverly suggested that secondary school students might like to take the afternoon off and join them – a move heavily criticised by those opposed to the demonstration – but thousands of students had come and their early arrival had inspired everyone.

Vincenzo Rinaldi's office was in William Street, which should have been an easy walk from my rooms in Lonsdale Street, but the crowds were both impenetrable and strangely alluring. I too was against the war in Iraq. George Bush the Second and his feeble Coalition of the Willing had based their case on weapons of mass destruction that nobody thought were real. Saddam Hussein may well be a murderous tyrant, but he wasn't behind the attack on the World Trade Center. Didn't anyone read the newspapers? Hans Blix, the highly respected Head of the UN Verification Commission, had pleaded for more time and proof and why wouldn't they want to give him that? I decided to join there and then, and took my mobile out of my handbag.

'Vince, it's Jane. I'm going to be late. The crowds down here are impossible. Why don't we reschedule to Monday?'

'No, get here when you can. It's Friday night and I'll be in the bar at chambers. Phone me when you're downstairs and I'll buzz you up. I need to brief you with a view to seeing my client tomorrow if poss. So, keep your head down and battle on through. And don't let the lefties win.'

Rinaldi was a top criminal lawyer and, however much I disagreed with his views on politics, I was one of his favourite consultants and did not want to let him down. He had a habit of attracting high-profile cases, which were inevitably the most rewarding, and I knew he wouldn't involve me unless he had a particularly challenging problem.

So on I pressed through the gathering crowd, trying to suppress the feeling I was moving in the wrong direction. The throng had my sympathies if not my physical presence, though I knew the numbers in any demonstration would be crucial in affecting public opinion. But, once again, work wins out ahead of personal desire. I wonder how often I'm guilty of that.

I'd been to Rinaldi's chambers across the road from the County Court on multiple occasions but never to the private bar on the fifth floor. It was packed. Most people were blaming the demonstration for preventing them from heading home, though I suspected they found an appropriate excuse every week. Queen's and Senior Counsel rubbed their privileged shoulders with prominent instructing solicitors and I had to admit I was flattered by the number of people who said hello.

An expert witness is highly dependent on perception as well as performance and this wasn't a bad place to be seen. But the noise was intrusive, so Rinaldi and I took our glasses with us to his chambers.

'What can you tell me about false confession?' Rinaldi began.

'How long have you got? It will take more than one of these,' I responded, holding up my glass of the excellent red. 'Not that I can stay for more than one. It's Valentine's Day after all.'

'Oh, shit. Is it? Too late for flowers, I suspect. Or a restaurant booking. It will have to be chocolates. Again.'

I imagined Rinaldi's wife, probably his second, somewhere in an inner city mansion, juggling her young kids and Rinaldi's difficult teenagers from his first marriage while she weighed the benefits of a bountiful income against the absence of its provider – but it was only an intelligent guess.

'Robert Millard. Accused of murdering his parents. A crime to which he initially confessed before changing his mind and insisting it was a murder–suicide and he simply came across the bodies and the gun.'

'Which is presumably covered with his fingerprints because he picked it up?'

'Got it in one. So, I need to get rid of the false confession.'

'Whichever one it is.' I could tell Rinaldi didn't like my answer. 'You prefer the murder–suicide version?'

'It's the easier one to defend.'

'Provided I can make the confession go away.'

'So, tell me. Why do people make false confessions? The single-glass-of-pinot version.'

'Because they're protecting someone else. Because they feel responsible. Because they know they are the reason it happened.'

'I'm going to ask that no plea is taken before a full psychiatric assessment.'

'Which you want me to do this weekend?'

'Jane, I'm sorry. But I wouldn't ask if there was any alternative.'

Of course he would. He's a Senior Counsel.

'Vince, at best it will be preliminary. Very preliminary. Without knowing anything, it already sounds complex. A false confession? This is tip-of-the-iceberg time.'

'I'm here all day on Sunday, prepping witnesses for next week's case. You can phone me at any time. I'll take the call.' Which he managed to make sound like a sacrifice.

Poor second wife, or long-suffering first. How many years? How many boxes of chocolates?

But I should have been worrying less about Rinaldi's situation and more about my own.

I got to Ben's on time, so the evening at least was intact. But I had to find a way of explaining why I wouldn't be joining him and Zoe for the weekend with friends at Torquay. His Valentine was well advanced on the stove: a man who can cook can give no better present. Unlike his, I hadn't made mine myself, but hopefully it was equally as thoughtful.

Ben had given Zoe her bath and she was waiting excitedly in her pyjamas for me to read her a story and put her to bed. Ben and I had been going out for almost a year, the first relationship I had had in some time that wasn't with a cop or a lawyer, which I hoped was a sign of maturity. Ben was in the music business: a session musician and maker of fine guitars; he counted Mark Knopfler and Eric Clapton among his clients, and was something of a celebrity himself. The rock 'n' roll world had been great for me – a welcome escape from the intensity of forensic science – and the weekend at Torquay would be one long party and jamming session between swims in the surf. Only a party-pooper would find a way to avoid it.

I read Zoe a story from her favourite book and told her another, as I usually did, made up on the spot. Telling her to close her eyes and hold onto my thumbs like the controls of a spaceship, I counted down from ten to blast off and shook her vigorously as we lifted up through the g-forces to a world beyond the stars. I never quite knew where we were going, but we always got there in the end. And safely back to earth. An amandapan tree was usually involved, which took on increasingly magical powers. Zoe loved it – and so did I – though Ben thought it was not the way to put a six-year-old to bed and only served to hype her up. He was probably right, as she would often re-emerge, asking for more until Ben finally had to do the task himself. Well, a girlfriend couldn't be good at everything.

Ben's seafood paella was wonderful: proper bomba rice (God knows where he found that in Melbourne) unstirred as much as possible so it could caramelise on the bottom, and seasoned with kosher salt. The wine was Spanish. He had chosen a tempranillo where I would have gone for a verdejo, but who was I to quibble when I couldn't put a six-year-old to bed?

After dinner I gave him my Valentine, a hei matau, a Maori pendant carved in the shape of a fish hook.

'Greenstone?' he guessed.

'We call it pounamu. But yes, it's jade from the west coast of the South Island. It represents strength and prosperity. And safety when travelling over water.'

'Jane. I don't know what to say. It's beautiful.'

'And I can't come away this weekend. Sorry.' After so much careful rehearsal, I ended up blurting it out.

'Oh. That's a surprise. But it's still a very beautiful pendant. Work, I suppose?'

'Isn't it always?'

'Unless you take the uni job.'

Our romantic Valentine's dinner was not going the way I'd hoped. Why hadn't I had the courage to enjoy the evening and tell him my bad news in the morning before we left? I could have faked a last-minute call.

The uni job was Professor of Forensic Psychiatry at Melbourne University. It was an honour to have been offered the position without the need to apply and Ben couldn't understand why I wasn't snapping it up. It would have fitted into our complicated lives much easier than the demands of private practice, or more correctly, fitted in easier with Ben's complicated life, both here and overseas. But I wasn't ready to make that decision or, indeed, such an implied commitment to him. It had taken nine hard years of graft to build my reputation as an f.p. and I was not about to give it up until I had thought through the ramifications. I was flattered to be asked – of course I was – but was teaching the right place for me? I was a woman of action and liked being at the rock face. It was where I performed at my best, under pressure, or at least that's where my thinking was taking me. Or was it to cover a fear of commitment? At thirty-nine, I was taking my time.

Somehow I rescued the evening, changed the subject and initiated the intimacy both of us were craving. I'd be there to make breakfast in the morning and see them off and tell them

I would rather be with them at the beach. Only part of me wasn't telling the truth.

I understand why crime fiction is such a popular genre. The criminal mind can become an addiction, an insight into aberrant behaviour in others, and sometimes, by reflection, in ourselves. Most people, given the choice, would choose the beach and a weekend of rock 'n' roll. So why was I checking myself in to the Melbourne Remand Centre with a such a heightened sense of anticipation?

Robert Millard was twenty years old and, like most young people who hadn't experiencing jail before, exuded a mixture of fear and bravado.

'Hello, Robert. I'm Doctor Jane Halifax.'

'Can you get me out of here?'

'Well, that's not really up to me. I'm here to make an assessment. You'll need to discuss that with Mr Rinaldi.'

'Who?'

'Your barrister.'

'I haven't met him yet. Only the solicitor. He'd better be as good as they say he is.'

Good enough to send others to do the heavy lifting while he had other things to do that weekend. 'There's some confusion about your name, Robert. They have you listed as Robert Van Meulenbelt.'

'I changed it to Millard by deed poll, but nobody takes any notice. When you have parents as famous as mine are, you're branded with their name for life.' Said without emotion, he could have been referring to strangers.

'Since you've mentioned your parents, maybe you could tell me what happened?'

'Well, what can I say? I came home, found the bodies. And the gun – which I stupidly picked up. God knows why. To put it somewhere safe, I suppose. My father had just shot my mother then turned the gun on himself. I guess I wasn't thinking straight. Maybe for a moment, I thought I would use it too.'

'On yourself?'

'For a fleeting moment. Until I thought of Luna.'

'Luna?'

'My little sister. I guess I couldn't do it to her. I'm all she's got and I'm sure she's terrified. You've got to get me out of here.'

'Where's Luna now?'

'With our grandparents. But they'll be no use to her. They'll be in shock.'

'As I'm sure everyone is.'

Robert could see I was watching him closely. Was he in shock as well?

'So, you made a statement to the police?' I asked.

'Two statements to the police. One in a state of madness followed by one closer to the truth.' I had read them both but wanted to hear it from him.

'And in the first statement you confessed to killing your parents?'

'Yes.'

'Can you tell me why?'

'Because the police are fools. They took what I said hook, line and sinker. I couldn't believe how gullible they were.'

'Did the police pressure you to make a statement, Robert?'

'No.'

'So, I'm not sure you can blame them for what you said.'

'I knew that I was innocent, Jane. I knew the truth would protect me. I guess I just got carried away.'

'Do you often tell fanciful stories, Robert?'

'You might say that.'

'And do you know why you do this?'

'Because it makes me laugh.'

'And after discovering your parents' bodies – brutally dead from gunshot wounds – laughing is what you wanted to do?'

'Can we do the analysis stuff some other time? Just get me out of this fucking place!'

I had encountered fabulists before and their motives were complex. Usually it was a confluence of not wanting to face reality and a desire to escape to somewhere safe. But it was clear from our very first meeting that Robert Millard's relationship with his parents would be the key to everything.

12.

It was late afternoon on Sunday when Rinaldi had finished prepping his witnesses for the week ahead and was ready to see me. I got the feeling he'd been there most of the weekend.

'So how was Valentine's Day?'

'A disaster. I got breathalysed. Instead of leaving my car in the carpark and catching a cab like I usually do, I drove off in search of chocolates.'

'I hope you're not blaming me?'

'Of course I am. Late for dinner, probably a six-month suspension and no chocolates. It's commercialised nonsense anyway.'

'Is that what your wife thinks too?'

'Girlfriend. No. She was impressed I went to the trouble.'

'Then it's not all bad.'

'You haven't met my girlfriend. Do you give advice on how to get back with your wife and three unforgiving teenagers?'

'Mercifully, it's not my field. I can recommend someone if you like. But it is going to take more than chocolates. Shall we talk about Robert Millard?'

'Yes. You go first since I'm yet to meet him.'

Rinaldi's chambers were old school and plush with shelves of law reports and legal tomes. But the books were just for show; it was his associate and the solicitors who prepared the brief and did the research.

'I would describe your client as a fabulist. Literally a person who composes fables. Someone with an imagination unfettered by the laws of logic or probability who delights in telling dishonest stories – the more fanciful and elaborate the better.'

'A compulsive liar?'

'It's more complicated than that. It's usually a question of *why* the patient avoids telling the truth. Sometimes, it's just for effect. Robert admitted to being amazed at how far the police let him go.'

'They'd let him talk as much as he liked. It's in their interests.'

'Sometimes a story takes on its own momentum and you run with it until someone says stop.'

'And you think that's what happened here?'

'Well, that's Robert's version.'

'And yours?'

'I'm still on the fence.'

'The police walked him through a reconstruction. They sent me a copy. Want to see it?'

'You bet.'

Rinaldi slipped the video into a player and pressed play. Robert stood in a big white room with two dummies on the floor to represent the victims. There was a wooden rifle as well, to serve as the weapon. A group of detectives stood nearby, watching with their notebooks in hand.

'So is this how you found the bodies?' asked a senior sergeant. 'Roughly in these positions?'

'Mum was more over there. With her head towards the door.'

A female detective moved the dummy. 'More like this?'

'Yes,' said Robert without emotion. 'But the gun was closer to Dad.'

Adjustments were made again until Robert was satisfied.

'God, he looks so young,' said Rinaldi.

'He is. He's twenty. You should meet him. He can't wait to meet you as well.' I couldn't resist the opportunity.

'Okay, Robert,' said the sergeant on the video. 'If you're happy with that – go outside and come in and do everything you did when you found your parents as accurately as you can remember.'

I watch with Rinaldi as Robert goes through eleven versions of coming in and discovering the bodies and picking up the rifle – each one with little adjustments until he is satisfied he has got it right.

When the video finished, Rinaldi waited for me to speak.

'Why do so many versions?' I ask.

'I guess Robert wanted to get it right.'

'Or rehearse it until it sears itself into his brain. Do anything often enough, and it becomes its own reality.'

'Is that what you think's happening here?'

'I'm not going that far. Just allowing for the possibility. Do you have a recording of the other confession?'

'Not yet. It's still being assessed by the DPP as they consider whether they'll upgrade suspicion of murder to murder.'

'And when will you know that?'

'Before court in the morning, I hope.'

'Will you apply for bail?'

'Yes, but we probably won't get it. Not with things so fluid.'

'When do you actually get to meet your client?'

'When I know what I'm defending.'

'But it's all right for me to see him now?'

'Your assessment doesn't depend on what he's charged with, does it?'

'No.'

'And in my experience, Jane, you need time to come to a conclusion.'

'After all these years, Vince, you've been listening.'

'I hate to admit this, Jane – and my fees will not reflect it – but in a case like this, you will be far more crucial to the outcome than me.'

'I will take that as a compliment and reconsider my charges.'

'If this goes where I think it's going, I won't be putting Robert on the stand but I will certainly be putting you on.'

'So, I will need to get it right?'

'Yes, Jane. You will.'

Ben had built an electronic cello for his friend Tim de Serville. I knew Tim as someone who played bass guitar and had no idea of his background as a cello player with major orchestras. Like Ben, Tim was a session musician and an electronic cello was something he wanted to add to his repertoire. The electronics did the work but Ben had built a futuristic body inspired by the classical form. It was sculptural rather than something that enhanced the sound, but its aesthetics were superb. Tim was about to give the cello its first test run,

As I settled in to Ben's studio with a cup of lemon and ginger tea, it was hard not to stare at Tim – his features were mesmeric. His nose was large and straight and perfect from any angle, his jaw broad and strong beneath high cheekbones and dark, hooded eyes. His limbs were long and thin and instead of bending at their joints, seemed to flow as he moved. He seemed unaware of his beauty and the effect it had on others, but could he be so ingenuous? It had to be deliberate; another string to his allure.

His first notes were dramatic – something from Elgar's Cello Concerto, I thought – with some flourishes of his own. The cello is a dramatic instrument with a deep, soulful timbre, and the electronics only enhanced its effect. Ben couldn't have been more delighted and surprised. I wanted to jump up and cheer. But Tim played on, moving from classical to impro to rock with ease as he explored the range of his bow on the strings. By the end of the session, we were clapping and shouting with joy – for Ben as well as Tim.

I slipped through to the kitchen and returned with three flutes and the bottle of champagne I'd had the foresight to bring. The birth of a new instrument needed celebration. But I had work to do, so I left the men to their fine tuning and the rest of the bottle and took my glass back to my briefcase in the dining room, where the Millard file was spread out on the table.

Vincenzo Rinaldi may yet to have flexed his adversarial muscles, but his solicitors had done their homework. This wasn't the first time Robert had been in trouble with the police. Or the first time he'd been psychologically assessed. Charged with various offences since the age of sixteen for passing dud cheques and 'fraudulent misrepresentation', a clever psychologist had managed to have most of them dismissed for something she termed 'Elevated ADHD' (which seemed a hyperactive description to me) plus full reparation from an indulgent father.

But Robert's fabulism and extravagant stories were at the base of it all, each one more fanciful than those that went before: shares in a start-up a major internet company had supposedly taken an option on (sold to the parents of his schoolmates, no less); a valet-parking scam for the Arts Centre that undercut the cost of onsite parking by thirty per cent, where the valets went joyriding in the cars until the performance was over; reselling product in a parallel pyramid selling scheme that depended on buying unsold product from disgruntled participants for the cost of removing the goods; and accepting deposits for a non-existent expedition up the Sepik River to discover a lost tribe of headhunters.

Ben popped his head in through the doorway. 'We're going out for dinner. Want to come?'

'What about Zoe?'

'I'll get Alina from next door to come over. She'll only be doing homework or watching TV.'

'No. You guys go. I'll stay with Zo.'

'Come on. It's a celebration.'

'Sorry, Ben. I have to work.'

'You have to eat.'

'There'll be something in the fridge. I'll make an omelette. Go on. I'm sure you've got things to talk about.'

'It was pretty damn good, don't you think?' says Ben. 'Though it's not finished yet.'

'It was beautiful. From you both.'

The men contented themselves with the compliment and headed for the door. They'd be talking about the cello all through dinner. I was better off here with the brief.

When Ben returned two hours later, I started to pack up my bag. Tim had headed home from the restaurant and I could tell Ben was feeling amorous.

'Stay over. You can't go home now.'

'Yes, I can. I've an early meeting with the barrister before court and I don't want to be late.'

Ben deflated. 'It's happening again.'

'Pardon?'

'You're taking on a new obsession.'

'Ben. That's not fair. You work all night when you need to finish a guitar.'

'It's not the same.'

'Why not?'

'Because I don't disappear on you.'

'Ben, my clothes are at home. My makeup's at home. I didn't come prepared.'

'I wouldn't mind if there wasn't a cost to you.'

'What do you mean?'

'This work you do, Jane. These all-consuming cases on the dark side of the road. How long can you keep doing this? How long before it all adds up?'

'To what? Burnout?' It wasn't the first time he'd said it. 'I don't have the energy for this tonight, Ben.'

'If you took that job at the university . . .'

'Or that. Not now. Please?'

'I'll ring you a cab.' He flicked his mobile open and dialled.

'How was dinner?'

'Great. How was Zo?'

'Didn't hear a peep.'

'Well, you probably didn't tell her a story.'

I smiled and crossed to kiss him. He held me tightly.

'If we lived together . . .'

'Shhhh.' I put my finger on his lips. It was something else that would have to wait for another day.

13.

The original confession was damning and was not going to go away. The prosecution had upgraded the charge to double murder and, as Rinaldi had predicted, bail had been refused. I had allocated all morning for this session – or as long as Robert could handle. We were literally fighting for his freedom.

Robert was now in a single cell, under protection and suicide watch. With all the interview rooms booked for shorter sessions, the remand centre had let me use a staff recreation room and Robert was taking full advantage of the extra space. As he moved aimlessly between the table-tennis table and the kitchenette, I watched as he toyed with the paddle and ball, made tea he never drank and searched for biscuits that weren't there.

'Have you met your barrister yet?'

'Yes. He looks expensive. Not expensive enough to get bail . . .'

'Well, that was always going to be problematic. Once they reverted to your first confession.'

'Or make that go away. That's two strikes already.'

'Let's start with your change of name by deed poll. Can you talk me through that again?'

'You've obviously never met my parents. They were both the best and worst thing that ever happened to me. Always on television, constantly in the papers. It was impossible to escape the label.'

'Did the name change help?'

'No. Nobody ever used it. Apart from me.'

'Why was being your parents' son so awful?'

'They were larger than life on every level. Famous, infamous, careless, overweening.'

'That's a word you don't hear very often.'

'They gave me a good education, if nothing else. And for a couple of cooks, they gave me a love of the arts.'

'Describe your childhood?'

'Privileged, indulgent, unsupervised. Endless parties with celebrities and all sorts of shady characters. It was very exciting.'

'Boundaries?'

'What are those? My parents never said "no". Just "stay out of trouble".' Robert stopped his fidgeting and at last sat down with me. 'What's going to happen to me, Jane?'

'That depends on a number of things. Beginning with whether you killed your parents.' It was a deliberately loaded question, but I wouldn't be the last person to ask it.

'I didn't.'

'Then let's start with your confession.'

'Haven't we been through this already?'

'Apart from the police giving you all the rope you wanted, why did you feel the need to say what you did?'

'Because I can't lie straight in bed, Jane. Because I find the truth banal. Because I like leading people up the garden path to all the skeletons in the shed.'

'And what skeletons are they?'

'All the stuff nobody talks about. Like how morally loose my parents were.'

'And how did you feel about that?'

'I detested it.'

'Enough to kill them?'

'Only in my dreams.'

Robert liked to talk – and he talked too much. The police would have had a field day. But a fabulist is not only performing for his audience, leading them on outrageously and delighting in every step on the way; he is, more than anything, entertaining himself.

'We need some safe words. So I know when you're telling stories and when you're telling the truth.'

'*Safe words*, Jane. I didn't realise it was that sort of relationship.'

'Which is a good example. You know what this relationship is. So why the need to joke?'

'Sorry.'

'This is not a joking matter, Robert. We get this wrong and you will go to jail for the best years of your adult life.'

'Sorry.'

'Shall we use "sorry" as our safe word? I don't have time for bullshit, and more importantly, neither do you. When I want to know if you're telling tales or not, I'm going to say "sorry". And you're going to give me the truth. You may well find this amusing, Robert, but I don't. And neither will the jury. If I can achieve only one thing before we go to court, it will be to stop you being so fucking self-indulgent.'

'Well, that's not very nice.'

'Sorry.'

'I hear you. You're right. I'm sorry.'

'Good. Now, let's start with your first encounters with the police. And how your parents reacted.'

For the next two hours, we talked through his teenage years and where things had begun to go wrong. Gone was the flippancy and easy one-liners as Robert stuck, as far as I could tell, to the truth. One could only wonder if the course of events might have been different if his parents had taken a firmer hand. Or his psychologist had not indulged him with easy-out labels like 'Elevated ADHD'. What he probably needed was what he told me his exasperated teachers had recommended in their many reports: a well-directed kick up the arse. Not that his condition could be written off as bad behaviour. But even mental health clients respond to limits, no-goes and boundaries. The 'sorry' had given Robert and me a way to move forward.

But how can you tell when a liar is telling the truth? Everything Robert had told me would have to be corroborated. He was his own unreliable witness. His parents were dead and there would not be much his eight-year-old sister would be able to verify.

The range of possibilities was wide. From those with a pathological condition to fabulists who live in a world where they like the truth to be blurred; from compulsive liars to grandiose narcissists; from fabricators who only want to bolster their self-esteem to those with an acquired brain injury; from intentional dissimulators who are trying to conceal genuine symptoms of a psychiatric condition to those who lie on principle. Fibbers, frauds, fakers, phoneys and liars come in many and varied colours.

I knew research had shown that compulsive deception could be embedded in the structure of the brain. People who habitually lie and cheat appear to have much more white matter in the prefrontal cortex than normal people. The white matter speeds communication between neurons. In one study I read, the compulsive liars in the control group had twenty-six per cent more white matter and fifteen per cent less grey matter than the non-liars. The difference may affect the portion of the brain that enables people to feel remorse, learn moral behaviour and plan complex strategies. Those with more white matter may be more adept at the complex neural networking that underlies deceit. Lying is cognitively complex and is certainly more difficult than telling the truth. It's hard work for most people, and a liar's brain may be better equipped to handle it.

But none of this was going to help Robert or sway a jury. A court didn't want conjecture, it wanted precision – and it would be my task to discover where Robert belonged on the spectrum of possibilities.

I headed to my favourite place, the State Library of Victoria, stood in homage for a moment beneath the high dome of the Reading Room, then got a librarian to set me up with a selection of microfiches on the Van Meulenbelts' very public lives.

The blanket exposure that *Top Cook* gave Robert's parents was probably more than any child would want to endure. The program had made them celebrities and the magazines and tabloids couldn't get enough. The big white kitchen in their home, which had been replicated in the TV studio, appeared to give anyone who wanted it open access to their lives. Not only was it the setting for the cooking show and countless promotions for their many spin-off products, the house was also host to extravagant dinner parties for anyone famous who passed through town. Film stars, celebrities, sportspeople and musicians – there wasn't a photo op missed. Even those on the wrong side of the law were frequent guests, in particular nightclub owner and 'colourful racing identity' Morrie Latal. It seemed like a house that never slept, and that Skyla and Herman were everywhere. Herman was photographed with models and actresses who seemed to be more than passing acquaintances, and Skyla's life was equally as ambiguous.

Skyla and Herman also had a vineyard on the Mornington Peninsula with a winery, extensive gardens, guest accommodation and riding stables. There was an artificial lake for kayaking and a skeet-shooting range. The sprawling farmhouse had commanding views of Western Port Bay and was yet another venue for their lavish parties. Various run-ins with the tax department probably meant the Van Meulenbelts' were living beyond their means, but their generosity was never in question.

How could an impressionable young man not find that life destabilising? Robert didn't need to create a fantasy world: he was already living in one.

Most of the photos focused on Skyla and Herman, but Robert was often there in the background, wearing his distinctive waistcoat and Fedora, posing with celebrities and, no doubt, telling about wild adventures. It was unlikely the milieu had created the fabulist, though it would have provided a ready-made audience.

I kept returning to the photographs that featured Morrie Latal, a man I had encountered before. He was someone around whom rumours swirled, though the police had never been able to secure a conviction. I first came across Morrie when he had been tried for assaulting his wife. His defence was based on non-insane automatism, where he argued the attack had taken place while he was sleepwalking. I appeared as an expert for the prosecution and although his case had little merit, the trial was eventually dismissed when his wife folded under cross-examination, withdrew her complaint and confessed she had concocted the entire story. Despite his reputation, Morrie was a likeable rogue and had probably won the jury over even before the case was aborted.

In many of the photos, Morrie was shown with or nearby Robert, and I wondered what effect the underworld figure had had on the impressionable young man. Famous celebrities have a certain unattainable aura but miscreants like Morrie lead lives that seem much more achievable.

His bar in King Street was open all day but it was at night when the place came alive. I got there at 5 pm before the after-work rush and took a table under the mezzanine near his office. I knew Morrie literally lived at the place and it wasn't too long before he emerged and came over to buy me a drink.

'Doctor Halifax. What a pleasure.'

'Hello, Morrie. How are you going? Or am I talking to you in your sleep?'

He gave his hearty smoker's laugh and summoned a hostess. 'Same again for my guest and the usual for me, darls,' he ordered without asking as he looked me up and down in that way some older men do. 'What brings you to the wrong side of town?'

'Tell me about Skyla and Herman Van Meulenbelt. Good friends of yours, I believe.'

'God, was that shocking or what? Do you think the kid's to blame?'

'I hope not. He's my client.'

'Oh, shit.'

'You know him pretty well?'

'Yes, I do. Nice young man, though mad as a snake. But, boy, can he tell a story.'

'Do you think he's capable of shooting his parents?'

'We're all *capable* of anything. Ask the wife.'

'What did you make of Robert's relationship with his parents?'

'Are you going to put me on the stand?'

'Probably not. I'm just trying to get some background.'

'Well, he was no madder than they were. God, did they know how to burn the candle. This joint stays open most of the night, but if you wanted fun, you went to their place. Girls, booze, more booze, more girls. And the kitchen cranking out food you could only get in a top flight restaurant. I don't know how they got anything done.'

'And was Robert always there?'

'Unless he was looking after his little sister. Somebody had to. Though there was a nanny as well, I think.'

'How well did you know them?'

'Skye very well. Herm not so much. Probably saw me as some kind of threat.'

'But Skyla?'

'She was a sweetie. Too good for him. The bastard worked her to death. She was gentle by nature. Nowhere near as driven. She only worked as hard as she did to keep the prick under surveillance. Which she failed to do on numerous occasions until he pleaded to be taken back.'

'A volatile relationship?'

'Totally volcanic. Made me feel like a homebody. Couldn't wait to go home to bed and beat the wife.'

'I am not going to laugh at a joke like that.'

'I wasn't joking.'

'So, you did beat your wife?'

'Only the once. And I wasn't sleeping.'

'At least that's cleared something up.'

'She saved my arse. Like Skyla saved Herm's on numerous occasions. Us blokes don't deserve you, Jane.'

'At least we agree on something.'

'What else can I tell you . . . That I'm not surprised the young fella snapped. His father rode him like an unbroken horse. And at no time was the fight a fair one. Herm was an overbearing Dutch bully.'

'Is his nationality relevant?'

'Dutch as in big and tall and physical. Robert's finer, more like his mum.'

'Did she try to protect him?'

'She could barely protect herself.'

'Did she ever talk about leaving?'

'None of your bloody business.' His eyes were suddenly moist as he downed his beer and called for another. 'My wife up and left me in the end. For a bloody stockbroker. If she'd done it sooner – who knows? I might have rescued Skye myself.'

The hostess arrived for our order.

'Want another?'

'No thanks, Morrie. I'll sit on this.'

'Robert worked here while still at school. Work experience in the hospitality industry, they called it. Jesus. He was down in the basement changing kegs. He was convinced a squatter was living down there like *The Phantom of the Opera*. Complete with a mask and damaged face. And madly in love with a singer who performed on that stage over there. She liked going down there for a smoke sometimes and Robert would shoo her away, terrified the bloody phantom would get her. I think Robert wanted to get her himself.

'So, we started calling Robert the Phantom and it became a kind of a joke. But after he left, we discovered a squatter with this birthmark all over his face. We thought it had been one of Robert's bullshit stories, but he'd been telling the truth all along. That's the trouble with people who tell tall tales – you never know when they're on the level.'

'I'll keep that in mind.'

'Please do. I like the kid and I hope he didn't do it. I'm glad he's got you in his corner.'

'Anything else?'

'If my wife hadn't pulled the plug and taken the blame, would my sleepwalking defence have worked?'

'Probably not. But the jury was on your side.'

'Yeah, I know. Pity the wife lost her nerve.'

'Or that you hit her in the first place.'

'Yeah, that too. Well, she had the last laugh on that one.'

'Thanks, Morrie. I might talk to you again.'

'Any time. Look after the kid. He needs you.'

'Yeah, I know.'

As if I wasn't under enough pressure already.

14.

Skyla Van Meulenbelt's parents lived in a modest cottage in Coburg. Not much of their daughter's wealth had trickled down here, though a fierce migrant ethic and independence had probably had a lot to do with that. The ageing couple were broken, the recent tragedy imprinted on their faces, the pride of their lives reduced from four to one in whom they were both now invested.

They insisted on making tea, which they served with krakelingen while their granddaughter played on a swing beneath a towering gum outside.

'Have you seen Robert?' asked the old man.

'Yes, I have.'

'And what's he got to say for himself?'

'That he discovered the bodies and picked up the gun.'

The old man grunted his disbelief.

'He's in shock, Mr Koetsveld. As much as anyone.'

'The police don't believe his story.'

'You should visit him and hear for yourself.'

'That's not going to happen.'

'He needs your support.'

'He confessed. The police told me so. He should have turned the gun on himself.'

'I understand your loss, but Robert's in pain as well.'

'Self-inflicted.'

'That's very harsh. These things aren't as simple as they might appear. If Robert did this – and I am not saying he did – he would have had his reasons, however difficult that might be right now for you to understand.'

'I don't need to listen to this.' Mr Koetsveld got up and headed deeper into the house and his anguish.

'Skyla was our only daughter, Doctor Halifax. Our pride and joy,' said Mrs Koetsveld.

'And Robert's your only grandson. You have to deal with what you have, not with what might have been.'

'He should have shot us. We would have swapped places. Our lives are nearly over.'

'We don't know what he's guilty of, if anything. If he did come across the bodies – of his parents – can you imagine how terrible that would have been?'

'If you want to talk to my granddaughter, I'll get her now.' Mrs Koestsveld headed outside, sustained, like her husband, by a bitterness towards her grandson that somehow made life's calculus make sense.

Their healing would be long and hard.

Mercifully, eight-year-olds are made with more resilience. After raiding what was left of the biscuits, Luna took up her dolls and introduced them, one by one. 'This is Kimba. She's very beautiful. This one's Cindy. She likes to play in the dirt. This one's Erica. Nobody likes Erica, so she has to play on her own. I'll put her over here.'

'Poor Erica. Why does nobody like her?'

'Because she's stupid. She always gets everything wrong.'

'Very strong personalities. Which one's your favourite?'

'Kimba, of course.'

'Did you name them yourself?'

'No, Robert did. He wrote a poem.'

Kimba is very beautiful,
Cindy's heart is cold as stone,
Erica is very stupid,
Which is why she plays alone.
But whenever they have a birthday,
They swap their party hats,
And become anyone they want to be,
Cos dolls can be like that.

'Do you think Erica's stupid?' I asked the girl.

'No.'

'Or that Cindy has a heart of stone?'

'She's a doll. She doesn't have a heart.'

'So it's just a poem?'

'To show that everyone is different.'

'That was very clever of Robert. Did he have anyone in mind?'

'Only the dolls.'

'Do you know where Robert is at the moment?'

'On holiday. With my parents. I'm staying here because I have to go to school.'

I hoped not. The playground would be the worst way for her to discover the truth, as she undoubtedly would. I needed to explain to her grandparents that Luna was better off knowing what had happened – without the violent details. Though understandable, their bitterness and lies were making things worse. It was going to be a very long and heartbreaking day.

I agreed to stay for dinner and after the little girl was put to bed – her school uniform all clean and pressed for the morning – I sat the Koetsvelds down in the lounge room.

'I want you to try to believe that this is what happened. That Herman, for whatever reason, maybe in a state of psychological crisis, shot Skyla and then himself. And that Robert discovered the bodies and, probably in a state of shock, took up the gun. Until we know what happened that remains the most plausible explanation. Robert's confession might be explained in a number of ways but none of those explanations are relevant now. And Luna needs to know the truth.'

'She's only eight.'

'I know, Mr Koetsveld, but delaying it is not going to make it easier or better. For her or either of you. We can explain it as a terrible thing in which both of them died. That we don't really know what happened.'

'Isn't that another lie?'

'At this point in time, it's the truth.'

'I wouldn't know where to start.'

'I can be here to help. If you like, I can do the talking.'

'Would you?'

'We can wake her up now or I can come back in the morning. But either way, she shouldn't be sent to school. Everyone there will know what's happened. It's been on television and in all the papers. And children can be very cruel.'

'Let's do it in the morning. Can you come back at eight o'clock?'

'Of course.'

The Koetsvelds started to cry and seek comfort in each other's arms. I had thrown them a lifeline that they had grabbed without hesitation. Their healing had finally begun and their burden passed to me. Of course, I was trained in this work and had built up years of callus. But I couldn't help thinking of why Ben wanted me to take that job at the university. This territory I had chosen to work in certainly came at a cost.

When I arrived the following morning, Luna was dressed in her school uniform and eating breakfast, her lunch already packed in her lunchbox beside her. I asked her to sit on the couch between her grandparents and hold their hands.

'A sad and terrible thing has happened and your mummy and daddy have died. It is very, very sad for everyone, but Nanny and Granddad are going to look after you and they love you very much.'

As the Koetsvelds held her tightly and started to cry, the little girl had only questions.

'What happened?'

'We don't know, but it involved a gun.'

'Does Robert know?'

'Yes. He's helping the police. To try to understand what happened.'

'Can I get my dolls? They need to know as well.'

'Of course you can.'

She crossed to her dolls in the corner and whispered her own explanations and kissed them each on the lips and held them close to her heart. Then, returning to the couch, she hugged her grandparents and told them that she would look after them and that they would be all right.

No-one can predict how a child will react to a tragedy like this, but I knew this was only the beginning.

I asked Luna if she had any questions and answered as simply and honestly as I could, suppressing my emotions, if not my tears, like I had a thousand times. Road accidents and sudden unexpected death are hard enough, but homicide is a new dimension for children. I avoided euphemisms or suggesting her parents were 'in a better place'. I knew such concepts could be confusing for a child, even scary, and sometimes worse than the actual event.

'Do you think we could get some flowers from the garden to show how much we miss them and love them?' I said.

Luna thought that was a good idea and, when we were outside, suggested we put the flowers beneath her favourite tree. While Granddad found a vase and collected rocks to build a cairn, her grandmother got some krakelingen from the kitchen so they'd have 'something to eat on their journey'. The birds, of course, thought the biscuits were for them, but at least it made everyone laugh.

'The birds must be angels,' said Luna as the old woman clutched her crucifix.

The old man dropped a rock on his finger, which started to bleed, but his pain was inconsequential and his clumsiness another excuse to laugh. How far away this simple tableau in a suburban garden seemed from what had happened in the big white room.

Afterwards, we went inside for tea and treats the birds couldn't get and I sat with Luna for the rest of the morning while she filled page after page with her crayon drawings. Most were happy memories of her parents and the good times they had enjoyed. But there were darker depictions as well, troubling images in black and red it was too soon to interrogate, though they would be on my mind when I sat down with Rinaldi the following day to discuss where Robert's case was at.

15.

Rinaldi was tired. His current case wasn't going well, and he needed to re-energise. A defence of diminished responsibility is tricky at the best of times, but at least he wasn't blaming his expert witness, a respected colleague of mine, as some barristers are wont to do. I hoped he'd be as generous with me.

'If you want me to give you a list of reasons why Robert would murder his parents, I could write you a book. An excruciating life in the public eye with endless accounts of his parents' bad behaviour. A bullying father, a distracted mother, too much money and freedom, and exposure to drugs and alcohol. As much licence as he wanted interrupted by moments of fury and rage. Constantly bailing him out for his misdemeanours and chewing him out for doing so. Rage one moment, an open cheque book the next. And all this for someone barely equipped for a normal life, who lives in a world of make-believe.'

'You think he did it?'

'I'm not saying that. Just that he had the motive. The forensics are going to be interesting.'

'We haven't got them yet.'

'Won't ballistics tell us a lot?'

'I hope so. Angle of entry, distance, powder burns. Evidence of a struggle.'

'Why wouldn't the police have waited for that before laying charges?'

'Because they had a full confession. Because they like us on the back foot.'

'It's not a bloody game, you know.'

'I'm sure they don't think that.'

'Do you think they know what the forensics are saying?'

'Probably got a fair idea. And checking to make sure they're right.'

'So you don't buy the reconstruction?'

'Do you?'

'Vincenzo, I might be the only one, but I'm keeping an open mind.'

'Good for you.' Rinaldi had more pressing problems. At this stage of the Millard case, he was relying on me. 'We'll need more than provocation, you know. To get an acquittal.'

'Provocation only reduces murder to manslaughter.'

'Correct. Though if it's all we've got, I'll take it.'

'I'm expecting something more psychologically complex.'

'Like what?'

'I don't know yet. I'm only at the beginning.'

'Well, you've probably got a year.'

'My God, is that how long it takes these days?'

'The courts are chock-a-block.'

'Must be good for business,' I suggested blackly.

'I'd rather have half the cases and two holidays a year instead of one.'

But my thoughts were with Robert. Would he survive a year in jail? 'When things are clearer, can we revisit bail?'

'You're worried about him, aren't you?'

'You know he's on suicide watch?' I asked.

'Would he be any safer outside?'

'In the right facility, yes. Can we get him moved to the Thomas Embling Hospital?'

'If you can support it – yes. Is he that psychotic?'

'He might be.'

'Then give me the evidence and I'll apply straight away. I'm sorry, Jane . . .'

'But you've got other things on your mind.'

'Too many crooks and too many crazies. The system's bursting at the seams.'

'You do your job and I'll do mine.'

'I think that's how it works.'

'My boyfriend wants me to give this away and escape to academia. Take a cushy job at the university and teach.'

'You'd hate it.'

'Maybe.'

'And the hourly rate.'

'Unlike you, my fees aren't set by the Bar Council.'

'And, besides, who would I use for a case like this?'

'Maybe I could do a bit of both.'

'Are you workshopping your future with me, Jane?'

'No. Just thinking aloud.'

'If you want my advice – stay where you are and put up your rates. You're worth it.'

'*Bringing in the fees, bringing in the fees, We shall come rejoicing, bringing in the fees . . .*'

'You're singing my favourite gospel song.'

'Just as well you're good at what you do, Vincenzo. Otherwise, you might be misunderstood.'

'Let me know how you go with Robert. I can lodge an application within the hour.'

'Do it. I'll give you a report by tomorrow.'

'Consider it done. Now, if you've finished, I've got other fish to stop from frying.'

'Have you thought about stand-up?'

'No, Jane. The one-liners are all for you. Bye-bye.'

———

I hoped it would be the last time I would see Robert at the Remand Centre. I couldn't get him to the Thomas Embling soon enough. He would be more comfortable among the deluded who only thought they were aliens, cannibals or prophets. Affectionately known as the Zoo, it was a kinder place for a fabulist to be than the chafing edges of the criminal world.

Robert liked hearing I had seen his grandparents and his little sister. I mentioned the drawings she had done for me – in particular the worrying ones in black and red – but he said they didn't surprise him, that Luna always hated it when her parents argued, which seemed a plausible explanation.

I took him back to his first confession and his state of mind at the time. I needed to understand the context for this and everything that had led up to the killings. It's the last thing he wanted to talk about. The reconstruction was his truth; why wasn't I concentrating on that? But the police had based everything on the first confession and I needed to know why he had made it.

'There had been worse times between me and my parents. The last few weeks had been comparatively peaceful. We'd been discussing me studying viticulture in Italy, which I thought was a great idea. I'd never found anything I'd wanted to study before, but given our winemaking plans, it made a lot of sense.'

'Did you want to move away from the family?'

'Escape them, you mean? There was a bit of Stockholm Syndrome, I suppose. You get to love your captors after a while. I wanted to take Luna with me. To go to school over there and learn a second language. She needed rescuing too. But Mum thought that was preposterous and said she belonged with her.'

'Had you argued about that?' I asked.

'Not really. I knew it was preposterous as well. I guess I was more afraid of being so far away on my own, in a country that doesn't speak English.'

'Weren't there other places you could have studied?'

'Like South Australia? Not in Herman's mind. Life had to be hard and challenging. The path of most resistance.'

'Tell me about your father.'

'Brilliant, cruel, harsh, weak.'

'Loving?'

Robert spluttered a laugh. 'In his own way, I suppose he was, though he spread it around too much.'

'With other women?'

'There was just too much of him to go around.'

'And how did your mother cope with that?'

'By trying to match fire with fire. But she didn't have the constitution. I must admit the first thought I had when I found them is that she had shot him then herself. It would have made more sense.'

There was no need for a safe word today. Robert was speaking calmly and rationally. If this was a fabulist's performance, it was a very good one. But then that's a fabulist's primary skill: utter plausibility. I had to find a way to rattle his cage.

'So why become the executioner? Why confess to doing it yourself if those thoughts were in your head?'

'Fuck off.'

'Robert. It's a serious question. The first thing you did after phoning the police was to make a full and unqualified confession.'

'Because that's what I do. I show off. I make shit up. I like to shock. I confess: I'm immature.'

'Or is this what you've learnt to say? To get yourself off the hook?' I could tell from his reaction that my assessment was close to the truth. 'Did part of you want your parents dead?'

'Not in the real world.'

'In your private world?'

'Doesn't everyone?'

'No, Robert. Everyone doesn't.'

When a fantasy world becomes this pervasive, it almost becomes impossible to discern the boundaries between what is real and what is imagined. When Oliver Sacks saw a man who mistook his wife for his hat, it made perfect sense to the man. But try explaining that to a jury.

That night I wrote a report and, with Rinaldi's help, had Robert transferred to Thomas Embling the following morning.

I was having a cheap and cheerful with Ben and Zoe at the local Thai when my mobile rang. I didn't like taking calls outside business hours but it was Rinaldi so I accepted and headed outside.

'Are you sitting down?' he asked.

'Not anymore – but go on.'

'The police have just shared ballistics on the Millard case.'

'And?'

'Predictable angles and distances and proximity of victims. Some contestable stuff but it's pretty much as expected.'

'Except?'

'They found some of Robert's clothing with residue gun powder from a recently fired weapon.'

'Shit.'

'So there goes your false confession defence. We're back to establishing his state of mind.'

I thanked Rinaldi for his call and stood on the footpath as the traffic flowed by, its noise and impatience adding to the jangling in my head. Was it stubbornness or instinct that told me that something was wrong, that despite appearances there was much more to this case than ballistics? They say a judge when sitting alone gets an instinct early in a case about the guilt or innocence of the accused and that their judgement is in many ways a justification of their initial position. Was I, as a forensic psychiatrist, doing the same thing? If I couldn't, at this early stage, prove there was far more to this case than was obvious, why was I so convinced there was so much more to be discovered?

As the traffic streamed past and my meal got cold and Ben waited inside before asking, as I knew he would, if I had made a decision about the uni job, I could only think of where Robert was right now and which fantasy world he was in. For his sake, I hoped it was somewhere more comforting than the evidence lining up against him.

PART FOUR

March 2023

Erica was a rag doll
Made up of bits and pieces.
She always felt alone in the world,
Without nephews or nieces.
Though she had both and parents too,
Doesn't matter how hard you try,
You're lost without a special friend
On whom you can rely.

16.

Though my memory of the last few years is still a blur, my former life is coming back. I am no longer afraid of the woman in the mirror and I remember my occupation. Though I have moved back to my apartment, I still feel like a stranger there but am beginning to recognise possessions I brought with me from the old house in Brighton.

We all take memory for granted, but its loss is catastrophic. It manifests not as a personal terror but as an objective fear – as if it is happening to someone else. The brain adjusts to keep your world sane and everything else unreliable. Because you think you can see the truth and lies around you, you convince yourself you are not the one going mad. It's the world that has wobbled off its axis – not you.

I have no memory of the accident or the night at Peter Debreceny's. The restaging of that evening seems phoney – like something I walked through for the benefit of others. I mistrust now that I remembered the meal, which feels too trivial to be of consequence. But I remember being with Ben, I remember how happy we were . . . Poor Ben. And poor Zoe, who came from New York to sit beside someone who didn't know who she was. I remember Ben has died, though mercifully not the details.

Memory – or rather the lack of it – can work in your favour sometimes.

And I remember his good friend, Tim de Serville, but I remember him from then. The electronic cello Ben made for him and how beautifully Tim played it. And their enduring friendship and the great times we all had at Brighton. But not anything more recent with Tim and certainly not anything one might call intimate. That part of my life is still numb.

Most of all, I remember Robert Millard. Going back through my files on Robert has been the most tangible thing I have done in reclaiming the past. I had kept the files in my office at the university, which I recalled when I remembered I still kept an office. It was like reliving every day of the investigation. I remembered the day of the protest against the war in Iraq and my meeting with Vincenzo Rinaldi; I even remembered the weather and what I was wearing: cream slacks, a striped top and navy jacket. Not bad for someone who can't remember what she had for breakfast. And I remembered Robert and his fabulism, his two confessions and the one he wanted to disavow. And the devastating ballistic evidence of the gunpowder residue on his clothes.

Going through the prosecution files helped as well and I could see why Peter had been so reluctant to let me see them. If someone wanted to reopen the case, what the Crown had chosen to withhold could be seen as a potential obstruction of justice. Well, at least by today's standards. Back then the presentation of forensic evidence wasn't so exacting. Who can forget 'a dingo's got my baby' and the conviction of Lindy Chamberlain based, in part, on evidence of blood that turned out to be a sound deadening compound.

I had sat down with Luna every week since she had visited me at Elizabeth's. I had agreed – again – to help her find her father. I reported to her and she reported to me. Today is our fourth or fifth meeting.

'I went to see Anna Leckie, who was a friend of Mum's,' says Luna. 'She said Mum hated Dad's affairs and, contrary to what people thought, didn't do the same thing herself. She said that despite the nanny we had, Mum had her hands full with me and Robert. Not to mention the show and inventing recipes and everything else she did.'

'So why are you so convinced that Herman isn't your father?' I ask.

'Because Robert insisted he wasn't. He said Mum had confessed as much before demanding he keep it a secret. And why would he fib about a thing like that?'

Well, Robert fibbed about most things, but she doesn't need me to remind her.

'And have you seen the photographs? Robert looks like his father but I certainly don't.'

'That's not unusual.'

'Herman had an olive complexion. So did Robert. My skin is parchment white.'

'Again—'

'If I didn't have my mother's eyes, you'd think I'd been adopted.'

With Luna's immediate family all deceased, I can understand why the possibility of a living biological father had become so consuming. But I'm concerned she's overinvesting in her quest, that it is becoming a fixation to the exclusion of everything else.

'Do you hate the genes you've been given?' she asks me.

'I'm sorry . . . ?'

'My parents betrayed each other and my brother killed my parents. That's my biological inheritance.'

'Of all the things that define a person, I think that's the least important.'

'Easy for you to say.'

'My father committed suicide, Luna. Do you think I should worry that's in my DNA?'

'Probably.'

'Then we've got some serious work to do, you and me. Apart from being scientifically and psychologically untrue, that kind of thinking is unhelpful and potentially worse than that. You need to be prepared for the fact that we may not find what we are looking for. That this search for your father may not find anything. Or, instead, that it confirms that your father is Herman. Are you prepared for that?'

'Yes.'

'And how will you feel if that's so?'

'Devastated.'

'Then we need to work on reconstructing your parents, Luna. And Robert too. I don't think he hated them and I don't think he murdered them either. And whatever they did in life, you need to remember your parents for the good they did. And the love they gave you. And celebrate that.'

Luna remains silent.

'So, here's the deal. I will do everything I can to help you, Luna. But only if you stop making these black-and-white judgements. Like Herman's bad and real Dad's good. It can only blow up in your face.'

'Okay. Deal.'

'And, please, no more talk about genes. You don't know how silly that is.'

Luna grabs me and holds me tight. It's a better way to seal our agreement than words, though she might have let go just a little bit sooner to hide her desperation.

There is work to be done as well with Tim, who feels more like my brother than my lover. Since I moved back into the apartment, he is showing more understanding than I would have shown had our roles been reversed. Not once does he question why it is the last few years I don't recall and the seeming expediency of that. How convenient to remember the Millard case, twenty years in the past, yet not recall our first date or our time together in the Margaret River. How random to retain the happy times at the house in Brighton but nothing after Ben had died. Before the accident, I knew I had negotiated Ben's violent death and the sorrow that followed, so why am I blocking it now? I don't buy the concept of selective memory or the 'index card theory' – whoever's theory that is. It's one thing not to remember the accident: that kind of thing is common. But to project that trauma back into the past – almost two years – suggests something else. Precisely what, I do not know, but I've retrieved enough of my psychiatrist's brain to know the block is real and awaits further analysis. 'Doctor, heal thyself,' you might say, but I'm in no shape to do that yet.

I'm grateful Tim has gone away on a tour of Japan with his chamber–jazz fusion group. He thinks the time apart will be good for us both but for me it is simply a welcome relief from the pressure. Though he hasn't put a foot out of place, his sexual longing is all-pervasive.

On the other hand, I miss the security of Tim staying over in the apartment from time to time. Even Doctor Zhou has urged me not to be on my own and that advice is medical. Yet here I am, flying solo with my flanks exposed.

With Bathgate out there on the prowl or whoever it was who'd been watching the house when I was staying at Elizabeth's, the police have got me rattled. Though the man disappeared when the police increased their surveillance, the worry remains. The PSIO against Bathgate was precautionary and his messages and texts stopped as soon as it was issued. And while I do my best to keep my paranoia in check, the thought of someone out there, watching me, maybe even wishing me harm, doesn't disappear because I can't remember being threatened.

Needing company, I shout my girlfriends to dinner at the Lilian Terrace on Collins for minute steaks and orange roughy. It's a way of thanking Elizabeth – who everyone now calls Ming Zu – for all she has done since my discharge from hospital, and Virginia for letting me appropriate her identity, which she says she found quite flattering and not nearly as alarming as it had been for me. (More grist for the analysist's mill when I feel well enough to unpack it.) Jasmine is her usual outspoken self, wondering aloud how I can stand being with someone as beautiful as Tim.

'You've got the self-confidence to pull it off,' she says, 'but I always feel drab in his presence. I don't blame you for keeping it a secret.'

'I did not keep it a secret,' I insist, much to everyone else's amusement.

'You're the most secretive person we know,' roars Virginia. 'The last time we were here, you were in the middle of those awful Torture Murders and you didn't tell us a thing.'

'That's different. That's work. What do you want? Blood and gore from the crime scenes?'

'Yes!' they shout in unison.

'You get it from me,' adds Jasmine.

'You're a midwife. Your stories are life-affirming.'

'Not always, Jane,' she answers ruefully.

But the point is made. The work I do is hard to discuss, hardly restaurant conversation. It was why Ben had urged me to do some teaching, to give myself a break. 'Burnout,' he called it. Is my selective recall a delayed reaction to that?

The girls tease me some more about 'keeping separate residences' and 'not being able to commit'.

'You call yourself a serial monogamist but you're really a commitment-phobe,' says Virginia.

'Come on. I was with Ben for seventeen years.'

'Because you fell in love with his daughter.'

Everyone laughs and we order another bottle. It's the best fun I've had in ages.

'Now tell me about that awful rug in your apartment?' says Elizabeth, who never criticises anyone.

'That's Tim's. But it's not there anymore. I insisted he take it back.'

'And does it look better in his place?'

'No. It looks even worse – if such a thing is possible.'

'I like it that Tim has no idea about soft furnishings,' adds Jasmine. 'Means he's not perfect after all.'

The wine arrives and the laughter continues. As the others talk among themselves, I pick over the day I spent with Luna. I'm hardly entitled to accuse her of being obsessed. I'm so fixated on her brother that I'm using him as the principal tool in my recovery. Am I going on this journey with Luna not only to find her father and recover my memory, but to right the imagined failures of my past?

'You think about things too much,' said Eric Ringer somewhere in my memory. And what would the good inspector say to me now if he could listen in on these thoughts? I need to talk to my psychologist. This self-diagnosis is sending me crazy. How can I even begin to help Luna when I can't even help myself?

17.

My physical recovery is almost complete. Nadia has hired an exercise bike, which she placed on my balcony, overlooking the botanical gardens, but it only reminded me of the freedom I didn't have. I used it as motivation to improve my strength, and am now riding every morning along the cycle track beside the river. Not yet with the confidence I had once enjoyed, but that's slowing returning.

My consultations with Doctor Zhou are less frequent. He is delighted with my neurological progress but keeps asking if I've seen my psychologist yet. Marion is overseas in Norway, seeing her parents after three years of Covid-imposed isolation, and he wonders if I should see someone else. I still have a distance to go in recovering my memory and the doctor, being a surgeon, isn't able to help me with that. But Marion knows my history and I can't face briefing someone new.

'If one of your patients gave you an answer like that, what would you think?'

'That they were stalling.'

'Well?'

'Marion helped me understand my father's death. And I think my current block could have something to do with Ben's.'

'Your diagnosis?'

'It's not totally uninformed.'

'You're such a soloist, Jane. Sometimes it's better to play in a group. It doesn't mean you can't contribute . . .'

That is a surprise. Musical allusions from a brain surgeon. 'I didn't know you had a musical background.'

'I was a child prodigy. On pianoforte.'

'What happened to that?'

'My parents thought surgery was a safer path.'

'Can I ask what they do?'

'Commercial cleaners. Still are. Work longer hours than I do. Of course, I want them to stop, to live with me, but they value their independence. Stubborn. Like you are, Jane. I can't tell them what to do either.'

As stubborn as a commercial cleaner. I haven't been called that before. I only hope they hadn't crushed a brilliant career.

'Zoe.'

'Jane, how are you?'

'I'm doing okay. It's great to see you.'

'Even if it's only on Facetime. Welcome to my messy loft.'

'It looks very *creative.*' There would be no crushing of musical careers from me. 'How's the album going?'

'Still mixing. And adding tracks. And redesigning the cover. All the usual procrastination.'

Like not seeing a psychologist. I hope she didn't get it from me.

'But, more importantly,' she says, 'how are you really doing? It was scary when I came to Melbourne.'

'I'm getting my memory back, in random stages – 2003 is really clear. And your ninth birthday party for some obscure reason, though I can't remember your last one.'

'Something to do with what you made? A Stevie Nicks cake, remember? You took me to her show at the Rod Laver Arena. It changed my life.'

And here she was in New York City, chasing her dreams instead of studying for a sensible career. The choices we make on our children's behalf. Are we pursuing dreams of our own? Did I make them for Zoe just as the doctor's parents had done for him? To what extent was Robert Millard formed by his upbringing and his parents' decisions?

My analyst's brain is in overdrive and I have to force myself back to the present. 'How are you going for money? Are you eating properly? Tell me about your friends.'

Zoe prattles on with ease, her chatter balm to my soul. Silly talk about her crazy friends and the bar in the village where she played once a week. She's been asked to write a soundtrack for a Western and was soaking up Ry Cooder and Ennio Morricone. Her father would have been beaming with pride.

'I am so proud of you, Zo. I'll come see you as soon as I can.'

'And money. Yes. That would be nice. Is there anything left in Dad's trust fund?'

There isn't a trust fund. Ben had died with an outdated will and his 'fund' had been invented by me so Zoe could ask for help without feeling she was asking for handouts. It was a white lie she wasn't abusing; she was entitled to more from her father's estate. But the thought still jags, another example of the way parents, for better or worse, can't help but influence their children's lives.

Luna has nothing to contribute when we next get together. She has exhausted her contacts and is starting to believe her search is futile. Her interactions have been limited to her relations and her mother's friends and others who have maintained contact after the trial. I have other sources of information, and one in particular, but is Luna ready for Morrie Latal?

Morrie is in his seventies now and still a crook. He operates these days from his pub in Carlton where he surveys the comings and goings in the street below from an apartment on the second floor. It's a step down from his King Street nightclub days, but Morrie is a survivor. He had been up to his gills in the gangland wars, which had ended in 2010, but had never done time himself. He managed his affairs so his underlings did that for him, for which they were handsomely paid. Morrie has the reputation but his record was Teflon clean.

Morrie had been a constant guest at Luna's parents' place in the days when gangsters were glamorous. He was seen as a 'fixer' or a 'scaffolding consultant to the building industry' but they were euphemisms for murderer and drug-dealing thug.

I could have seen Morrie alone, but thought Luna should hear what he had to say first-hand. I warn her that it would be a mixture of bravado and bullshit laced with seams of truth, but two antennae are better than one.

Morrie is no longer in the drug trade. The gangland wars had put an end to that and the outlaw motorcycle clubs had taken over. Gone were the public revenge killings: the bikies kept those to themselves. Violence wasn't good for business and, these days, troublemakers simply disappeared.

Despite his reduced activities, Morrie remains wary of

visitors and has his bar manager pat us down. As she feels for listening devices in our underwiring, Morrie watches on, no doubt wishing he was doing the task himself. Though Luna clearly felt it invasive, it is an apt reminder of the world we've entered, one run by different rules. Whether or not the cops are still out to get him, Morrie isn't taking any chances.

His apartment is dark and plush with leather couches and Italian lamps as you imagine a gangster might have. There are video screens on the walls linked to CCTV in the street outside. He's more paranoid than the last time we met. Old gangsters fade away, but not before becoming jumpier.

'A long time between drinks, Doctor Halifax?'

'Twenty years. Which is the last time you would have seen Luna. She was only eight back then.'

'Hiding under the table and eating chocolates when she should have been in bed.'

At least my post-accident hallucinations have some connection with reality.

'But you're not here to talk about that?'

'No. We'd like to talk about Luna's mother, who I think you knew very well?'

'Skye. What a sweetie. Too damn good for your father. Sorry. But she should have been with me.'

'Was she?' asks Luna, unable to hide her shock.

'No. That was never going to happen. I lived on the wrong side of town. I was surprised they let me in their house.'

'Why did they?'

'Because everyone was welcome. From celebrities to me. And everyone in between. They were never discerning. Which was why they were so much fun.'

'How well did you know my mother?'

'We trusted each other.'

'Meaning?' I ask, sensing more.

'She did things for me and I did things for her.'

'Like?'

'She'd give me advice on the nightclub menu . . .'

'And what would you do for her?' asks Luna.

'None of your business.' Morrie is looking hard at Luna. Was it a mistake to bring her?

'Did Skyla ever ask you to check on Herman?' I ask.

'What makes you ask that?'

'She hated that Herman had affairs. It wouldn't have been an unusual request.'

Morrie looks at me as if I was straying into forbidden territory. 'Once or twice, perhaps.'

'Did Dad ever ask you to do the same? To check on Mum?'

'No.'

'Why not?'

'Because he thought if anyone was having an affair with Skye, it was probably me.'

Luna can't take her eyes from Morrie. Is this the man she was searching for, a broken-down crook in his seventies with a shady past and emphysema on the horizon?

'You're looking for your father, aren't you?'

'Did Skyla ever say anything to you?' I ask.

'No.'

'Did anyone else?'

'Only Robert. And who believed a thing he said? It was while he was doing work experience with me.'

'The Phantom of the Nightclub.'

'Exactly.'

'But didn't that turn out to be true?' But Luna was out of that loop and we needed to get back to her father. 'Just tell Luna what Robert said about her dad.'

'Robert was obsessed with organ transplantation. He reckoned it wouldn't be long before they could actually build a Frankenstein – as long as they got the matching right. He said the South Africans had already tried it, but they didn't have a big enough data bank and none of their experiments survived. But he said it would all be commonplace one day and that we'd all have to go on a register. And that then we'd know who our matches were and our real parents in the process. And that it'd be a terrible way to find out if your father was really your father. Then he told me what he reckoned Skye had told him. Because if something happened to Skye, then someone would need to know.'

'Know what?' Luna is barely keeping up.

'That if you were involved in a medical emergency and needed a transplant or some shit like that – that Herman wasn't your father.'

'Morrie, can we dispense with Robert's theories and focus on what he told you about Luna? And what his mother had said to him?'

Morrie addresses his answer directly at Luna. 'That Herman isn't your father.'

'Did he know who is?'

'No. She never gave Robert a name.'

Luna seems crushed, but there remains one obvious question.

'What about you, Morrie? Can you think of a likely contender?' I ask.

Morrie looks at me, then at Luna, then back at me again. 'Yes, Jane. Yes, I can. But he's not going to want to hear from either of you.'

18.

Eight o'clock is a busy time at the apartment building as people leave for work or breakfast at one of the nearby cafés. To make matters worse this morning, removalists have commandeered one of the elevators to move in a new owner, increasing demand on the other lift, so I decide to take the stairs. My fitness still isn't what it should be and, as Nadia would say, 'exercise every day', so taking the eight floors down to the carpark seems like a sensible option. I'm not the only one with that idea.

As I make it to the fifth-floor landing, someone enters behind me. Male, I think, with a heavier step and in more of a hurry than me. As he draws closer, I quicken my pace, though not for any coherent reason. Do I not want someone judging my cautious progress or am I matching my fitness with his? Or worse than that, do I think I'm being followed? Bathgate is never far from my mind nor the man who'd been loitering outside Elizabeth's house before the police increased their patrols.

I try to match my foot-fall with his, but he is moving more quickly. The doors on each landing only open one way – into the stairs and not back into the building unless you have a pass-key for that level. There is no way out until I reach the ground floor. Suddenly, squeezing into a crowded lift seems infinitely preferable to my self-imposed entrapment. If only another person would enter the stairs to prevent us being alone.

The man behind me is gaining. He seems to be taking two treads at a time. I remember Bathgate was a big man and how he used his size as a form of intimidation when I assessed him. I start to plot a strategy if we come face to face, how the right attitude will keep him calm and the wrong one, provoke his aggression. I should have been paying more attention to my progress.

With a rising sense of panic and my timing half a beat out, I round the landing on level four and lose my footing. The strap of my handbag is tightly wrapped around my left arm, so there is no way I can grab the nearest banister and the other is too far away. As I pitch forward down the unforgiving concrete stairway, I know it's going to hurt.

The moment of impact or how long I lie there for doesn't register. Struggling to keep my panic under control, I strain to hear any sound above my breathing. Has my pursuer, if that's who he is, stopped to assess my situation? Or has he fled?

A middle-aged woman enters the stairwell, sees my predicament and hurries to my assistance. She confirms we are alone and that there is no sign of anyone else. As my pain begins to register, I am thankful I've managed to protect my head. Any sort of concussion is the last thing I need so soon after my surgery. But my shoulder hurts and my jacket is ripped and there's blood soaking through my slacks.

Helped by my rescuer, I limp back to my apartment and reschedule my appointment. Without giving an explanation, I say an hour later would suit me better and the message comes back that is fine. I should have given myself more time. My left shoulder is heavily bruised and will need manipulation. How my leg has been cut is a mystery and it takes time to stop the bleeding. I bandage my leg, shower again and put on a whole new outfit. With my confidence severely shaken, I order a cab, wait patiently for the lift and set off on my journey once more.

Joe Wasserman is a self-made man. His trucking and logistics company is one of the best known in the country and his wife, a prominent conservative politician, someone marked as a future PM. Why he agreed to see me without any explanation of my purpose is a reflection of his self-confidence and curiosity. I would not have extended the same indulgence to someone I didn't know, but was that a reflection on me or him, or a distinctly female caution?

As I wait in the reception area of the headquarters that bore his name, I'm overcome by a wave of tiredness and wonder if I have hit my head after all.

'Doctor Halifax. What a pleasure to meet you. My wife's a genuine fan.'

Ah, Sally Wasserman, I should have guessed. We had met at a conference on family violence where we had both been keynote speakers. Our politics were at the opposite ends of the spectrum, but we were united on what had to be done.

'She said I should definitely see you but warned you were probably after money.'

'I'm sorry . . . ?'

'For a new Chair at the university.'

'Oh, that. Well, I'm on leave at the moment, but if you're in a mood to give I can point you in the right direction.'

'Come on in. Take a seat.' He ushers me through to his expansive office with its expensive Danish furniture, not a file or sheet of paper on his desk, the lack of clutter in stark contrast to my study at the university.

His assistant asks if we want refreshments: he orders an espresso and I, water and two Panadol. The pain in my shoulder is getting worse.

'So – to what do I owe the pleasure?'

'I would like to talk to you, if I could, about Skyla Van Meulenbelt.' I'm doing what cops like to do: springing a name then studying the subject for their reaction.

'Ah, Skyla. Now there's a blast from the past.' There's a fondness in his reaction, but a guardedness as well, his open smile replaced with a searching look that demands more information.

'I have a client. Skyla's daughter, to be precise. We are trying to find her father and have reason to believe it wasn't Herman.'

Wasserman moves to a panelled cupboard that conceals his bar fridge and gets himself a bottle of water. He removes the cap, takes a long draught and recaps the bottle.

'So why have you come to me?'

'I'm told you knew the Van Meulenbelts, back in the day. And Skyla in particular.'

'Who told you that?'

'Morrie Latal.'

'That broken font of wisdom. He loved Skyla more than I did.'

'So he said.'

'You've been getting yourself around.' He returns to his desk and sits down. 'Jane, I had an affair with Skyla, but her daughter– she's not my kid.'

'How do you know?'

'Because Skyla would have told me.'

'But you were married.'

'So was she.'

'To a jealous man with a famous temper.'

'She would have told me.' His certainty seems unshakable.

'Was Skyla afraid of Herman?'

'Yes.'

'Were you?'

'No. But I was afraid of Morrie Latal.'

'Well, I wouldn't be. Not anymore.' It was time to ask the big question. 'Would you take a DNA test, Joe?'

'No.'

'Why not?'

'You've met the wife.'

'A future PM.'

'It's not because of politics. Something far more personal. We tried to have kids for years and years. IVF. It left us emotionally exhausted. If the girl was mine—'

'Luna.'

'If Luna was mine, it would break Sally.'

'You may be surprised. If you took the test and it was negative your wife wouldn't need to know.'

'And if it was positive?'

'You would still have that choice. And Luna would have her answer.'

'Doctor, you're asking me to play Russian roulette.'

'No. You did that way back then.'

A wry grunt acknowledges the truth of that, but it doesn't change his mind. 'The answer's no. And don't even think about taking that coffee cup.'

'I wouldn't dare.'

'You had the balls to walk in here.'

'Yes, I did. But I did that for Luna. After that, it's up to you.' I stand up and place my card on his desk. I have to steady myself for a moment.

'Are you all right?'

'I took a tumble on my way here this morning. All my fault.'

'Please, sit down and take your time.' He refills my glass with water and gets another bottle from the fridge, at the same time moving his coffee cup away in case I change my mind. 'Can you even get DNA from a coffee cup?' he asks.

'Probably. Depends how much you slobber.'

Joe Wasserman grins and sits down to wait for my dizziness to pass. He isn't a bad man. In fact, he holds no animus for what I've brought into his comfortable, well-ordered life. It's Luna's interests I'm invested in, not his, though they're not necessarily mutually exclusive. But how could I blame him for putting his wife first after all that they had been through together?

Doctor Zhou is furious. I haven't seen this side of him before, and he isn't holding back.

'Jane. You're a doctor. A specialist. You should know better. Six weeks ago you didn't recognise yourself in the mirror. Now you're tumbling down stairs and self-diagnosing and telling me you didn't have a concussion.'

'Did I have a concussion?'

'Of course you did. You know the symptoms.'

'I'm sorry . . .'

'What were you doing? Why wasn't Tim driving? Where were you going?'

'Tim's away. I was using the stairs to try and please Nadia.'

'Nadia is ready to quit. You keep referring to her as your "physio" as if that doesn't equate with "psychiatrist" and that she should somehow be listening to your suggestions.'

'God. Am I that appalling?'

'Apparently.'

'Have you found me like this yourself?'

'Are you asking me or Doctor Two-Bob?'

I want the ground to swallow me up.

'Jane. You have had a serious brain injury. And for that I will make allowances. You still haven't told me where Tim is.'

'You asked three questions at once. He's away in Japan. With his group.'

'And Ming Zu?'

Does he have to remind me of that?

'I can't keep asking her for help.'

'Why not?'

'Elizabeth has a young family. I'm not helpless. And until I fell down the stairs, I was doing okay.' I'm determined not to cry but Two-Bob knows I'm close.

'Breathe, breathe.'

'I'm sorry?'

But Two-Bob is talking to himself. 'My apologies, Jane. But somewhere in there, I think I lost my bedside manner.'

'Don't apologise. It's me that should be doing that.'

We both calm down and he makes some tea and discusses my situation. My first instinct after the fall had been to go to sleep on the landing, so we conclude I'd hit my head on the stairs.

I'd done a bad job of dressing my leg which should have had stitches and would leave a nasty scar. I hadn't lost enough blood to warrant a transfusion, but if my rescuer hadn't helped me to keep moving, like a rugby player after a head clash, and I hadn't staunched the flow, who knows what might have happened?

'Where were you going that was so important?' Doctor Zhou asks.

'We're trying to find Luna's father.'

'We?'

'Me and Luna. Robert Millard's sister.'

'Oh, that.'

'It's important.'

'Why are you pushing so hard?'

'Because I want to get my memory back. And right now, Robert is all I remember. So I'm using that – yes, as hard as I can – to unlock everything else.'

His silence says everything. It implies I should think about what I'd just said, which I do, as my fragile confidence finally collapses. I'm a disabled person, with a concussion on top of a serious brain injury and no memory of anything – apart from my greatest failure. It's inevitable the tears would follow.

I had given myself six minutes to cry after Ming Zu had hidden the toilet. Now, I really am going after the record. As the doctor hunkers down and checks his tissue supply, I could have told him he'd need more than he has. The flood gates are open. There is no holding back. I sob and I cry and I bawl. I cry for what I remember, for Robert and his poor dead parents and for Ben and my father. And I cry for what I can't recall, for the gaps and the blackness, and friends that are strangers, for lovers whose kisses feel like an assault. For the pain in my shoulder, the scar forming on my leg and the bump on my head too weak to bring me peace. For the misery of being Jane Halifax.

Two-Bob flees his office and his assistant takes over. She hurries in armed with two boxes of tissues, which is a bit of a challenge, but I'd do my best to give it a go.

Jane Halifax, f.p., an intrepid warrior of the transgressive mind, but could she conquer her own? I have never felt so alone in my life, so abandoned by the one thing on which I could count: my once infallible memory.

19.

I meet Luna at a coffee bar in St Kilda over the road from the design studio where she works and tell her how things had gone with Wasserman. She isn't surprised his first reaction to a DNA test was 'no', but like me is hopeful he might reflect and change his mind.

'Or discuss it with his wife?' says Luna.

Against my advice, Luna has been googling furiously, and who could blame her? Urbane, rich and happily married, who wouldn't want Joe Wasserman as a father?

'I've been stalking him,' she confesses. 'Well, not exactly stalking him – but I had to see him in the flesh. So, I hung around where he lives in Toorak and asked him for directions.'

'Did you say who you were?'

'No. But he was looking at me sideways. And I wasn't that convincing about being lost.'

'He'd know your approximate age. And you do have your mother's eyes.'

'Do you think he knew?'

'More importantly – did you?'

'I think he did,' says Luna, 'but it may have been wishful thinking. I should have gone to see him with you.'

'No. Nice, easy stages. This is just as big for him. One step at a time.'

As if on cue, my phone goes *bing* and I check my messages. It's Wasserman.

OK. I agree. I will take the test. But at a laboratory of my choosing and Luna will have to sign a non-disclosure agreement.

'A non-disclosure agreement?' says Luna, screwing up her face.

'He's being cautious. And taking advice. Anyway, an NDA is probably not enforceable in paternity cases.'

'Then why bother?'

'It's an attempt to control the narrative. Probably more to do with his wife.'

'Do you think he's told her?'

'I have no idea. Let's do the test and take it from there. One step at a time.'

But Luna can barely contain her excitement. To be honest, neither can I. Which is the opposite of what I should have been urging, but it's hard not to be invested.

'So, what happens next?' Luna asks.

'You sign the agreement – unless you want to run it past a lawyer . . .'

'No.'

'And go to the lab and they'll take a swab inside your mouth.'

'As easy as that?'

'Apart from the waiting.'

'I've been doing that for twenty years.'

Tim returns from Japan; the last part of the tour was cancelled when he and the others got Covid. It has knocked him around quite a lot, but pales in comparison to my latest concussion and tumble down the stairs. To see me depending on a walking stick again has made him feel guilty for going away, but we find comfort in each other's arms – within the limits of my still tender shoulder. It's good to feel physically close to another human.

Tim insists on staying at the apartment until my balance returns and immediately escapes to the kitchen to whip up a meal from what he can find in the fridge. Ben had been a great cook as well; it must be something I look for in a partner. Tim talks about Japan and its fascinating culture and promises to take me there for a holiday. I fill him in on my time with Luna and how much of my memory I've recovered working through the Millard case.

'I've had the files to help me, of course, but ask me anything you like about 2003 and prepare to be amazed.'

'Okay. Who was the Governor of Victoria?'

'John Landy.'

'Best group and single artist?'

'Powderfinger and Delta Goodrem.'

'Well, I wouldn't know. You could be making it up. Who won the Melbourne Cup?'

'Pass.'

'The AFL Grand Final.'

'Collingwood.'

'Close. They were beaten by the Brisbane Lions by fifty points. See – you're not infallible.'

We laugh and enjoy the game some more. It's good to be silly and frivolous. Life had been hard since the car accident and my surgery, and not only for me. It was easy to forget that those around me had been hugely affected as well.

'Thank you, Donis,' I say. His nickname had caught on too.

'For what?

'For hanging around – when I didn't know you from Adam.'

'Adam Gilchrist?'

'What?'

'Australia's wicketkeeper, 2003.'

'Shut up and serve me my meal.'

After dinner, we talk until we're tired. I hope he will go home, tonight at least, until he can collect his things, but Tim has other ideas and is clearly not going anywhere. I stall as long as I can and, much to my shame, even feign a headache. He gets me some Panadol and a glass of water, packs the dishwasher and turns out the lights.

I change in the bathroom. I still can't undress in front of him. I feel self-conscious, as if I'm getting into bed with a stranger, that I'm acting out a role like a character in a play. Tim by contrast is uninhibited, almost brazen in his nudity. I avert my eyes and rub an anti-inflammatory into my shoulder, overplaying my disability like some childish ruse to keep him on his side of the bed. But he doesn't complain. To Tim, this is progress. He is exactly where he wants to be.

I lie beside him, rigid with fear, awaiting his arm, which I know will come – reaching out beneath the sheets to hold my hand. Such a simple gesture; how can I take offence? How can I tell him all I want to do is run away to the guest room and lock the door and go to sleep alone? I have abandoned instinct in favour of a pretend intimacy. I would rather have been on the moon. My pulse is pounding in my temples, my hands are sweaty, my mouth dry. Please God, let this only be a panic attack and not let Tim find me dead in the morning.

I awake with my head buried under a pillow to block out the low eastern sun. I'm lying on top of the bedclothes, my pyjama top unbuttoned so I can warm my uncovered back. I feel like I'm alone in the room but am too afraid to peek. Surely Tim has gone home during the night like the sensitive person I knew him to be, surely he intuited my discomfort and left without waking me, leaving a loving note in the kitchen: *Jane, I love you, Jane, I understand, Jane, take as long as you like.*

But the aroma of freshly ground coffee and sizzling bacon tell another story. I get out of bed and button my top – which I hope I've undone myself – draw the curtains halfway to reduce the glare and plump the pillows for what I know will follow.

Tim comes in with breakfast: freshly squeezed orange juice and flat-white coffee (full cream, with three-quarter milk, exactly how I like it). Soft poached eggs with carrot-coloured yolks to show they are straight from the farm, grilled vine-grown tomatoes with pepper and basil and bacon crisped like crackling. Ciabatta, cultured butter and English marmalade. Even a single flower in a finger vase. He wouldn't have found much of that in my larder. He must have been up bright and early to shop, so why is he dressed in my silk dressing gown with his long hair rolled up in a bun and looking like a geisha? I decide it's best not to ask. I am tempted to ask for a tea ceremony – but don't.

The breakfast is superb. What a beautiful, thoughtful androgyne. I must be blessed.

Late that afternoon, I get a call on my mobile which is quite unexpected. My psychologist, Mette-Marit Walters – better known as Marion – ringing out of the blue from Oslo. Well, not exactly out of the blue. She'd received an email from Doctor Zhou, who had hoped she was back from visiting her parents.

'Hello, Jane. How are you doing?'

'Hello, Marion. I thought you were in Norway?'

'I am. But I'll be back next week – I thought we should make an appointment.'

'Someone been talking out of school?'

'Only because he's concerned.'

It was nice of the doctor on one level, though not much of a vote of confidence. I couldn't blame him for that.

'I'm sorry I've been away so long, but Mum and Dad are getting old, and it's hard when you live on opposite sides of the world. What felt like an adventure in my twenties had consequences I didn't think through.'

'I hope you're not coming back for me?' I ask.

'No. We're coming into autumn here and I've promised to come back next year. Anyway, how are you doing, Jane? Not so good I hear.'

'I expected some amnesia after the accident, but mine seems longer than usual. An acute case of post-traumatic amnesia lasts days or weeks: my blank is the last several years.'

'Then we've got some time to spend together.'

I was sure the good doctor had been very thorough in his report and Marion could tell I was outwardly calm and rational. But her offer to help me through my fog is instantly reassuring. She knows my history and she knows the blocks I've had in the past. I didn't tell her how paranoid I'd been about threats unknown, but one thing at a time.

'I am putting you in for Monday week. How does that sound?'

'Cheering and comforting.'

'Then consider it done.'

'And enjoy those northern lights.'

'Have you seen them, Jane?'

'Only from Scotland.'

'Oh, ours are so much better. But the Scots do better whisky, so I will bring you a single malt. Aquavit won't do it for you. Or me.'

'You make me sound like a lush.'

'Friends and whisky. It will be good to see you again.'

I was lucky to have someone like Marion. Regular supervision is best practice in counselling, but forensic psychiatry has no clear guidelines and operates under ad hoc rules. Cops have a worrying tendency to see therapy as a weakness, and when you work in that world you can get lulled into thinking the same. I'm grateful Marion has been given a nudge from Doctor Zhou and am already looking forward to Monday week.

In the meantime, I had Luna to attend to. I take her to the laboratory where she signs the paperwork and they take her swab. Then we walk around the bay from the Kerferd Road Pier to the café at Port Ormond for lunch. Whether the paternity test is positive or negative is, to a large extent, irrelevant. Luna has to resolve her feelings towards Herman, who had been her father until she was eight. Discovering a different biological parent now isn't going to change any of that. Settling her feelings about Herman is the only way I can protect her against the outcome, whatever the result.

The walk is good for my recovery, though I can't help checking any man on his own who might be following us along the path. My time with Luna gives us plenty of time for reflection, which continues over our sandwiches. Herman had a lot of good attributes which Luna concedes have been passed on to her. A drive for perfection, a strong sense of ambition, a desire to succeed. I keep her focused on the positives. She has spent too much of the last twenty years dwelling on the opposite. Herman's larger-than-life personality meant that everything was exaggerated – the bad along with the good. But where was the upside in the negatives? Certainly not peace of mind.

'Herman loved to build us stuff and made this amazing treehouse at the vineyard. It was full of trapdoors and drop-down ladders and had a lookout with a real telescope he'd got from a second-hand shop. We'd spend hours looking for pirates out on the bay.'

'You and Robert?'

'No, he was twelve years older than me. But I was always allowed to bring friends for the weekend. And we'd ride the horses as well.'

'Not a bad childhood?'

'No. But it finished too soon.'

'Yes, that I'll concede. But even Joe Wasserman can't change that.'

'It finished too soon,' Luna says again, 'but up until then it was magic.'

Luna is starting to say the right things. The challenge will be keeping her there.

20.

Joe Wasserman phones me as soon as he knows the outcome. He asks how Luna had taken the result and I have to confess I hadn't heard. She had promised to contact me immediately, whichever way it went. The fact the test was negative explained why she hadn't. I worry she has taken the results badly.

Joe seems genuinely concerned about Luna and asks if I could arrange an introduction. 'I was very fond of her mother and it would be great to meet her daughter.'

I promise to get back to him and ring off to phone Luna, but all my calls go unanswered.

It's half past six before Luna phones. She isn't keen to meet but I insist and we meet at St Kilda Pier. As the sunset's orange curtain descends on the bay, we walk the beachside path towards Middle Park. My need to walk is becoming obsessive and I hope Luna doesn't mind.

'I knew what the result would be,' she says. 'It wasn't a surprise.'

'It doesn't stop you being disappointed. But would it have changed your life?'

'It would have meant that at least one of my family wasn't a victim or perpetrator of murder.'

I give Luna a doubting look and she manages to laugh at herself.

'I know. I'm being melodramatic.'

'Just a touch. But it's not a bad emotion sometimes – as long as you know what you're doing. Why do you think Robert was so convinced Herman wasn't your father?'

'Because of what Mum had told him?'

'But why would Robert tell you? You were only eight years old.'

'So I wouldn't get upset when Herman was mean.'

'In what way was he mean?'

'Herman was tough on everyone. He could always find a way to make me cry.'

'And by telling you Herman wasn't really your father – how did that make things better?'

'I suppose it made me rely on Robert more. That I'd have someone to go to when I was upset.'

'Brotherly love and protection?'

'I guess.'

'Was Robert afraid of Herman?'

'Probably more than me.'

The Van Meulenbelts were an usual family and it wasn't surprising their dynamics were unusual too. But using information his mother had sworn him to keep to himself seemed a strange way for Robert to interact with his little sister. And wasn't it an enormous risk for Robert to take? It seemed a disproportionate burden to impose on a little girl. If Luna had blurted it out – as children are wont to do – wouldn't it have made matters worse?

'Looking back on it now after all these years,' I ask, 'does it seem strange that Robert entrusted you with such a secret?'

'No. We kept secrets all the time.'

'What kind of secrets?'

'You know – childhood stuff. Secret places and secret words and stories we would only tell to each other.'

Robert Millard had had an unusual psychology with his ability to replace the truth with fantasy as easily as turning a light on and off. Had the story about Luna's parentage been just another of those tales, a way of comforting his little sister by taking power away from her father? But if that was all it was, why share it with Morrie Latal? In all the time I had spent with Robert, I never knew his stories to be cruel or hurtful. Constantly far-fetched and inevitably outrageous, but they were never manipulative or designed for personal gain. So why did I think there was more to this father thing than met the eye? And why was I still so convinced that Robert did not commit the murders of which the court had found him guilty?

We take the tram to Chez Bagou, my favourite French restaurant in Bridport Street, where we treat ourselves to les huîtres naturelles, cuisse de canard confit, frites and haricots verts and wine by the glass as recommended by Aurelien, our host. Luna agrees to meet with Joe Wasserman. She appreciates his concern for her welfare. The non-disclosure agreement aside, he had done everything he could to resolve the situation – all in the name of her mother, Skyla, who he remembered so fondly. Why wouldn't he like to get to know her daughter? I'd arrange a meeting as soon as I could. But mostly we talk about Luna's concerns – bordering on an obsession – about her genes.

'My brother murdered my parents, who were cheating on each other. Why wouldn't I want to discover someone outside that family? Someone with less dodgy DNA.'

'Luna, you already know what I think about that. And your parents did have an open relationship which they pursued, for better or worse, without pretence. But what if I could give you your brother back by proving he wasn't a murderer? By proving he didn't kill your parents, despite what the court decided?'

'Is that a promise?'

'No. A challenge directed at myself. A pledge, if you like. To do everything I can to prove to you I'm right.'

Luna raises her glass and clinks it with mine. The deal is sealed.

All I have to do now is prove my instincts.

When I sit down with Marion Walters in her Hawthorn garden, I feel the tightness easing in my neck and shoulders. It isn't only the effect of the roses and sunflowers or the water running silently over a Japanese water feature, Marion has one of those soothing personalities that's perfect in a psychologist. She had been my supervisor since I began in forensic psychiatry and apart from my time away in academia, she continued to be the person I came to when I needed to decompress. I'm very lucky to have her.

As she reverentially pours green tea from an iron teapot, her manner is calm and unhurried, as if I could take all day if I wanted to talk through my issues. Like any good analyst, Marion is a listener. Her opening gambit was to get me to ask my own questions.

'Have I been overdoing things? Yes. Have I been pushing too hard? Absolutely. Is my doctor concerned? Well, I am sitting here with you.' I explain how terrifying it had been to lose my memory and how gradual and piecemeal its return had been, of my delight in remembering the Robert Millard case and how I was using those memories as a tool to recover the rest.

'And is that working?'

'Yes, I think it is, though the last two years are still a blank.'

'Which you and I both know is unusual.'

Marion doesn't need to remind me of what post-traumatic amnesia involved. Like any trained clinician, I'm well aware of its attributes. That it was not unusual to remember nothing of the accident or the events leading up to it or immediately following. That it was not unusual to have hallucinations and balance and movement problems or be hypersensitive to light and noise. That it takes time to become orientated again, recall memories or remember day-to-day events; to recognise familiar faces or learn new ones. That the most commonly used medications for a traumatic brain injury, such as sedatives and opiates, can actually mask recovery and cognitive functioning and impair the return of memory. But we both know that a retrograde gap of two years was unlikely to be attributable to the physical trauma of the accident alone, that something more 'psychological' was a more likely explanation, something I or my brain didn't want to face.

I tell her about the index card theory, and that while I didn't think it was necessarily sound, psychologically, it seems to be working for me, that remembering the Millard case and 2003 in particular was beginning to spread – both before and afterwards – to everything else.

'Except the last two years?'

'Yes,' I agree. 'Except the last two years.'

'And why do you think that is?'

'Because I'm still dealing with Ben's death?' I'm giving her the answer I think she wants.

Though Marion and I had had multiple sessions after Ben was murdered, I know as well as she does that a relapse was always a possibility. Sitting in a car beside the person you love only to have his blood and brains explode all over your face after someone shoots him with a high-powered rifle is an incident you can never expunge.

'Do you remember the work we had to do regarding your father?'

'Of course.'

'The first of the big traumas in your life: his suicide. And then to top even that, Ben's appalling murder.'

'Yeah,' I agree. 'I am all done with trauma.'

'Not to mention the car accident. And now a third one: Robert Millard.'

Her words, though softly spoken, are like a detonation. To equate my father's death with Ben's or even include the accident was one thing, but to add Robert Millard to that list? It doesn't make sense.

'Didn't you once describe his case as your greatest failure?' she asks.

'Well, that was a figure of speech. I thought he was wrongly convicted.'

'Which in turn led to his suicide. And we know what a big word that is for you.'

Marion knows me better than I know myself. Suicide is indeed a big word in my life. For years I had blamed my father for leaving me as a child until Marion helped me understand it from his point of view, that I was probably the last thing on his mind at the time and that if I had been in his thoughts, he quite possibly wouldn't have done it. Had I done the same thing with Robert? Taken it as my failure, instead of trying to understand where his head was at? Embarked on this journey with Luna, which led to an accident which the police hadn't ruled out as deliberate to find myself where I am now?

'Do you worry about the accident?'

'Of course I do. But until the police have concluded their investigations . . .'

Marion doesn't comment. She doesn't need to. I have mulled over the situation a thousand times.

'If the collision had been deliberate,' I continue, 'then they weren't after Peter's files in the boot, which no one tried to retrieve. And if someone wanted me dead, then running me off the road was a clumsy way to go about it – so I've dismissed that as well.'

'Very sanguine of you, Jane.'

'I've tried to keep things in proportion. It's easy to jump at shadows. I don't have any obvious enemies – at least none I remember. Which is a worry in itself. Why don't I remember? Because I really do have enemies? Is that why I'm blocking things out? I couldn't remember Paul Bathgate until the police told me who he was.

'Who?'

'Someone I did an assessment on a few months ago, someone who didn't like my conclusions. He tried to persuade me to change my mind and I had to take out an intervention order.'

Marion is watching me closely.

'The other day, I thought he was following me in the fire-stairs at my building. Which was totally irrational: how would he have a pass-key? But my panic got the better of me and I started to rush and fell.'

'Are you alright?'

'I'll have a scar on my leg, but like most things, it will fade.'

'Have you told the police?'

'He's already on their radar.'

'About him being in your building?'

'I am not sure he was.'

'And you don't want to look foolish.'

'I've had panic attacks before.'

'But what if it wasn't a panic attack? What if it was real?'

'If I allow myself to start thinking like that, where does it end?'

I wasn't even convincing myself.

'Tell them, Jane. They'll want to hear. You're not helping anyone by being so valiant.'

Valiant? Is that what I am? With Tim away, I am feeling more afraid than I'm prepared to admit. I promise Marion I will inform the police – imagined encounter or otherwise.

'So, back to your theory . . .'

'I don't have any theories, Jane. Just questions. Things for us to discuss and for you to think about. If you want to.'

Which is what a good psychologist does. But despite her reasoning, I know I'm not doing this for ego or to correct the results of a record on which no-one but myself kept score. I'm doing this for Robert Millard, to clear his name for his sake – and for Luna's. And if the only thing in it for me is recovering my memory, then I will pursue that without apology.

PART FIVE

October 2004

I like telling porkies,
I do it all the time.
From tiny little white ones
To the outrageously sublime.
Everybody does it,
It makes the world go round.
The truth can be too harsh sometimes,
Make-believe's a kinder sound.

21.

I gave Robert a reassuring glance as I took the stand and swore I would tell the court the truth, the whole truth and nothing but the truth – within the limits of my fallibility.

Rinaldi submitted my report as an exhibit and began his examination. 'Doctor Halifax, in your report you refer to the accused as a "fabulist". Would you like to explain this term to the court?'

'It's not a psychiatric term. It doesn't describe a mental condition such as schizophrenia or delusional disorder. It is not histrionic. It is not unintentional. It is a behaviour that some people exhibit where they exist in a world of make-believe where the truth and fantasy are deliberately distorted.'

'Do they tell the truth?'

'Sometimes.'

'Do they also tell lies?'

'Yes. Though they would probably describe them as exaggerations.'

'And why do people choose to "exaggerate" in this way?'

'That's more complicated. Sometimes it's because they find the truth unpleasant. Or a threat. Or too traumatic to face. Or sometimes because they find they can get away with it. Or they like to entertain others – or sometimes just themselves – with their deliberately outlandish stories.'

'And you would describe the accused as such a person.'

'Yes. I would.

'So, a difficult person to believe – one way or the other – when he makes a statement?'

'Yes.'

'Or a signed confession to the police?'

'Yes.'

'And in this case, as we know from evidence already before the court, he has made two – two diametrically opposed confessions.'

'Yes.'

'A common occurrence?'

'Objection.' The chief prosecutor, Simon Baragwanath QC, was quick to interject.

'In your experience, doctor, would you say this phenomenon is common?'

'I haven't encountered it in a criminal setting before, but I am reasonably familiar with this behaviour through clients I've seen in private practice.'

'"Clients", doctor?'

'"Patient" presumes a medical condition; "client" doesn't. These days, it's the preferred description.'

I noticed that Baragwanath's assistant was assiduously taking notes. Sometimes this is a deliberate ploy to unnerve the witness; sometimes it's a sign of the barrister's lack of confidence – like a first-year student trying to write down everything the lecturer says rather than distil the essence of what's being said. I would have to wait and see which one it was.

Rinaldi continued. 'In your report, doctor, you examine both confessions signed by the accused and conclude that the first of these is a "false confession". Are you suggesting the police obtained this confession unfairly?'

'Not at all.'

'That they pressured the accused in some way into making the statement he did?'

'No. I think he was a more than willing participant, trying his best to convince them what he was saying was true.'

'Despite the fact that, in your opinion, the whole thing is a fabrication?'

'Yes.'

'So why would he do this? What's in it for the accused?'

'Being the centre of attention. Pleasing the police. Telling them what he thought they wanted to hear.'

'Even though he is confessing, according to your contention, to something he didn't do?'

'As I say in my report, there are many reasons for this.'

'Then I think you might need to explain them to the court. Could we start with what you call his state of mind, the fact that he was in shock.'

'Both of the accused's parents were dead as a result of fatal rifle wounds. He was in a state of shock and, on one level, simply wanted his nightmare to be over as soon as possible.'

'By confessing to the crimes himself?'

'As improbable as that sounds.'

'But why would he do that?'

'Because he knew the truth and felt protected by it. That the investigation would eventually prove what really happened and that his confession would be rendered useless.'

'Not something a normal person would do?'

'The accused is not a normal person.'

'Could you elaborate?'

'This confession should not be seen as a one-off incident but as part of a pattern of behaviour going back to childhood. The accused lives in a world embellished by his imagination – where fact and fiction are constantly blended to make him seem remarkable. Robert receives a high degree of gratification from telling elaborate stories with himself at the centre – usually the more fanciful the better. It involves a degree of narcissism and is often accompanied by a sense of superiority and an impatience for those he would see as "lesser beings".'

'In this case the police?'

'Yes. On one level the accused would be amazed by the extent to which the police seemed to believe him; while on the other, he'd be waiting for them to stop him, to call his bluff and challenge what he was saying as patently wrong or absurd.'

'And if they didn't?

'He'd just keep going.'

Rinaldi led me through the rest of my report, giving me the chance to explain medical and technical matters for the jury, but I knew my crucial testimony was to follow in cross-examination. Baragwanath's junior had stopped his incessant writing, which had probably been designed to distract me, and was now studying me closely with unblinking eyes. Clearly it would be he and not his senior who would question me.

It would be the first but certainly not the last time I would engage with Peter Debreceny.

'Doctor Halifax.'

'Mr Debreceny.'

It might have been something to do with the tone we used, or in our fixed but paper-thin smiles, but I think we both knew that the battle lines had been drawn. We were both in our late thirties; old enough to know better but young enough to make mistakes. We were building careers and reputations. Individually, there was a lot at stake.

'Doctor Halifax, it's a big call, is it not, when you dismiss one confession and promote another?'

'Not when you look at the reasons.'

'But one is completely damning to the accused while the other is a get out of jail free card, is it not?'

'If you focus on the outcome, you could come to that conclusion, but not if you look at the underlying reasons.'

'Can I remind you, doctor, that while you are engaged by the defence to present this evidence, as a professional expert you also have an obligation to the court?'

'You can remind me, Mr Debreceny, though you don't need to. I am well aware of my responsibilities of impartiality as an expert witness.'

'Maybe I was stating that, doctor, for the benefit of the jury?'

'Then maybe, Mr Debreceny, you should have addressed your comments to them and not me.'

I knew I was making things worse for myself. But sometimes you have to draw that line in the metaphorical sand and see what happens.

'Doctor, do you place any significance in the fact that what you term "the false confession" was the first statement the accused made to the police?'

'Yes, I do.'

'Could you elaborate?'

'Because that was the statement made in the heat of the moment, when the accused was still in shock from finding his parents' bodies.'

'His shock aside, would you describe your "client" as an intelligent man?'

'Are you referring to the accused, Mr Debreceny?'

'I'm only using a word you used yourself, doctor.'

'To avoid using the term "patient", which pre-judges his condition. When I am asked to undertake a psychiatric examination, it's the term I prefer to use.'

'But not anymore?'

'As you have already pointed out to the jury, I have a wider responsibility as an expert witness, an obligation to the court. So now we're in a judicial setting, I think "accused" is the more appropriate term.'

'But isn't he still your "client", doctor? Isn't his defence still paying your bills?'

'Mr Debreceny . . .'

'Yes, Your Honour.'

'I think you could use your time more productively than getting bogged down in this.'

'Yes, Your Honour.'

Round one to me.

'Doctor Halifax, you have stated that the accused has no known psychiatric conditions such as schizophrenia or a delusional disorder . . .'

'Yes.'

'That he is of above average IQ?'

'Yes.'

'And has successfully held down a number of jobs, including producing and directing a documentary.'

'Yes.'

'When he confessed to murder in the first confession, would he have had any understanding of the consequences of what he was saying?'

'Probably.'

'Specifically, the seriousness of the crimes to which he was confessing?'

'Yes, I think so.'

'And the likelihood of the consequences if found guilty, that is, a very substantial term of years in prison?'

'Yes, he would.'

'Then why on earth would he do it?'

'Because it made him the centre of attention. Because for the very first time in a life dominated by his parents, it gave him, however briefly, a sense of power and control.'

'Or, to put your theory aside for a moment, Doctor Halifax, he could have been telling the truth?'

'As I've said, I did not come to that conclusion. But only after weighing the circumstances carefully. I'm not spinning some kind of . . . psychiatric chocolate wheel.'

'I put it to you, doctor, that that's precisely what you're doing.'

An own goal if ever there was one. Round two to Debreceny. I resolved to keep the clever comments to myself.

'You have presented lots of reasons why the first confession is wrong and the second confession is correct. But couldn't you use the self-same arguments and swap them over and come up with the opposite result?'

'No.'

'Why not?'

'Because of the order in which they took place. The second confession is more thoughtful and considered. It involves a police reconstruction. It is an attempt by the accused to repair the damage of his erroneous first confession.'

'Or come up with a defence?'

'No. I don't believe so. Yes, he's had time to reflect on what he told the police, he's had time to reconsider and recant. But each confession has its own unique features and characteristics, its own psychological setting. Those elements aren't random and interchangeable.'

'And if the confessions had been reversed, doctor, what would you say then?'

'Well, they weren't reversed, Mr Debreceny, so that is just speculation. But for argument's sake, if they were reversed I would always take more notice of the second confession, when a person with the accused's profile has had time to think. So, if he had said in the first confession that he had found the bodies and picked up the gun and in the second, that he had used the gun on his parents, I would be inclined to believe his confession to murder. But that's not what happened.'

Never ask a question in cross-examination to which you don't know the answer. Jane, two; Debreceny, one.

'Doctor Halifax, there's not much science in your assessment, is there?'

'Well, there's no pure maths.'

'And not much psychiatry either? By your own admission, the accused has no formal psychiatric condition as might be defined, for instance in DSM-IV?'

'No.'

'So, is anything less than that useful to the court?'

'Yes, it is. As I have said, the accused's fabulism is a form of pathological lying and as such can be seen as a symptom of narcissistic or histrionic personality disorders.'

'But you stop short of making those diagnoses?'

'He exhibits aspects of both disorders but they are not what I would term full blown. He sits somewhere on the cusp, where he is capable of telling the truth. And often does.'

'As, you would argue, was the case with the second confession?'

'Yes.'

'A fairly convenient diagnosis, doctor? When you want to dismiss one confession and promote another?'

'I could have said they were both false – but that is not my diagnosis.'

'So how do you decide when he's lying and when he's telling the truth?'

'By looking at context. By looking at the entire psychological landscape.'

'But can't a pathological liar, once they have realised their lies have got them into trouble, lie again to try to repair the damage?'

'Objection, Your Honour. The question asks for the witness to speculate.' Rinaldi was sensing danger.

'On the contrary, Your Honour, I am asking Doctor Halifax, as the only expert before this court, to help us understand what a pathological liar is capable of doing.'

'Objection overruled.'

'Thank you, Your Honour. I will put the question again. Doctor Halifax, in your professional experience and as an expert before this court, is it plausible to say that a pathological liar, once they have realised their lies have got them into trouble, could lie again to try to repair the damage? Yes or no?'

'Yes, that's plausible.'

'Thank you. I have no further questions.'

Rinaldi rose for his re-examination, but the damage had already been done.

22.

The court adjourned and we hurried across the road to Rinaldi's chambers to weigh the day's proceedings.

'What a disaster,' I concluded, happy to accept the blame.

'It's not the worst thing I have to contend with,' said Rinaldi.

'Ballistics?'

'Gunpowder residue on the sleeve of his jumper. That's not going to go away after "a spin of a psychiatric chocolate wheel".'

'Yeah, apologies for saying that too.'

'Leave the one-liners to me, Jane. And never say them in court.'

'I knew it was foolish as soon as it came out of my mouth.'

'The problem is he fancies you.'

'Debreceny?'

'Have you considered wearing a wedding band in court? Or an engagement ring?'

'What do you mean?'

'Might provide you with some protection.'

'Come on, Vincenzo. It's 2004.'

Rinaldi produced a bottle of wine and two glasses.

'No, thanks. I need to go see my client.'

'Yeah, he made mileage with that as well. But I set you up for that one.'

'No, you didn't. No-one would have objected to patient. I should have called him that from the start.'

Down in the holding cells, Robert was agitated. He knew the week had not gone well. He had followed every twist and turn of the case and his initial confession was looking more and more plausible with every witness – myself included.

'Can I ask you again about the ballistics report and, in particular, how gunpowder residue might have got on your sleeve?' I asked him.

'It's bullshit. It was a very hot day. Why would I be wearing a jumper?'

'I know Rinaldi has asked you this before, but we need to do a better job of establishing what you were wearing. Who were the last people to see you before you went to the house?'

'How can I be expected to remember that?'

'Robert, you're on trial for murder. You need to remember everything. When you put on your jumper. When you took it off. The last time and place you can remember wearing it . . .'

'I can't remember.'

'Sorry. Yes, you can.' I had to use the safe word, I had to call him out when he was deliberately avoiding the truth. 'What were you doing, Robert? Before you went to your parents' house?'

'Watching *Beavis and Butthead*.'

'Where?'

'At my place.'

'On your own or with someone else?'

'With Luna.'

'Then maybe she remembers.'

Robert's emotions flared. 'I don't want her involved in any of this, do you understand?'

'Even if it could change the outcome of this case?'

'Even then.'

I could understand Robert's desire to keep his little sister away from his trial. After all, he was charged with their parents' murder. But his reaction seemed disproportionate, as if he was troubled by something else.

'Can you get this to Luna?' he asked, handing me a sheet of paper. 'It's a poem.'

Robert had been scribbling away in court during the day's proceedings. I'd wondered what he'd been doing. I folded the sheet to afford him some privacy.

'You can read it if you like.'

Georgie Porgie, picklety pie,
Kissed the girls and made them cry.
When Georgie Porgie comes home to play,
It will be a long and sunny day.
Jack be nimble, Jack be quick,
I give you a stone, you give me a stick.
Keep our secrets alive forever,
And that way we'll be together.

'It's my promise to Luna. That I'll be back when this is over.'

'Not unless we can explain that jumper.'

'Isn't it obvious? It's been planted by the police.'

'Sorry.'

'I know you don't believe me. Nor does anyone. What's the point?' Robert's belief had become so entrenched that he couldn't get beyond it. He wasn't wearing the jumper, ergo, the police must have planted it. End of story.

But without evidence, it wasn't an explanation we could prove. Rinaldi had done his best to challenge the logging of the forensic evidence, but even the jury could sense he was relying on technicalities that probably weren't there. Most damning was the fact that Robert had agreed to wear a jumper during the police reconstruction. It implied that was what he was wearing when he had entered the house. If he thought the police were introducing a planted item, why didn't he object at that point? He had been meticulous in his desire to get every detail right.

Luna was living with her uncle and aunt in Sydney. I promised I would send her the poem as soon as I could. I asked Robert to think again about the jumper, but had no confidence that he would.

Peter Debreceny was the last person I wanted to run into as I left the court after the prison van had taken Robert back to jail.

'Hey, Jane. I'm going for a drink. Want to join me? I promise not to talk about the case.'

'Peter,' I stalled, hiding the naked fingers of my left hand, 'maybe some other time.'

'No. I insist. If only to show there's no hard feelings. We have long careers ahead of us, hopefully. Surely that's worth a solitary drink?'

We found a corner table in a noisy bar and Peter struggled back from the counter with two glasses of wine and a bottle of sparkling water. Technically it was one drink a piece, red for him and white for me, though the water would bulk out the time. Was that Sade singing 'Smooth Operator' on the sound system or only in my head?

Peter Debreceny wasn't a tall man but his presence was commanding. Confident and intelligent, he fixed the person he was talking to with a flattering intensity. A natural advocate, he would probably end up on the bench one day or Director of Public Prosecutions.

'We have a case coming up where we'll need an expert. Can I give you a call when this case is over?'

'Of course. I'm in the book.'

'I've appeared against Rinaldi before. He's very good.'

How to talk around a case but never mention it.

'I've got to write a paper for the Law Reform Commission,' he continued. 'On Expert Evidence. I wonder if you'd consider cowriting it with me? I could send you the extract and you can have a think.'

'That could be timely,' I admitted. 'I'm considering an academic position. Professor of Forensic Psychiatry at Melbourne.'

'Congratulations.'

'I'm yet to make the decision.'

What was I doing, sharing personal information with a virtual stranger? Trying to lessen the bruises he had given me in court? And what was I doing here, having a drink with a member of the other side? Even if my part of the case was over.

I should have been talking about my boyfriend and the meal he was cooking for me at home. Ben had been my most successful long-term relationship, although I was yet to make that final commitment. I knew my father's suicide had a lot to do with it. When someone you love to the moon and back leaves you without explanation, you can find it difficult to believe in permanency.

'If you take the university position, will you be able to give expert evidence?'

'Yes, but probably less frequently.'

'Well, as long as you take on mine.'

I finished my drink, declined the water and consulted my watch without displaying my unbanded fingers. 'Thanks for the drink, Peter, but I have to go. My boyfriend's cooking dinner.'

At least I got that in.

Ben and I tried our best to keep the weekends clear. Sometimes he had a guitar to finish making, sometimes I had a court case to prepare, but we considered our downtime as important as work, though there was always the unexpected. As we packed the car for a weekend with friends at Mount Macedon, my mobile vibrated in my pocket. My first instinct was to ignore it, though I couldn't resist checking who it was. So when he rang again, I accepted.

Rinaldi didn't even bother to introduce himself. 'What did you say to our client yesterday when you saw him in the cells?'

'Nothing in particular. Why?'

'He wants to change his plea. To guilty. He informed his solicitor this morning.'

'Oh, shit.'

'I'm at the farm so I can't see him till Monday. Can you?'

'I've got plans as well, Vincenzo . . .'

'Well, sometimes the best of mice and men . . .' Though Rinaldi wasn't hurrying back from his stud farm to see our client.

Ben gave me his blessing, though not before asking where my thinking was at with the offer from the university.

'A lot more tempted than I was before,' I admitted.

He seemed to take some reassurance in that.

'You and Zoe go on and I'll join you later,' I said without predicting when. 'I'll come as soon as I can.'

23.

Barwon Prison is a modern facility but not somewhere anyone would choose to be. It maintains a mood of grim formality, which must take a toll on the warders as well as the inmates, though at least the staff get to go home. As I checked into the protection unit, which was separated from the rest of the prison, the wind became sharper and the sun lost its warmth, not that there had been any change in the weather. A prison has a desolation that modern architecture can't obscure: the hopelessness of incarceration, the long minutes and months and years marking time, the efficacy of deterrence.

As I waited for Robert to be escorted to the interview room, I could only speculate how a change of plea would reflect on my evidence and the confession I was so convinced was false. Without understanding the legal ramifications, I knew a change of direction at this point in the case would not be routine. Perhaps my time in the witness box and my battle with Peter Debreceny was destined to continue.

I was not the person Robert hoped to be meeting.

'I do not need another psychiatric assessment. I want legal advice. I want to change my plea.'

'Hello, Robert. Mr Rinaldi's not available. He asked me to see you. I'll be reporting to him after this. We want to understand why you've changed your mind.'

'With two confessions, one was always going to be wrong.'

'Are you saying the first confession is true?'

'Yes. I shot my parents. Someone needed to.' He was speaking without emotion, as if following a script he'd prepared.

'What do you mean someone needed to?'

'For not protecting Luna. For not protecting me.'

'What about the police reconstruction and your second statement?'

'I was attempting to come up with a defence.' Which was fairly close to the words Debreceny had used in court.

'Well, I know the confession, I believe,' I said with a quiet conviction I hoped might be contagious.

'That's not going to be enough.'

'I can understand why you're anxious, Robert. Criminal trials can be very frightening but you have to let them play out. It's not for you to influence the outcome.'

'What's the point? You're not going to make my first confession go away. Or the gunpowder residue either. I just want it to be over.'

'Robert, did you get any sleep last night?'

'No.'

'Then I'm going to give you some sedatives to calm you down and help you sleep. What you are experiencing is not unusual. You are having to revisit very traumatic events—'

'Why won't you listen to me? What do I have to say to convince you? I shot my parents and I'm glad I did. And I am happy to admit it.'

'For not protecting you and Luna?'

'Yes.'

'For not protecting you from what?'

'From their . . . appalling behaviour.'

His choice of words was unconvincing; they seemed random and lacked belief. It was as if Robert had made a decision and was determined to follow it for reasons that remained opaque. Short of taking a lie-detector test – in which I had little confidence but was seriously considering for the first time in my career – I was faced with a genuine dilemma. How does one discern when a pathological liar is lying or telling the truth? How can anyone drill down and find the truth when the subject is confused himself?

As things stood, it was my expert evidence versus the Crown's ballistics. It would be up to the lawyers to convince the jury which argument was more persuasive. But now Robert was threatening to change his plea and turn everything on its head.

'Robert, when did you decide to change your plea? Yesterday in court, when I saw you in the cells, last night, this morning . . . ?'

'What does it matter?'

'Because I need to know your thought processes in order to understand them.'

'I'm tired.'

Which was understandable, but not a good reason to change his mind.

'I'm sick of lying.'

Unlikely too, since lying was his raison d'être.

'Because I don't want Luna involved.'

Ah, the jumper. That's what had sparked this whole thing. Asking him what he was doing before he went to his parents' house. And who he was doing it with. Trying to look for something that might explain away his jumper. Trying to get someone – anyone – to corroborate his insistence that he wasn't wearing it.

'Robert, the system is very good when dealing with children. Luna is not going to be dragged into court.'

'No.'

'She can be interviewed in a non-threatening environment by someone like me . . .'

'No.'

'All we want is the truth.'

'I want to change my plea. And I have a perfect right to do so. Unless of course you think I'm insane. In which case, you should have me committed.'

It is hard when an accused has to sit in court and endure the ebbs and flows of proceedings and descriptions of themselves that are harsh and unflattering. It's inevitable they will weigh the evidence and speculate on the outcome. It's explicable when the stress gets too much and they just want it to be over. Robert's desire to protect his nine-year-old sister was also understandable. So why did I think there was more to this than he was prepared to tell me? And how could I keep his case on track in the meantime?

'Let's meet with Rinaldi before court on Monday morning and see what he recommends.'

Robert agreed and we left things at that. I phoned Rinaldi, who took Robert's situation better than I expected. He implied that he would have more authority with Robert than me and could 'settle him down on Monday' and hoped my sedatives would do the rest. He didn't want to dwell on things and was clearly more adept in protecting his time at his stud farm than

I had been in keeping my weekend intact. Maybe men are better at that.

I arrived at Mount Macedon in time for the barbecue and to enjoy the beauty of our friends' expansive gardens. As the sun went down, I swam in the heated pool and watched with pride as Ben and Zoe delighted the others with a guitar duet. Barwon Prison seemed a long way away, but it was never far from my thoughts. Nor a little girl not much older than Zoe called Luna and the promise her brother had made.

When Georgie Porgie comes home to play,
It will be a long and sunny day.

An hour before proceedings resumed on Monday, Rinaldi led me down to the holding cells beneath the court. An imposing figure in his wig and gown, his approach was unambiguous. While I had tried to understand Robert's change of heart and his readiness to confess, Rinaldi was blunt and to the point.

'You are going to lose me my case.'

Robert was as shocked as I was. Was his barrister even interested in his reasons?

'So, tell me, Robert – what's going on?'

'I've had enough. My case is hopeless. I just want it to be over.'

'The case isn't hopeless, Robert. I've hardly begun. Beyond reasonable doubt is the standard here, and the prosecution is a long way away from that.'

'That's not how it feels.'

'It's not your job, Robert, to assess how we're doing. It's mine. Yours is to sit in the dock and do a better job of not looking so goddamn guilty.'

'But I am.'

'After eighteen months of waiting for this to come to trial, are you telling me I've been wasting my time?'

I was uncomfortable with Rinaldi's bullying. Robert was calmer than he had been on Saturday, but he was still subdued and defeatist and I doubted if such a front-on attack was helping.

'You're not the first person to lose his nerve during a trial and you won't be the last,' continued Rinaldi.

'I want to change my plea.'

'Which you are perfectly entitled to do, but let me tell you what will probably happen. In the first instance I will ask for an adjournment and get Doctor Halifax to do a detailed psychiatric assessment. It's not your guilt or innocence I'm concerned with at this point but your fitness to stand trial. And if I hold that concern, so will the court. And if the doctor here shares those concerns, then this case could well be abandoned and the jury dismissed and we will have to start all over again at some point in the future. So instead of hastening a decision, you'll be prolonging it. Do you understand?'

Robert was silent.

'This isn't an easy case, Robert. For me or the jury. But in the end it's a simple choice between two confessions. And, with the doctor's help, I know the one I believe. I apologise in advance for being direct, but given your history, maybe you don't know the truth yourself.'

While I didn't agree with Rinaldi's tactics, I was observing an interesting dynamic. Robert was being dominated by a male authority figure. It was easy to imagine his father in a similar position. It was also easy to see it as a possible motive for murder.

'Do you want my opinion, Robert?' I interjected, to Rinaldi's displeasure. 'Let's ask for a short adjournment and spend some time together. I'm concerned about your welfare and I'm not sure I understand your thinking.'

'You're not helping, doctor.' Now Rinaldi was bullying me. 'If we seek an adjournment, we will be risking abandonment and a brand-new trial. And if that happens, I cannot guarantee that I'll be available.'

Rinaldi was no doubt acting in what he believed were his client's best interests; it was his tactics I found hard to accept. Showing confidence and holding the line is one thing, threatening him into submission quite another, and I was prepared to risk Rinaldi's disapproval to make it clear where I stood.

Rinaldi looked at his watch and then at Robert. 'I need your instructions, Robert, and I need them now. I have told you what I think, but the decision's up to you.'

'I don't want Luna involved in this.'

'What?' Rinaldi didn't understand.

'To verify what I was wearing.'

'Who's suggesting that?'

'I think that may have come from me,' I confessed, earning another stormy look from the barrister. 'I was only trying to help.'

'Robert, I can promise you we won't involve your sister. You have my word on that.'

Robert seemed torn between our positions although I was in no doubt which way he'd decide. 'Okay,' said Robert. 'Let's stick with the plea I've made.'

'Thank you,' said Rinaldi, relieved his authority was intact, despite my attempts to undermine it.

As we left the holding cells, Rinaldi steered me into an interview room and closed the door firmly behind us. I had never seen him so angry.

'You stick to your field and I'll stick to mine.'

'You're a bully, Vincenzo, and I don't approve.'

'I do what I need to do.'

'What? To protect your precious case?'

'I am running this defence, not you.'

'Yes, you are, but the accused's state of mind is my business. I am the expert on that.'

'Are you saying he's not fit to stand trial?'

'No. But there are too many unanswered questions without you eliminating a possible source of answers who might be able to tell us what he was wearing – Robert's sister.'

'You let me worry about ballistics, Jane. The prosecution is not going to win on that. If he's fit to stand trial then I'm fit to defend him. And your evidence, despite the odd stumble, is still my ace in the hole.'

There was no point in restating my position. The case was minutes away from resuming. 'We shouldn't be arguing before you have to perform. I'm sorry I interfered.'

'You were right to express your opinion, Jane. And I am a bully. No hard feelings?'

'What is it about you barristers that you hate to be challenged?'

'A certain thinness of skin, I suspect.'

'Good luck in court this morning. And to Robert too.'

'It's not up to him anymore.'

Whatever my feelings about Rinaldi, I couldn't question how seriously he took his case. Like any good advocate, he was in this to win.

'Go break a leg, Vincenzo.'

'Or if not mine, somebody else's?'

24.

My spirits lifted as I headed across the south lawn of Melbourne University. I had inhabited the court case all weekend and was resigned to leaving it to Rinaldi to deal with.

Nicholas El Masry was waiting by the clock tower of the old building, chatting with two of his students. He peeled away as I approached and met me with a wicker picnic basket and a big Arabian smile.

'Such a beautiful day, I thought we'd skip the club dining room and eat out here.'

We found some shade and he spread out a rug and opened a bottle of pinot grigio. Vine leaves, hummus, maqluba and bread; falafel and olives and a selection of cheeses; real plates and cutlery and pre-chilled wine glasses. He had rendered the club dining room mundane.

I had presented the odd lecture for Nicholas and helped him with his doctoral students, but I was concerned I wasn't a natural teacher like he was. Like his picnic, his lectures were inspired.

'That will come,' he assured me. 'You don't want to be too serious. It's about mystery and curiosity.' He talked me through the salary package and how I could continue in private practice. 'We encourage our staff to keep a foot in the real world.'

I told him about the approach from Peter Debreceny to cowrite a paper for the Law Reform Commission.

'Perfect,' he said. 'What starts out like that can end up as a book. We want you to write and be published.'

I had to admit I was tempted.

'So, what's the problem?' he asked.

'I've put in a lot of effort to build my practice. It feels like I'm quitting just as I'm getting started.'

'Won't you be able to pick and choose more?'

'I'm not sure I'm established enough for that. There'll be those who'll think I've abandoned it all to teach.'

'What does your boyfriend think?'

'Oh, he's all in favour. He thinks I'm burnt out already.'

'Are you?'

'No. He's thinking about himself. He would like to see more of me and he has a daughter who could probably do with a mother. When a case is on, it's all-consuming – and I won't pretend I don't get lost in it. But I like cops and lawyers; I like their world. And I'm very good at what I do. The transgressive mind is my addiction, Nicholas, my compulsion to figure things out.'

'Maybe you'll find that passion in teaching?'

'Maybe.'

'Why don't you take a short-term contract and see how you go?'

'No. I'm an all-or-nothing gal.'

'Well, you've got till the end of the month. Then I'm going to have to advertise.'

'I can't tell you how grateful I am for the offer.'

'That's okay, Jane. I'm being as selfish as your boyfriend.

I want you in my department and I know the students will love you.'

I thanked Nicolas for the picnic and headed back towards the city. I considered swinging by the court to see how Robert was doing, but opted instead to collect Zoe from school to make up for Saturday's absence. Family life, the ultimate juggle; that balance between self and others. Was that a looming decision as well?

Sometimes I felt like a cop with a busted relationship who ends up married to the job, not because she liked it so much but because she couldn't quit.

'*Hello, my name's Jane and I'm a workaholic.*'

'*Hello, Jane.*'

'*This is my first meeting. I've tried to come before but I've always been too busy.*'

As I waited with the other parents outside Zoe's school and gossiped about how the winter holidays had gone and asked questions to which I didn't want the answers, I could see that part of my life was slipping away. Did I lack the quality most people had to sign on to daily routines? Home, hearth and children; was that really me? Or was a pathological liar of much more interest, or patricide or matricide, or an accused who couldn't make up his mind about which way to throw the dice? Even teaching seemed to lack colour and movement. *Do young minds really need to be fed that much water or do they flourish better in more arid ground like grape-vines? Discuss.*

Zoe was pleased to see me. She had made a drawing of herself and Ben playing their guitars at Mount Macedon. There was an admiring audience to one side with me in the background, swimming alone in the pool. Kids – they notice everything.

I attended court the following day. Robert was doing fine. Rinaldi had recalled the ballistics expert for further examination and was scoring points with the jury. Baragwanath QC had challenged the recall on the grounds that Rinaldi had brought no new evidence before the court, but the judge wasn't interested in technicalities; she had a murder trial to run. Peter Debreceny re-examined the witness, but couldn't plug the gaps Rinaldi had exposed. Things were beginning to turn in our favour.

I arrived at Ben's house as the babysitter was settling in with Zoe. We were going to a birthday party for Ben's friend Tim at his parents' mansion in Kew. It took the form of a progressive concert with different instruments placed around the garden. Most of the guests were his friends from the orchestra. They performed in groups of four or five supported by singers and jazz musicians with jugglers and people on stilts and an enormous elephant operated by puppeteers. The pageant told the story of Tim's life through music from his early years in South Africa, his time at the Conservatorium and his triumph at the Newport Jazz Festival. 'Wimoweh', *Boléro*, 'Take Five', *Rhapsody In Blue*, Habanera, Dvorak's Cello Concerto, 'Money For Nothing' and your chicks for free. And Tim's electronic cello version of the Miles Davis classic 'Venus de Milo'.

It was one of those nights you never forget. And as Ben and I sat in the garden with long glasses of soda and lime, Tim circulated among the guests. Like the other performers, he was still in costume. With long, thin antlers, black and white stripes on his face and a bared torso, his gazelle seemed exposed and vulnerable.

‘Can a gazelle outrun a cheetah?’ Ben joked as he observed a flautist looking hungrily in Tim’s direction.

‘No. But I can outmanoeuvre her,’ Tim replied.

‘Why would you want to do that?’

‘Because she’s married to the baboon.’

The baboon, a timpani player, sat at the outdoor bar, determined to consume as many free drinks as he could.

‘It’s been a magical evening, Tim,’ I said. ‘Thank you for including me.’

‘You’re almost family, aren’t you?’ he said before moving on.

It was an innocent enough response, but it made Ben uncomfortable. Had he been talking to Tim behind my back? I got the impression that Ben had brought me to this remote bench in the corner of the garden for a very particular purpose.

‘How did your meeting go at the university?’ Ben asked.

‘The offer’s still there till the end of the month.’

‘Will you take it?’

‘I really don’t know. Probably not. Though he suggested a short-term contract so I can see if I like it or not.’

‘So, what’s the problem?’

‘Other people’s expectations.’

‘Then will this help or make things worse?’ He took a small box from his pocket and opened it to reveal a ring.

‘Is that what I think it is?’

‘An engagement ring; a friendship ring. Anything you want it to be.’

My commitment-phobe’s heart was taking flight. I felt cornered with no means of escape. It wasn’t the first time I’d received a proposal and those occasions hadn’t ended well.

‘Oh, Ben, it’s not that I don’t love you . . .’

'Then what's the problem? Zoe?'

'No, I love her too.'

'So . . .'

'I'm not very good with surprises.'

'You wanted to discuss it first?'

'Probably.'

'Is that a "no"?'

'Do I have till the end of the month?'

His laughter relieved the pressure and he placed the ring beside him on the bench.

I gave him a kiss. 'I think I need a proper drink.'

Ben headed off to the bar as I sat in the dark, feeling foolish. I'd had counselling to deal with my problem, but it hadn't helped. My position was too entrenched. I didn't believe in the institution of marriage. As far as I could tell, it didn't guarantee anything. Relationships either worked or endured or they didn't. And I still resented the fact that my mother was expected to wear a ring while my father never did.

Would a ring bring me protection? According to Rinaldi, it would.

Ben returned with two glasses of riesling. We kissed again, clinked glasses and toasted the future, whatever it would be, while the ring sat between us, hiding in its box.

25.

I took a seat behind Rinaldi as Inspector Bryan Tregonning filed in with his 2IC to sit behind Baragwanath. Tregonning, known in the force as the Silver Fox because of his prematurely greying hair, was a rising star in the Homicide squad and a celebrity case like this would probably define his career. He had been cross-examined by Rinaldi with the same vigour as Debreceny had examined me. Each of us was seen as our side's greatest strength and potential weakness. It seemed surreal that a man's freedom could finally turn on the evidence we had given.

Rinaldi's and Baragwanath's closing addresses were predictable summations of the evidence for and against, and then the judge gave her final instructions to the jury. After weeks of evidence and testimony and argument from highly skilled lawyers, experts and policemen, everything now was down to the competence of twelve good men and women.

Rinaldi's task was done until the jury was ready to deliver its verdict and he hurried back to chambers to work on an upcoming case. His solicitors were similarly 'occupied elsewhere', so it was left to me to visit Robert before the prison van took him away.

His response was unexpected. 'I should have pleaded insanity.'

'But that would assume you were guilty, Robert. Insanity's a defence to murder.'

'I'd rather spend the rest of my days at Thomas Embling than Barwon Prison.'

'But you weren't insane. That option was never available.'

'No. Not insane. Just a pathological liar.'

He was clearly wounded by the expression used throughout the trial. But after years of unchecked fabulism, maybe it was time he faced the truth.

'Will you be here when they deliver the verdict?' he asked, like the child he still behaved.

'Of course.'

I resisted giving Robert a prediction, for in truth I was as anxious as he. It was hard not to recall the words of the great American poet, Robert Frost: 'A jury consists of twelve persons chosen to decide who has the better lawyer.'

As events transpired, I was not there when the verdict was handed down. After three days, the jury had been unable to agree and the judge sent them back for further deliberation. She said she would accept a majority decision of eleven, though she urged unanimity if this could be achieved. In the constant toing and froing between judge and jury for further clarification, Rinaldi had left me alone.

'Guilty as charged on both counts,' he informed me on the phone, sounding as surprised by the verdict as everyone else.

'You're joking.'

'I will appeal, of course. Misdirection on "beyond reasonable doubt" for a start. It is always a minefield when a judge tries to say too much.'

'Was the decision unanimous?'

'Yes. In the end. I think she bullied them on that as well.'

Well, it takes one to know one. 'How did Robert take it?'

'Like someone who was guilty all along. I think he was expecting it.'

'He did not murder his parents, Vincenzo. I will stake my reputation on that.'

'It's too late to revisit the facts, Jane. All I've got is misdirection. That and forensics. The judge should never have allowed the gunpowder residue evidence. It was never properly recorded.'

I crawled my car over the Westgate Bridge with the rest of the rush-hour traffic. At this time of day it would take an hour to get to Barwon Prison. Plenty of time to think. It was hard to believe I couldn't have been warned the jury was about to deliver its verdict, though my office was not as close to the courts as Rinaldi's. And as he liked to remind me, it was 'his' case and not anyone else's – Robert included. He was probably right. I needed to learn how to be an expert without becoming so involved.

I had phoned ahead to let the prison know I was coming but when I got to the reception area, the staff seemed evasive and I was ushered through to the chief warder's office, where I was made to wait for almost an hour. It was obvious something was seriously wrong.

'Doctor Halifax, I am sorry to inform you that the prisoner Robert Millard is deceased. He hanged himself in his cell two hours ago. We called a doctor to do what he could, but he was unable to save him. I'm sorry.'

'Wasn't he under observation?'

'Yes. This is an observation unit. There will be an investigation. It shouldn't have happened. I'm sorry.'

The chief warder was sorry. The entire Department of Corrections Victoria was no doubt sorry as well. And the minister and the premier and the government and the opposition and everyone else in between. Sorry, regretful, remorseful but finally unrepentant, for it had happened before and would happen again until prisoners – especially those declared as vulnerable and therefore at risk– received the care and special protection they deserved. What a miserable place a prison is.

The traffic leaving the city hadn't eased as I drove back to Melbourne. Alone in my car, I seemed inconsequential among the grey masses swarming home. Was I being idealistic to put such a high value on a single human being who, whatever I believed, had been found guilty of the murder of his parents? Or was suicide the concept I couldn't process?

I am a psychiatrist. I deal with depression as part of my job. I know how persistent it can be, how mulish to treat. I have suffered the tragedy of suicide myself. My father left me and I still don't know why. And now Robert had confounded me, too.

I soaked in a bath while Ben prepared dinner. I had some decisions to make. I was not suffering from burnout as Ben liked to suggest. He misunderstood the term. I loved my work and didn't lack enthusiasm. I didn't have problems sleeping. I didn't suffer mood swings or migraines. My libido was intact – very intact. My work–life balance could be better, but so could Ben's. But I had become emotionally involved in this case and I knew that wasn't good. I had set out to save Robert Millard and I had failed. I had taken him on as a cause. Had I misdiagnosed him? Were my boundaries in serious need of a survey?

I told Zoe a story and she held my thumbs as we blasted off into the heavens. 'Once upon a time there was an alien who couldn't tell the truth and it got him into a lot of trouble. He ended up not being able to describe himself, even when he looked in a mirror.'

'Was he blind?' said Zoe, eager to make sense of the story.

'No,' I replied, 'he just got lost in his lies. It's an easy thing to do when you don't tell the truth.'

'But a mirror can tell the truth,' said Zoe wisely.

'Not on the planet the alien came from. It wasn't like earth, more like *Alice In Wonderland*.'

'Was there a rabbit?' she asked.

'There's always a rabbit.'

'And a Mad Hatter too?'

'No. Aliens don't wear hats. Because their nostrils are on top of their heads.'

It was time to bring the rocket back to earth and calm Zoe down. Ben was right about me hyping her up before bed. But it's hard to assume motherly instincts when you begin with a six-year-old from a standing start.

'I've made some decisions,' I said after dinner as we took our wine out into the garden. 'You may need that little box.'

'Let me go and get it—'

'No, just listen. Before I change my mind.'

'Doesn't sound very considered,' said Ben. 'Doesn't sound very Jane Halifax.'

'I have decided to take the uni job. On a two-year contract, while maintaining my private practice. So, if anything, I'll be even busier.'

'So why does that involve the little box?'

'Shut up. They're not connected. You need to understand I will still operate as an expert witness. That I'll disappear from time to time, though hopefully on a less frequent basis. I may find the two things are inconsistent but I won't know that until I give it a go.'

'Great. Fantastic. I approve.'

'Before I tell you decision two, I need to tell you my conditions.'

'Now that's more like the f.p. I know.'

'I will wear the ring but it's not an engagement ring. I don't want to get married. I will come live with you and Zoe, if that's still on offer, but I am not going to sell my place until I know if this is going to fly.'

'Practical, analytical, extremely sound.'

'Romance will be limited to set times on Tuesdays and Sundays unless I change my mind, but masks and whips are still off the menu. Understood?' He knew I was joking about the last condition. Well, I hoped he did. 'Now, go see if you can find the little box while I write up the contract.'

No-one knows the precise moment a relationship begins. It is seldom to do with rings or proposals or other formal markers but with moments of affirmation, and this had been one of those. A relationship's progress cannot be predicted. Some flourish, some fade, some become a habit. Only the end of a relationship is certain. Until death us do part. Or unless one of us runs off with somebody else. Or changes their mind. Or falls out of love. Or was never in love in the first place.

At least I knew that wasn't me. I was in love with Ben. I was in love with Zoe. I hoped we would all live forever, though I knew that was only a notion. As my mother liked to say, 'No-one gets out of this alive.' The newborn replace the dying and the world goes round and round.

To what extent Robert Millard's death had prompted this moment was something I would never know.

PART SIX

April 2023

Luna is a silver moon,
Up in the sky she'd stay,
Going through her phases,
Until the light of day.
But Luna didn't fade for long,
She'd come back every night,
For that is when the magic starts,
And fantasies take flight.

26.

'*Take the northbound train to N. Hollow Rd. Then take the eastbound train to Atkinson Ave.*'

The voice is otherworldly and digitally stretched. It has become my early morning companion, an addiction to which I happily devote an hour every day before breakfast. But I'm not back in the spaceship. I'm on my computer.

An animated graphic of two trains heading in opposite directions appears on the screen. Remembering the direction of earlier selections, and without the aid of a compass (included only when the game begins) I'm required to adjust my orientation and make a choice. A friendly 'click' indicates success, a harsher 'beep' an error.

True North is a brain training exercise from brainHQ which tests quickness and memory. Widely used to recover from 'chemo brain', the fogginess many patients experience following chemotherapy, it's the perfect exercise for me.

Tim delivers my morning coffee and kisses me lightly on the head where my hair is growing back after the operation. Marion has helped him understand the pressure his expectations have created, and he's now happily sleeping in the guest room. It's like having a flatmate who does most of the shopping and cooking. Heaven! More and more gaps from the last two years are returning and Doctor Zhou is pleased with my physical progress. 'Staying away from stairs, I hope?' he'd said as he tested my balance.

It's still not back to normal, though I thought ninety per cent was a good result. I wanted him to lessen my medication, but he was much more cautious than me.

'It's holding me back from getting to the next level of brainHQ,' I'd quipped like a frustrated teenage gamer.

'If you took my advice, you'd be resting in a resort somewhere. But as you've said many times, it's not the Halifax way.'

I'm exercising with Nadia twice a week and ride the cycle track on the other days. Elizabeth had purchased a bike and comes with me when she can. At Marion's suggestion, I had started a journal to record things as I remembered them. Music was the most reliable marker, an instant recall of time and place.

'Something So Strong'. November, 1996. Following a particularly distressing investigation involving a child murderer, I had travelled up to Sydney for the weekend to attend the Crowded House farewell concert on the steps of the Sydney Opera House along with some friends and 200,000 adoring fans. When rain caused the concert to be delayed from the Saturday night to Sunday, I had to abandon my return flight and rebook on Monday morning. It was the last time I ever booked a non-flexible fare. But it was a concert I would never forget.

'Breakeven (Falling To Pieces)'. Christmas, 2008. How is it that breakup songs can define your happiest memories? Ben and I sang that song by The Script all through the holidays. We had never been more in love. Zoe was twelve.

'Solar Power' by Lorde. I remembered her striking yellow

dress and the video and the beach where it was shot, but nothing else. Not where I was or who I was with when I heard it. So, I look it up. August, 2021. Well, at least I remember the song.

My other aid to trigger the past is going to the State Library to read back copies of the newspapers. It's like living the past in the present. I could not recall the election or Scott Morrison's welcome defeat. I could not recall the Teal Revolution: surely I would have been involved in that somehow? I could not remember selling the Brighton house or moving into my apartment. I remember Zoe going overseas but not that it was semipermanent. I remember the one-year anniversary of Ben's death and how disruptive Covid had been to the memorial we held but I couldn't remember who had attended or where it was.

I've begun returning to my office at the university and Nicholas is eager to have me back. Like everyone, he's cautious about the accident and worries I'm overdoing things. Why I took my frustration out on him, I can't explain.

'Nicholas, I have a phalanx of people worrying about me. I don't need any more.'

'I'm your employer. It's my job to worry.'

'You reminded me of that when you forced me to take extended leave.'

'You were throwing yourself into your work as a way of coping with what had happened to Ben.'

'Probably . . .'

'Isn't that what you're doing again?'

It's an accusation I can't deny – the evidence was spread around the room. Peter Debreceny had generously agreed to lend me his files again and I had laid out his folders alongside mine. The whiteboard had my usual chart of keywords and intersecting connections. It's as if I'm in the midst of a major psychological investigation – and maybe I am.

'Perhaps you should do this at home,' says Nicolas, 'and think about other things when you come in here.'

'Ben – sorry, *Tim* – wouldn't approve . . . We try to keep work and home separate.' Or am I confusing Tim with Ben?

Nicholas picks up a thesis from my desk. He had asked me to read it the week before. 'Have you had a chance to look at this?'

'Not yet. For God's sake, it's almost a thousand pages. Why do people who have nothing to say feel the need to compensate with so many words?'

'I can give it to someone else if you like. All I want is a second opinion.'

'Sorry, Nicholas. Of course, I'll read it.'

'That is if you want to come back?' He returns the thesis to the desk. It sits there like a test; of my intentions and Nicholas's patience. If I was moving on, he needed to know.

'I'll read it this weekend,' I promise, placing the heavy document in my bag.

'I can send you a pdf?'

'No. I like to scribble in the margins.'

'I want you back when you're ready, Jane. But I want you full time, like it used to be. This part-time thing worked in the beginning but it won't work anymore.'

'Well, thanks for the ultimatum.'

Nicolas flinches.

'Sorry, that sounded worse than I intended. What I meant is I need to make a decision. And you need to know where you stand. Have I told you how grateful I am that you're giving me all this leeway?'

'If you want my honest opinion, Jane, I don't know how you're still standing.'

'Grit and denial,' I say with a crooked smile. 'It's on the Halifax coat of arms.'

The most obvious 'blocker' to the gaps in my recent past is the trauma of Ben's death. I'd had many sessions with Marion after it happened, but death and loss are ongoing, not a single event where you mourn and move on. It's as if my brain injury has wiped my memory banks of anything that had happened since his murder, as if everything stopped on that terrible night as he sat beside me in my car, squiffy and affectionate and full of his usual mischief.

'Of course you miss him, Jane,' agrees Marion. 'As you say, he's irreplaceable. But I'm not sure it adequately explains your post-Brighton amnesia.'

Post-Brighton Amnesia. My condition now has a name.

'When I read the newspapers at the library, I wonder where I was. Where was I during the bushfires and the last election? Did I volunteer to help the Teals? I can't imagine I didn't. And what did I do during Covid? Did I catch it? Did anyone I know? Maybe I was abducted by aliens for the last two years and sat it out on Mars.'

Marion keeps her opinions to herself. I can see she's as puzzled as I am but she isn't going to add to my anxiety.

'How is your journal going?' she asks.

'Jane's Greatest Hits? Most of the entries are songs I remember. And where I was when I heard them.'

'That's good.'

'When Ben was alive and when I lived with Zoe, music was part of our lives. Is that why I hardly remember any music since then? Did I stop listening to the radio? When I'm thinking clearly – which is only on Tuesdays and Sundays – I explain it away by my brain trauma from the accident.'

'Tuesdays and Sundays?'

'It was a joke between me and Ben.'

'From when?'

'The year he proposed. 2004.'

'Ah. Your favourite year.'

'No, that was the year before. Don't we all have one of those?'

'All right, 2003 – the year you just happened to remember Robert Millard?' Her tone is as close as Marion has come to challenging my theory.

'You don't buy it, do you?'

'Jane, if you had worked as assiduously on any other year, wouldn't that have worked as well?'

'Are you implying I should work as hard with last year?'

'Since that's where you are having most of your problems.' Marion isn't being prescriptive, just floating ideas. 'I am not saying that Robert wasn't a useful tool. And perhaps there's a lesson in that. That there's a methodology that worked for you and can be applied to other settings.'

'Well, I had other motives, didn't I.'

'To right the wrongs of the past?'

'And to find his sister's father.'

'All I'm saying is the technique worked with Robert. So, maybe it can work with . . . sorry, what is her name?'

'Luna. Except she's not answering her phone.'

The session concludes and we arrange to meet again the

following week. One step forward, two steps back, three steps to the side. There should be a dance or a song called that. The Post-Brighton Amnesia Blues.

Joe Wasserman had seen Luna a number of times after he'd had the DNA test. Although it confirmed he wasn't her father, he had taken a genuine interest. He said he owed it to Skyla. We had agreed to catch up for lunch at my favourite North Melbourne Italian, Amiconi in Victoria Street. I'd been going there for most of my teaching years. It was a great place to take my students after they'd completed their exams and if it looked like a celebration, Michael Cardamone would slip you something special, like a grappa or a port or a shot of something in the affogato. He only knew one way to welcome you to his restaurant: like you were a valued and life-long friend.

'How many times have you seen Luna?' I ask Wasserman, eager for information.

'Five or six. She's a lovely young woman. With a mother like that, who's surprised?'

'She's not answering her phone.'

'She said something about going away for a while. Tasmania, I think. Bushwalking.'

'What else did you talk about? If you don't mind me asking.'

'Her mother mainly. And what she was like.'

'And her father?'

'By that you mean Herman?'

'Well, yes.'

'She still doesn't think it's him.'

'Despite the DNA test?'

'As far as Luna's concerned, that ruled *me* out. It didn't rule anyone in.'

'Of course,' I say, hiding my foolishness for jumping to the opposite conclusion. 'Did you talk about other contenders?'

'Not really. We talked about her mum. And the happy times. And those crazy nights at the house. She was eight years old and remembers more than she should. She was a very precocious child.'

'With a very unusual childhood. Do you plan on meeting again?'

'No, but she knows I'm here if she needs me.'

'And you think she's still looking for her father?' I say, concerned.

'Absolutely. I don't know why, but she's utterly convinced it's not Herman.'

After lunch I walk back through the city, passing through my old stomping ground, the courts and legal chambers in William Street. The barristers flounce by in their wigs and gowns, strutting their self-importance, high on the status their theatre provided, whatever the outcome. It wasn't for them to take the court's findings to heart or be slighted by judge or jury. They were playing their part and nothing more. It's how the advocacy system works. To do the very best you can and leave the decision to others.

Why can't I do the same?

27.

When detectives Poulos and Abbas had interviewed me at the hospital, I was only beginning to recover my memory. Now that I was doing better, they had asked me to call by police headquarters. It's the first time I've been in the Police Centre since the Torture Murders – at least I think it is – but it feels like I don't belong anymore, like I was visiting a former life where I remembered feeling comfortable and part of a team. I'm not feeling comfortable now.

As we settle in to a meeting room with spectacular views of the bay, the detectives tell me what they've discovered about the day of my fall in the stairwell.

'Bathgate was at your address,' Poulos begins. 'You were right to be concerned. His image is there on CCTV both outside the building and inside the foyer. But since there are no cameras in the fire stairs, we don't know if he was there or not.'

'Wouldn't he need a pass key for that?' I ask.

'You'd be surprised how often people slip into buildings behind someone else,' says Abbas. 'Some people even pause to hold the door open. They think they're being helpful.'

'We interviewed Bathgate and he admitted he was there,' Poulos continues, 'hoping to bump into you in the street. He insists he only wanted a second chance, that he was uncooperative when you made your assessment and that he may have given the wrong impression.'

'Did you remind him about the PSIO?'

'We did more than that. We charged him for breaching the order and trying to influence a witness.'

'Is he in jail?'

'He was. He's been bailed, pending his trial. This is not going to help his cause.' Abbas is trying to be reassuring but it has the opposite effect.

'So, is it reasonable to suspect he was in the stairwell?' I ask.

'We can't prove it,' says Poulos. 'But we know he was in the vicinity. And we found something else: a tracking device that had been placed under your car.'

'Which is definitely true to Bathgate's form,' I add.

'Except this one has no fingerprints. When he's done it in the past he's generally been careless in that respect, used simple baggage trackers and similar devices. This one was more sophisticated.'

'So, he's getting smarter.'

'Or it could be someone else. There are cameras on the car-park levels of your building and there's no sign of Bathgate being there. But he could have attached the tracker somewhere else – when your car was at the supermarket, for instance. We're not ruling him in or out.'

'I am sorry, sergeant, I don't think I'm following what you're saying.'

'Bathgate is a suspect in your accident but we can't yet link him to running you off the road. The disposal of the car suggests a professional job as does the tracker under your car. What I am trying to say, doctor, is that Paul Bathgate may not be the only one taking an unhealthy interest in you at the moment. It's important we don't jump to conclusions.'

'Sergeant, are you telling me I should be worried about someone else?'

'Potentially. What can you tell us about Morrie Latal?'

I wondered when that would come up. 'This has nothing to do with Morrie Latal.'

'Can you tell us why you visited his pub last week?'

'I hadn't run out of drugs, if that's what you're implying. I thought you were keeping me under surveillance for my protection.'

The detectives don't respond.

'I'm sorry. That wasn't called for. I'm trying to help someone find their father. Morrie is a possible intermediary. That's all.'

'Do you usually spend time with criminals, doctor?'

'Only at work. And for the record, I get my drugs legally. From the chemist.' Why am I behaving like this? The police are trying to help me, investigating a suspicious accident in which I had nearly died.

'So, what are you suggesting I do?' I ask, assuming a less defensive tone.

'Take care. Try not to be alone. And inform us of anything suspicious. You can ring us at any time. You have our cards. I suggest you put us on speed dial. And Triple Zero as well.'

I thank the detectives for their efforts on my behalf, make some limp excuse about brain injuries and irritability, and pause at the door.

'There's something you could do for me,' I say. 'A former Homicide detective, Bryan Tregonning. You wouldn't happen to have a current address? I'd like to look him up if I could. We were on a case together. You know, old time's sake.'

'The Silver Fox?' says Abbas.

'That's the one.'

She grabs the phone and dials. 'No probs. I'll get it for you now.'

As I leave the police complex, I feel like a fraud. *Old time's sake?* I omitted to mention the Fox and I were on opposite sides of the case, that we'd barely exchanged so much as a nod in the courtroom corridor. I would never have said anything like that before the accident. Jane Halifax 2.0: acerbic and devious with a tendency to fudge the truth. Happy to exploit her boyfriend and treat him like a eunuch. Catty behind her doctor's back and petulant with her loyal employer. Happy to ignore her personal safety to obsess with a cold case she didn't win and addicted to theories like 'the index cards', which she knew were more than likely hokum.

Is this who I've become? Has my brain injury changed my personality and turned me into someone I don't particularly like? I cross the river and trudge back home. It had rained for most of the last two weeks and the Yarra is flowing upside down, its muddy waters matching my disposition.

The Silver Fox had lost his hair. What was his nickname now?

Former Inspector Bryan Tregonning is in his late seventies. Tall and thin with a beer belly he tried to hide by wearing his shirt outside his pants. It only made him look untidy. He's opted to shave his head as well but lacked the attractive cranium one needs for that effect. He's wearing a floppy hat, but that doesn't work for him either. Previously neat and natty, he seems diminished without his distinctive locks, like a man who has lost his identity.

I see someone letterboxing leaflets near Tregonning's house in Cheltenham and offer to do a block on the opposite side of the road. The day is hot and the volunteer grateful for the help. I say I need the exercise and was going in that direction anyway. It's advice I remember from my old cop mate Showbag who used any excuse to go undercover during the Torture Murders case. 'Undercover is not about being invisible but blending in,' he had said. 'Try and look like you belong and no-one will give you a second thought.'

The Fox is in his front garden, tending his roses. Like raw recruits, they stand in regimented rows, pruned to within an inch of their lives. This was a man who liked order and obedience and everything in its place. He pretends not to notice when I pop a leaflet in his letterbox, ignoring his 'No Junk Mail' sign.

'Lovely day,' I say. 'Your garden looks a picture.' Bland, polite and forgettable. Showbag would have been proud.

I buy a take-away coffee from the local shopping centre and find a strategic bench in the park at the corner of his street. I wonder where the Fox might go for lunch. His beer belly is the clue. At half past twelve, he heads for the local RSL, which I might have guessed a former cop could do on a Friday. Probably to catch up with mates.

I check myself into the RSL as a casual guest and go to the bistro. The Fox sits alone with a beer at a table in the corner. Maybe his friends would be along later. I sit at a nearby table and pretend to text a friend. Then, going one better, fake a call.

'Hello. Are you running late? No, I'm here now. What do you mean you can't make it? Oh, that's terrible. No, she's your mother – you need to go. Don't worry about me, I'm fine. And give her my love . . .'

I end the call. I can tell that the Fox had been listening. 'Excuse me,' I say. 'Do you order the food from the bar?'

'Yeah, that's the menu on the wall and the specials on the blackboard.'

I order Pad Thai and a bottle of sparkling water and return to the table with a wireless pager. The Fox sits on his beer. It's an unlikely place for a woman to go on her own, but scanning the news on my phone seems to provide me with some protection. The Fox goes to the bar for a second beer and returns with a pager for himself. He clearly isn't lunching with friends.

My pager buzzes and I collect my meal. The Fox does the same: his is a burger and chips. I wait another ten or so minutes.

'Excuse me,' I say at last. 'Are you Inspector Tregonning?'

'Used to be.'

'We worked on the same case together . . . Probably twenty years ago. The Robert Millard case. Or the Van Meulenbelt Murders, depending on which name you use . . .'

'No. Doesn't ring a bell.'

'When I say we worked together, I was on one side, you on the other. I'm Jane Halifax. I'm a forensic psychiatrist.'

'Sorry, lady. I don't remember. And I don't particularly want to.'

'Because of the case?'

'Because it's in the past and I've left the past behind.'

'I'm sorry. I didn't mean to interrupt your meal.'

'No harm, done. The chips are still warm and the beer's still cold.'

'I just wanted to say . . .'

'Can't you read?'

'I'm sorry?'

'No junk mail? It's a simple message. And what's a forensic psychiatrist doing delivering leaflets?' The Silver Fox may have been retired but he is still as sharp as ever. 'Now you eat your Thai and I'll eat my chips. Or I can find another table.'

So much for my undercover work. Ham-fisted surveillance followed by a front-on assault. Showbag would have been appalled. But I didn't know how else to do it. I could hardly reveal my sources; I could hardly admit I had seen the prosecution's files. Imagine what Tregonning would have made of that.

'How did you get my address?' he asks after a moment.

'From detectives I know at HQ.'

'That was wrong.'

'Yes, I know. And I apologise for them. And me. And I am really sorry for approaching you like this, but it's Robert Millard's sister, I'm trying to help her, and you are one of the few people I can turn to—'

'I have nothing to say to you.' The Fox takes up his glass and plate and moves away.

I've made a mess of things, but Tregonning's reluctance to engage spoke volumes. I can tell he remembered who I am. After all, it's easier for him than me. I hadn't lost my hair. And dismissing one of the most significant cases of his long and storied career was telling.

Given everything else that had happened, I needed something like this to keep me focused, to convince myself I wasn't stumbling around in the dark. My major cases had defined my career, and the Silver Fox's experiences would have been the same. You don't back away from significant investigations without a reason, you don't deny them unless you've something to hide.

What would Showbag do? Regroup and try again? So, I'd been clumsy in my first approach, which only reinforced how far below my best I was operating at, but I hadn't come away completely empty-handed.

I had touched a nerve and the Fox had run.

28.

My mind is on other things as I answer my mobile but the caretaker is still not making any sense. 'Doctor Halifax, I need the key to your storage room. I can't find mine among the masters – and you seem to have sprung a leak.'

Storage room? What storage room? And what storage room springs a leak?

'I'm sorry. Can you say that again?'

'I'll meet you downstairs if that's okay. Or I can come up and get the key. Up to you.'

'No, I'll come down. Where are you exactly?'

'At your storage room on the second basement level.'

Second basement level? I park my car on basement one. What was I doing with storage down there? I grab my keys and go down in the lift, wondering if he's confused me with someone else.

The caretaker meets me and I hand him my bulging keyring. I trail after him as he sorts through the keys and seems to find the one he's after. As we round the corner, he stops at a room I don't recognise. Water is running freely under the door. He opens the lock and turns on the light, filling the room with a dull red glow.

I follow him inside. It's like stepping into the past. The room is essentially my darkroom from Brighton. The benches and developing trays had been placed beside the sink with drums of fixing and developing chemicals underneath. Huge ghostly portraits of Ben and Zoe stare at me from the walls. The leak had been caused when a rubber tap extender perished. Otherwise, the damage is slight.

The developing trays are dry, the chemicals long evaporated. I hadn't had an exhibition since my participation in *Portraits in Black and White* in 2020. I have no memory of setting up the darkroom, which is not surprising: I have no memory of moving from Brighton. I examine a roll of negative hanging from a rack, shots taken at the anniversary of Ben's memorial, but not in the way I would have taken them, although someone seemed to have used my Hasselblad.

'No damage done,' says the caretaker. 'Though that tap extender and trigger nozzle was an accident waiting to happen. Best to turn it off at the wall next time. Can I take a copy of your key? I have no idea what happened to mine.'

The caretaker prattles on, unaware of my distress. The red light protects me, but only from him. I struggle to breathe and wipe my clammy hands on my dress. Ben's haunting face, enlarged and living, worries at me from the wall.

When Tim comes home from rehearsals, I tell him what had happened. He isn't surprised I had forgotten about the darkroom. My interest in photography had taken a back seat for some time.

'At the anniversary we had for Ben last year, did you use my Hasselblad?' I ask.

'Yes. Why?'

'I don't really lend it to anyone.'

'Then I guess I'm the exception.' Tim seems to take reassurance from this, as if it provided him with some kind of validation. For me, it feels impertinent, as if he had used my camera without my permission. Even Ben hadn't been allowed to touch my Blad, though who could rely on my memory anymore? Certainly not me.

'When we got together in WA – at the Margaret River – whose idea was that?' I ask.

'What's that got to do with photography?'

'Nothing. I'm trying to remember, that's all. Just piecing things together. Reconstructing the past.'

'I was there with the orchestra and you were in Perth for a conference. We ended up in the same hotel. It was one of those happy accidents.'

'I looked up the article about that shark attack on the beach. I did get a mention, but how did they know my name?'

'Probably from me.'

'We usually don't disclose that sort of stuff to the press. If there's anything to say about the victim, we say it to the family. Or the coroner.'

'Bit stuffy, isn't it?'

'It's the way it works.'

'Whatever you say . . .'

Musicians move to their own beat, but I'm surprised Tim doesn't understand my world a little better. Though who am I to criticise him after my adventures with the Silver Fox?

'Today, I remembered the nickname of a cop I used to work with. Showbag. One of the best. I remembered going to his wife's funeral in 2021.'

'That's recent.'

'Yeah. Things are coming back.'

'I'm cooking salmon tonight. With kale and dauphinoise potatoes. You can choose the wine.'

Tim goes into the kitchen as I select a bottle from the rack. Drinking isn't a great idea, given my medication, but it had been a ragged day, kale takes more than a little fortitude and one glass won't hurt. *If it's expensive enough*, as Ben liked to say, *it doesn't do any harm at all.* I select a 2019 Black Peak pinot noir from Central Otago and carry it through to the kitchen. Tim has put my playlist on to get him in the mood. Rag'n'Bone Man is singing 'Human' from 2016, a song Ben loved to sing, mimicking the rasping tones.

I pour the wine and smile at Tim, wanting to remember a song that placed us together. The concert in the vineyard is all that comes, but even that seems remote and out of range. Apart from random incidents, the recent past is such a struggle and I'm fearful it will never return.

The pinot goes straight to my brain and enlivens my medication. I'm going to regret it in the morning.

Before bed I open my journal and record the rediscovery of my darkroom and the joint exhibition where I had displayed my work in 2020. And Showbag, my favourite cop, the great *Rattus rattus* hunter, who had worked with me and Eric Ringer. His terrible fall from the roof of a building that had confined him to a wheelchair. Him joking about going to the Paralympics to compete in the Special Fishing section. Hopefully he was chasing Barramundi up in Broome.

Showbag had a song too. 'Rat Trap' by the Boomtown Rats.

Why can't I remember a song for me?

I'm back at the Victoria Police Centre. Poulos and Abbas have had a breakthrough. They had found CCTV footage of the Kia Telluride being stolen.

Two young men get into the car parked outside the owner's house. According to the owner, he and his wife were watching television when someone must have entered the house through the unlocked back door, found the car keys in a bowl in the hall and left without making a sound. The footage was taken from a neighbour's house along the road, too far away to distinguish the faces. One was big and overweight, the other small and wily.

'Did you get the impression of more than one person in the car?' asks Poulos.

'I'm sorry. It's all a blank.'

'There are a few possibilities,' continues the detective. 'That these were the two who were inside the car at the time of the accident or that they stole it for someone else.'

'Like who?'

'Someone who wanted to do you harm?'

'Like Bathgate?'

'He remains our most likely suspect,' says Poulos.

At least Morrie Latal appeared to be off their list.

'But Bathgate wants to change my mind, not cause me harm?' I respond.

'Or stop you from giving evidence?'

The suggestion is instantly sobering. A motorcar might be a very blunt and unlikely instrument of murder, but as a weapon designed to harm someone and stop them appearing in court, it made sense.

'Doctor Halifax, until we have evidence to the contrary, we have to assume what happened to you was deliberate. That someone tried to run you off the road, and when it happened, didn't stop to offer assistance. Are you sure you've told us everything you know?'

'About what?'

'About Bathgate? Or anyone else?'

'No, I am sure I haven't, Sergeant Poulos. I'm sure there are gaps in my memory you could drive a truck through. Or at least a Kia Telluride. Do you think I would deliberately withhold information?' Which is a bald-faced response since it was precisely what I was doing. But how can I tell them about Peter Debreceny's files, the precious cargo in the boot that Peter had managed to reclaim only to take the risk of lending them to me again? And why didn't Poulos and Abbas know about that? Was there nothing in the records of the Accident Investigation Unit? Had Debreceny's insistence that the files belonged to the DPP made any evidence of their existence miraculously disappear?

I had tried hard not to jump at shadows, but I'm jumping at them now. My medication clouds my judgement as my recovering brain limps along in second gear. I desperately want to share my burden with the detectives – no-one needs their help more than me.

'Guys, I would really like to help you. And I'm grateful you are keeping an eye on me. The thing is, I'm still getting over the accident and am a long way short of my best. If things were different, I'd be in there with you chasing down the villains. I'm sorry.'

'Have you considered going away? Until his trial begins.'

'As a matter of fact, sergeant, I have. I owe my mother a visit in New Zealand.'

'Then maybe this is the time to do it.'

I find myself at St Patrick's Cathedral, which was an unlikely place for a non-Catholic let alone a non-believer. I think I had made my way here to look for Father Keely, who had helped me after the Torture Murders, but when I ask I'm told he's away at a retreat somewhere. Even Jesuits need renewal.

I sit in the gardens by the Pilgrims Walk with its falling waters and hope they'll soothe my soul. Who was I before the accident? Why couldn't I remember the recent past? Why didn't I pursue my favourite activity and take photographs anymore? Why was intimacy so overwhelming? Why did I feel so alienated from the university where I had been happy for so many years? Why couldn't I be open and tell the truth? Why couldn't I remember people who wanted to harm me? Why did my boyfriend feel like a stranger?

I need to make an appointment to see Marion again; next week was too far away. And Doctor Zhou – perhaps my problem was neurological. I need to see if Luna is back. I need to take another crack at the Fox. I need to phone Zoe in New York and visit my mother in New Zealand . . . I need a haircut and a facial and a pedicure and a deep tissue massage. I need some serious retail therapy: my wardrobe looks like I do – all worn out.

I need to remember a song, a recent song for me, a passport back to time and place, somewhere, anywhere, nothing inspired or momentous. Just around the corner would do. The Post-Brighton Amnesia Blues simply isn't cutting the mustard.

Jane 2.0 is in trouble.

29.

I never take calls from unknown numbers but, hoping it was Luna, I make an exception.

'Doctor Halifax?'

The voice on the other end of the phone isn't hers though I recognise it immediately.

'How did you get my number?'

'From detectives I know at HQ.' The former detective is quoting me deliberately. 'I'm across the road from your apartment. They gave me your address as well.'

If the Fox was trying to make a point about how invasive it can feel to be approached by someone who has obtained your personal information improperly, he had succeeded.

'We should talk,' he says.

I don't want to meet in my apartment, but he's caught me on the hop and, before I can think things through, I'm opening the door – something I would never have done before the accident. But in my desire for information, my needs are up and my defences down and in less than three minutes I've let a virtual stranger into my home.

'Quite a place,' he says as people typically did when they take in the expansive views and expensive furnishings. It's said with surprise rather than envy, as if I was living beyond my means or, at the very least, above my station. His house in Cheltenham is humble by comparison, a three-bedroomed bungalow on a busy thoroughfare which wasn't good for his health or his roses.

The Fox looks around the apartment like a man who has never stopped being a policeman, assaying its owner as a tasseographer might read a teacup. He can tell I like to travel and collect mementos. He can see I like art (though not that I was reluctant to hang my own photography). He can see I like to entertain, with a drinks trolley as bountiful as the Queen Consort's. He can see I like fashion magazines, uncluttered coffee tables and designer chairs. He takes in the top-of-the-range exercise bike on the balcony beside an $8,000 stainless steel outdoor barbecue and kitchen. He can see that no expense has been spared.

'What I don't understand,' he says at last, 'is your sudden interest in a double murder that was put to bed twenty years ago.'

'As I tried to explain, it's Luna Van Meulenbelt I am trying to help. She's looking for her father.'

'Didn't her brother shoot him? Along with her mother?'

'She thinks her natural father is someone else.'

'And what's any of that got to do with me?' The Fox makes no attempt to hide his irritation.

In order to take the heat out of the air, I offer to make tea. He follows me through to the kitchen where I put on the kettle. He examines my impressive array of chef's knives on the wall.

'What this?' he asks, taking down a long knife from the magnetised rack.

'It's a yanagi ba. For making sashimi.'

He notes its sharpness and puts it back in the rack as I add hot water to the teapot.

'You were one of the last people to see Robert Millard alive,' I continue, eager to take his attention away from the knives. 'Did he say anything about his sister's real father?'

'Not that I remember.'

We take our tea back to the lounge room, where I offer him a seat. The Fox prefers to stand.

'You thought the accused was innocent, didn't you?' says the Fox. At least he remembered that. 'And that we had somehow "fixed" the evidence?'

'I am sure we didn't say that. The barrister interrogated ballistics in cross-examination. That's all.'

'If he wasn't guilty, why did he kill himself?'

'Inspector, do you really want me to answer that? To tell you the reasons why people kill themselves? He may have thought it preferable to spending a very long time in prison.'

'Is that what you think?'

'No, it's not what I think. I'm not into speculation.'

'You speculated about the ballistics.'

'We tested them in court. Which is perfectly normal.'

'And you think we selected the wrong confession, the first one, which you swore on oath was false.'

For someone who claims to have put his career in the force behind him, the Fox is displaying a very good memory – and a lot of emotion.

'Robert Millard murdered his parents. He told me,' the Fox says.

'When?'

'In the car, as I was taking him back to the station to make a statement. Later, when he was cautioned, I tried to get him to say it again, but for whatever reason, he didn't.'

'What did he say in the car?'

'That there had been a huge argument between him and his parents about Luna. About what his father was *doing* to Luna. And that his mother wanted Robert to take it back, to admit it was another of his outrageous lies and wasn't true.'

'Robert told you Herman was abusing Luna?'

'Not in as many words, but that was the implication.'

'And why did none of this come out in court?'

'Because I couldn't get it on the record.'

'But even if the argument was over Luna, it could still have been between Herman and Skyla. And Robert Millard could still have come across them and discovered the bodies.'

'Except Robert couldn't stand the situation anymore,' counters the Fox, 'which is why he killed them: to make things right.'

'And he told you this in the car on the way to the police station?'

'Yes.'

'And you never mentioned it?'

'It was hearsay. There was no-one else in the car. Just him and me. Imagine what your barrister would have made of that if I'd tried.'

I'm struggling to process what the Fox is telling me. A huge argument between Robert and his parents *about what Herman was doing to Luna.* That Robert had shot them because he *couldn't stand the situation anymore.* It explained why the first confession was suddenly more persuasive than the second. And it explained why Luna was so desperate to find her real father. Had my attempts to clear Robert's name and give him back to Luna backfired? Had my carefully considered 'expert' opinion to the court been totally wrong?

But none of that seems important now. Now, all I want is to talk to Luna.

But Luna is nowhere to be found. I discover she hadn't applied for leave to go on holidays but had resigned, which had taken her employer by surprise. She had been with them for three years, they tell me, and were very happy with her work. She didn't offer an explanation and said nothing about going to Tasmania. Joe Wasserman hasn't heard from her either. He says he'd given her some money to help with the trip, but she hasn't made contact since then. There is still no sign of her at her apartment, her mail mounting and uncollected.

I decide to pay Morrie Latal another visit.

'Do you know you're still being watched by the police?' I say as I settle into one of his plush leather chairs.

'They watch me and I watch them,' he replies, waving at the screens on his wall. 'It's a game we've been playing for years. But they won't find anything – they never do. You coming here will throw them.'

'It already has. They're watching me as well,' I confess. 'For my own protection. They think somebody tried to kill me when they ran me off the road.'

'Bullshit,' says Morrie. 'If someone wanted you dead, they'd shoot you.'

Which I have to admit felt strangely reassuring.

'Do you know a cop from the old days called the Silver Fox?'

'Never had the pleasure, I'm pleased to say. But I knew him by reputation. Straight as a die – which meant he was no use to me.'

'He led the Homicide team in Robert's case. Had some

interesting observations to make about Herman. Reckons he was interfering with his daughter.'

'Bullshit. Who told him that?'

'He says Robert did, before he was charged.'

'Oh, that's a reliable source,' says Morrie, his voice thick with sarcasm. 'Did he try and flog him the Harbour Bridge as well?'

'Not everything Robert said was untrue.'

'Herman was many things, but he wasn't that. He'd fuck anything with a pulse, but not children. And definitely not his own. We're talking about a lush and a root rat, but he was no Jeffrey Epstein.'

'I'll admit the sexual psychologies are different.'

'Then you've answered your question.'

Many paedophiles seek sexual relations with children in response to anxieties and self-esteem issues that inhibit normal sexual relations with adults. Incest with children had a similar psycho-sexual profile. Many had been molested themselves as children, and although I had no evidence of that either way, Morrie was right: Herman Van Meulenbelt did not fit the profile of a molester.

'So, what was Robert doing?' I ask, thinking aloud.

'Building his defence, no doubt. He was very good at that. Making up a story about his sister that would justify what he did.'

'So you think Robert was guilty?'

'He committed suicide, didn't he?'

'Not you as well, Morrie. Give me a break.'

Cops and crooks are generally uncomplicated people and often arrive at the same conclusions. But I was not expecting to hear the same thing from the Fox and Morrie Latal within twenty-four hours of each other.

'Do you remember much about Robert's trial?' I ask.

'I followed it in the papers. Everyone did.'

'Did you attend the court?'

'No. The place gives me the spooks.'

'And tell me, Morrie – honestly – what did you make of Robert's defence?'

'I thought it was bullshit. He makes two confessions which were diametrically opposed to each other. Then wheels in an expert to select the right one. What did you use? A water divining stick?'

The jury had probably used the same logic.

I leave Morrie's pub and head for the university to drop off the thesis Nicholas had asked me to read. There weren't too many margin notes, just my damning assessment at the end: *There's no way you can pass her on this. Doesn't prove the concept: quite possibly it does the opposite. And far too many words. C-.* I'm glad to relieve my bag of the burden, but there are other things weighing me down. Was the reason I was so obsessed with the Robert Millard case not because I believed an innocent man had been found guilty but because my meticulous, reasoned, expert opinion was, like the thesis I had just delivered, fatally flawed?

The human brain can only take so much damage. With severe traumatic injury, confusion and disorientation are predictable and memory returns in its own good time and not necessarily in the right order. Some memories may never return at all but those that do – and, in particular, those that persist and dominate to the exclusion of almost everything else – do so for a particular reason. That I believe implicitly.

My brain may not have been back to where it used to be, but my instincts were undiminished.

30.

Marion begins our session by reading my journal. Her face does not betray what she's thinking, but instead of scanning the entries as she usually did, she seems to be weighing every word. 'Not a lot about looking after yourself? Are you still riding your bike?'

'When I can.'

'And brainHQ. Are you still doing that?'

'Not a lot. Tim's in Sydney, doing session work on an album. I've been sleeping in.'

'When you're not playing detective.'

'I don't know why I write that stuff down. The ramblings of a recovering mind.'

But my attempt to minimise what I had written is not working on my therapist. 'You seem very harsh on yourself. Jane 2.0?'

'I know a brain injury can change a person's personality and I'm worried that's happened to me.'

'Yes, you've made that clear. But the more you angst about it—'

'Sorry. I will try and modify what I write.'

'Jane. That isn't the point. You are in recovery. Exercise and rest is what you're supposed to be doing. Not running around doing – this. Who's the Fox?'

'A cop. On the Millard case.'

'And Morrie Latal?'

I try to put what I've being doing in context, but can barely convince myself. Marion listens, watching me closely, resolute and concerned. I explain the dominant thoughts I had experienced after coming out of my coma: the big white house and the cops and crooks eating dinner and Robert's outrageous stories. How I had used these spectres – and I wasn't afraid to use the word – to remember who I was. How I had used Luna and the Millard case to begin with 2003. How recovering that year had cascaded back and forth to fill the gaps in my returning memory. How it wasn't in my nature to sit and wait, I needed to be proactive.

'But you hate that word – proactive. And "moving forward" and "reaching out"; all those glib, jargon-ridden management phrases.'

'I'm not sure I get your point.'

'Jane, you worry about a change in personality, but you're not giving yourself a chance. You're a doctor. Rest and recuperation. You know that better than most. If you keep running around like this, who's surprised you're going backwards?' Normally one to listen and interpret, Marion is not holding back.

'Is that what you think? I'm going backwards?'

'We agreed that your problems aren't only neurological. That there's a psychological obstruction in there as well, something that's blocking your recovery.'

'Like the recurrence of what happened to Ben.'

'*If* that's the problem. I think I'm changing my mind on that. After Ben was killed, we did a number of sessions together and resolved a lot of issues. And while something as profound and shocking as his passing will always return – you'd be inhuman if it didn't – I wonder if that's really your issue. Or losing a case that's twenty years old. Is your ego so fragile you can't take a loss, if indeed that's the right word to use? Your recent past is what's not returning and we have tried to understand that by relating it to Ben's death, the loss of your greatest love and soulmate. That it's the reason you find it so hard to remember anything since. Because the event was so defining.'

'But?'

'Jane, do you remember why we first got together?'

'Yes. It was after the Point Cook massacre.'

'A mass killing that made no sense, as mass killings seldom do. Do you remember you shot someone? In self-defence?'

'How could I forget that?'

'And do you remember who taught you to use a gun in the first place?'

'My father. At our farm. He saw it as a rite of passage.' I sense where Marion is steering the session and even now, after all this time, I don't want her to go there. I know what she wants to say.

'Now let's look at your "favourite" year.'

'I know the index card theory doesn't hold water. As you said, I could have selected any year—'

'But you didn't. You selected 2003. And Robert's case in particular. Do you see any connection between that and your father?'

'Guns?'

'No, not guns, Jane. A far bigger word than that. What happened the following year? Immediately after the trial?'

My reaction was primordial. I wanted to run out the door.

'The word you've struggled with all your life and still can't comprehend. Not that anyone can blame you for that. It may well be the most confounding mystery of all.'

Suicide. I tried to say the word though no sound emerged. *Suicide*. The legacy my father left me when I needed him most. *Suicide*. The bequest of the client I had failed to save when I was his only chance. The word I took so personally when I was surely the last thing on the mind of those who had made such a lone and desolate decision.

It was a golden afternoon. The fields were dry and bleached of colour. The sun had found a gap on the back of my neck between my hat and my collar and left its brand, but I was happy. You accept a little sunburn when get to ride your horse at such a mystical place, our farm in the Western Districts of Victoria. I was twelve years old.

As I brought Thistle back to the home paddock and let her cool herself in the dam, I could see cars at the house I didn't recognise and wondered who the visitors were. I wish I had never found out.

My father, John Halifax, was proud and ambitious. Being a lawyer suited his leonine personality. But Dunedin, where he grew up in New Zealand, was too small to contain him, so when I was nine we moved to Melbourne so he could parade his wares on a larger stage.

My mother had resisted the move. To Angela, any city of over a hundred thousand people was, by definition, too large. Dunedin had a town hall and a central square called the Octagon and a highly regarded university. And grand nineteenth-century bluestone churches and a bustling harbour and wild, white sandy beaches with kelp and sea lions and seabirds that rode the wind. And most of all, it had a golf links along the sandhills running from Tomahawk to St Clair where we lived and to which my mother had become addicted. It helped that she was a very good player, though winning trophies in Dunedin, the Edinburgh of the South, was hardly the same as winning at St Andrews.

I approved of the move to Australia. I found it big and brash and exciting. My mother's mother came with us too. A country girl, she didn't like the big cities either, but when we bought the farm near Clarendon, she was instantly won over and the score card was suddenly three to one. Any hope my mother still harboured of going back to New Zealand was over, though my father had promised we would if she couldn't adapt. So she played to her strength and gave in to her passion and filled her life with golf, repeatedly hitting a tiny white ball into eighteen small holes twice a week, the only equation that made any sense to her.

I removed Thistle's saddle and put it on the stile for Dad to retrieve later; it was too heavy for me to carry all the way back to the stables. Then, as Thistle sought the shade of a tree, I took her bridle and set off for the homestead. Two stern-faced men stood by the stables, watching my progress. I gave a friendly wave but they turned away. I wasn't inclined to interrupt them anyway, whatever it was they were doing. I needed a glass of water too much.

One of the cars by the house was a police car and my first thought was that something must have happened to Grandma. She had travelled to New Zealand for a Pioneer Women's Association reunion where she was to receive an award for her work with the Otago Early Settlers' Museum. I dropped the bridle and my helmet by the door, removed my boots and socks and headed inside.

My mother was in the kitchen with two policemen, tears running down her face. She enveloped me in her arms while the policemen looked away. It had to be Grandma. What terrible thing had happened to her? She was more of a mother to me than my mother had ever been. I couldn't stand it if something had happened. Grandma was my champion, my inspiration.

'What's happened?' I asked.

Nobody answered. My mother increased her crushing embrace. I had to break free, she was squeezing the life out of me. I reeled back, gasping for air.

'It's your father. He's dead. He did it to himself in the stables. I hate this place. I hate Australia. I wish we had never come.' My mother howled like a victim, like someone who had been deliberately punished by some unspeakable wrong.

I turned and fled. The younger cop came after me, but he couldn't keep up. The dry stubble of the emaciated grass punctured my feet, but if anything, the pain made me faster. He gave up as I vaulted the fence and vainly called for me to come back. 'Your mother needs you!' I think he said, though she was probably using him as a medium.

I made it to the dam and scrambled up onto Thistle's back. Kicking her flanks and steering her with her mane, she rose up over the fence like the jumper she had never been and headed west, in the direction I was pointing her. To where we'd been happy only moments before, enveloped by the wind and the thrumming of hooves, in our very own galloping time machine that, if we could only make it go fast enough, held the promise this day would never come.

PART SEVEN

May 2023

Dress me up, dress me down,
Dress me like a crazy clown.
Paint me yellow, paint me blue,
Kill the colours that aren't like you.

31.

The red light is comforting, its glow a cocoon. My darkroom had been transported in its entirety from Brighton to South Bank but I'm struggling to remember when, if ever, I had used it. I look through the negatives of the celebration we had held to mark the first anniversary of Ben's death. The faces are familiar but the event itself, like much of Tim's photography, was misframed or out of focus. How could such a beautiful musician, such a beautiful man, have so little sense of form? Surely design and euphonics go hand in glove, the one reflecting the other? Of course, Tim's rug disproved that theory. Was his music and his face enough perfection? Is there a maximum beauty quotient, overt or hidden, we all receive? Had Tim exceeded his allocation?

I know my musings are an attempt at avoidance but since my session with Marion, I couldn't get what she had said out of my brain. '*No not guns Jane. A far bigger word than that. The word you've struggled with all your life and still can't comprehend. Not that anyone can blame you for that. It may well be the most confounding mystery of all.*'

The manner of my father's death had been behind most of the major decisions in my life. My determination to defy him, even after he'd died, and do medicine instead of law. The repetitive patterns of my serial monogamy. My decision, still vehemently denied and conveniently blamed on others and circumstance, not to have children. And now Marion had extended my bogey word to someone else – to Robert Millard. Is my determination to clear his name and prove his innocence to Luna motivated less by my belief the court had made the wrong decision and more by the means of his leaving? Am I still galloping away on Thistle in wounded despair? Is the final inhibition to recovering my memory not Ben's death but a word I still can't say?

As I look through the photo negatives I recall the song Zoe and Tim had sung at the celebration. There are only shots of Zoe setting up to perform and the audience, which included me, as Tim used my studio Blad like a disposable camera. He would never have treated his cello like that.

Everyone knew how much Ben and I loved Mark Knopfler, but 'Romeo and Juliet' would have been a better choice than 'If This Is Goodbye'. Maybe it had been selected to feature Tim's sorrowful cello solo, but I never wanted to mark the sadness of Ben's passing like that. What the occasion needed was a love song with much more cheek. I wanted to shout the abundance of our time together. A resonator guitar would have been a better choice of instrument.

I head into the university, sticking to the busier streets to avoid being on my own. Since the police had warned off Bathgate, I am less concerned about him, but it's harder to remove enemies I can't remember from out of my head. I stop from time to time to make sure I'm not being followed: I pretend to check my makeup in a window while using the refection to check anyone who might look suspicious. It's one of Showbag's techniques: 'reverse surveillance' he called it. Watchful, ever watchful – and trying very hard not to be anxious.

Nicholas had been right. My office was no place for Debreceny's files and my forensic prognostications. If I was serious about coming back, my study needed to be what it had been before: a place for tutorials and stimulation.

I take my midday medication and examine my tongue in the mirror. It's no surprise it looks unhealthy. My treatment is a delicate balance, a juggle between making me better and keeping me stable. I would gladly abandon my pills to have a clear head. Or my sunglasses if I could tolerate bright light. Or my stick if I trusted my balance. Not yet.

As I gather up Debreceny's files and pack them into their boxes, I hesitate at the file marked 'Ballistics and GSR'. Should I read it again, one last time?

The ballistics report with its careful angles and calculations supported murder (Skyla's) and suicide (Herman's) but also allowed for Herman's death to have happened during a struggle (with Robert). The contentious element was the logging of Robert's jumper with the gunshot residue, which Rinaldi had focused on during the trial. There were thirty-five pages of tests, analysis and diagrams. Unable to content myself with the executive summary, I decide to read the whole thing. It's easy to get lost in the detail and I do my best to concentrate, but my meds made my thinking ponderous and heavy and I have to force myself to focus. *Take the northbound train to N. Hollow Rd. Then take the eastbound train to Atkinson Ave.*

The gun was Herman's, a Beretta 694 over-and-under shotgun designed for the competition shooter. Herman had a licence and stored it correctly in a gun safe: one at his home in South Yarra and another at the vineyard, where he had a shooting range and other guns for guests. It was always locked away safely, never left around the house, and only brought to South Yarra for cleaning and maintenance. He treated firearms with respect.

In his statement to the police, Robert maintained he didn't like guns. He thought shooting clay targets was pointless. Even with ear protection, he had a sensitivity to the sound and sonic pressure the gun produced. He wasn't sure where the key to the gun safe was kept. Or the ammunition. He was vague about how the gun was loaded. He said Herman had tried to get him interested, but he preferred to do other things. He said Luna had shown more interest than him, although Skyla forbade it because of her age.

It is often said that psychiatric reports can be fashioned to support the expert's conclusions. Was this supposedly scientific analysis any less vulnerable to interpretation? I had more faith in my assessment than what was outlined here.

I pack the file away. I'd return the boxes to Debreceny as soon as I could. Right now I need the exercise of the long walk home – 'reverse surveillance' and all. I need to clear my head and re-examine my motives. Is Marion right? Is the block to recovering my memory not bound up with how Ben had died but with how Robert had ended his life? Is my crisis still rooted in that word I never mentioned but, alone in my office, finally dare to say out loud?

'Suicide.'

It is Ben's birthday and I've laid white arum lilies on his memorial at Brighton Cemetery. As I walk back through the tranquil gardens, I'm aware of a gardener in a floppy hat, but don't pay him much attention. He's pruning roses and has his head down. He doesn't look up until I'm only a matter of metres away. It's the Silver Fox.

'Are you stalking me?'

'No. I've been placing flowers on my partner's grave. I didn't know you worked here.'

'I don't. I'm a volunteer.'

'Nice secateurs,' I say, making small-talk.

'They're Tobisho.'

'Yes, I know. I have a friend who loves to garden. Won't use anything else.'

'Sorry about your husband,' says the Fox. 'That's my wife over there. Beneath the Lady of Australia.' The Fox gestures towards a rose bush he's just finished pruning. Beneath it is a bronze plaque on a granite base dedicated to his wife. 'It's at its best with the autumn flush, in March. Spectacular yellow,' he says. 'You garden yourself?'

'No. But Marion's mad keen. Says it keeps her sane.'

'Well, nothing else makes any sense when you get to this stage of your life.'

'I'm sorry about your wife. Has she been here long?'

'This will be her first winter,' he says like a man who counted seasons rather than years. 'Lung cancer, though she never smoked. Blamed the traffic from living on a major road.'

'No-one gets out of this alive.'

The Fox looks at me sideways, as if I am being disrespectful.

'My mother's favourite saying. It makes her laugh.'

'It won't, when it gets to her turn.'

'Oh, I don't know. She's pretty resilient.'

'Does she garden?'

'No. Plays golf.'

'Works for some.' The Fox snips a branch off a standard rose and cuts it into smaller lengths, dropping the pieces into a bucket. 'Hand forged. In Japan.'

'I'm sorry . . .'

'The Tobisho. Your friend would know.'

I am waiting for the Fox to shoo me away so he can get back to his pruning. But, for once, he seems unhurried.

'My wife hated me being a policeman. Worried about me every day. And there she is, six feet under, and me still going around. I wish I had never been a cop. Worst decision of my life. Should have done something horticultural and lived a clean life in the country.'

'You should have asked for a rural posting.'

'Too ambitious for that. Had to go to Homicide, didn't I, and build the big career. Fat lot of use that was in the end. To man or dog.'

'You made a name for yourself.'

'The Silver Fox? That was more to do with my hair than my reputation. And now I don't have either.'

'I like cops. I like the work they do. I think it's honest toil.'

The Fox looks me up and down. I had tried to say what I wanted to say but my words sounded insincere. I feel like a fraud behind my props: sunglasses on an overcast day; the walking stick I still carried but needed less and less; the scarf I wore on my head to hide the fading evidence of my operation.

'I was a good cop. By-the-book correct. Took pride in doing things right. Never put a foot wrong until that bloody case,' says the Fox, returning to his pruning.

I hold my breath. Is he about to make a confession?

'It was the jumper, wasn't it?' I say.

'It wouldn't have made any difference.'

'Robert wasn't wearing it when his parents died?' I had no proof. It's a calculated guess, based on what I'd read in the file.

'He was guilty. He confessed as much in the car. There'd been a terrible argument and he just wanted it to go away.'

'You found the jumper afterwards?'

'I've said enough.'

'At the vineyard. It wasn't even at the house.' Now I was into speculation.

The Fox is silent.

'It could have been used at the clay target range. Even by someone other than Robert. It could have been borrowed if the day was cold. You had no way of proving it was at the house at the time the homicides occurred because it never was. Which is why the log was so deficient. It was introduced later. Then Robert wore a similar one during the reconstruction, an accused who was having difficulty knowing which day of the week it was?'

'I have said enough.'

'You planted evidence.'

'Yes, I did. For the one and only time in my life. And it's haunted me for the rest of my days – all the way to you.'

'It was the evidence that convinced the jury.'

'You don't know that. It was only one piece in the puzzle.'

'You don't even believe that yourself.'

The Fox snibs his secateurs and looks across at the plaque on the granite base. 'I'm not telling you anything I haven't already said to Jean.'

'Jean?'

'The wife. The Lady of Australia is her favourite rose. And mine. Bred here in Victoria. Won a gold medal. Named after the wives of the Governors-General.'

'And what did Jean say?'

'That what I did was wrong. And she was right. But sometimes you back your instincts. Isn't that what you were doing when you came to me?' His confession seems to give him some sense of release. 'So, what are you going to do?' he asks. 'Re-open the case?'

'No. Nothing official. I'm just trying to make a young woman feel better about her family.'

The Fox doesn't speak. His relief is palpable.

'I like your garden,' I say as I turn to go, removing my sunglasses so he could see my eyes.

'You should see it in summer.'

As I drive back to South Bank, I wonder if Showbag would approve of my undercover work. I know Marion and the doctor certainly wouldn't. I ponder what the Fox had told me. Had Rinaldi revealed in court what the Fox had admitted, the Crown case would have been contaminated and would surely have failed. But the jumper on its own didn't prove Robert's guilt or innocence. That truth still lay ahead.

I try Luna's phone but the call rings out. I don't leave a message. I had left so many already. I hope her Tasmanian holiday is going okay.

32.

Luna opens the door to her apartment and kills her cigarette. I'm pleased to see she's back, though I'm not sure she shares the same sentiment. I've caught her on the hop. She's looking anything but relaxed after her holiday.

'Sorry. I'm a bit disorganised. I'm in the middle of moving.'

'I thought you liked it here?'

'I do. It's the landlord who's the problem. Keeps putting up the rent.'

'Don't you have a lease?'

'He only does monthly tenancies. He says it's the market these days.'

'There's a tribunal you can go to . . .'

'Who wants the stress of that?'

The apartment is small and simply furnished, with a private garden. It's in a desirable suburb, but not without a proper lease. A bin sits in the middle of the room, overflowing with rubbish. Luna's possessions are half-packed in boxes or heaped in piles for disposal. It's hard to tell if the mess is recent.

'So how was Tassie?'

'Didn't make it in the end. They stuffed up my airfares. Got the wrong dates.' She lights up again and puts on the kettle. 'Instant coffee's all I've got. And no milk.'

'I'm okay,' I say as I start to wash the dishes in the sink.

'You don't need to do that.'

'I like to make myself useful. So how have you been?'

'Frazzled.' Luna shrugs a smile and draws on her cigarette.

I don't remember her as a smoker, though she wouldn't have smoked at Elizabeth's or the hospital. She seems weary and unkempt, but who doesn't get around at home sometimes looking a bit dishevelled?

'And you've left your job, I hear?'

'You sound like somebody's mother.'

'With Zoe away, I have to take it out on someone. Does your fridge need a clean?' I ask, opening the door.

'No. I'm leaving that. The new place has already got one.'

'I'll do it anyway,' I say, determined to fulfil the role I was playing. There's nothing in the fridge that hasn't exceeded its use-by date, so I open a new rubbish bag and start to load it up.

Luna watches from behind her coffee and cigarette. Looking small in an oversized T-shirt, she's slighter than I remembered. Without makeup, her eyes lack definition and her lips are pale and thin.

'Where's the new place?'

'St Kilda.'

'Maybe I can help you move?'

'You could help me with the bond. I'll pay you back, when I get the bond from here.'

'Not a problem. Tell the agent to give me a call and I'll put it on my card.'

'Thing is, there isn't an agent. I'm dealing with the owner and he'll only take cash.'

'No probs. How much do you need?'

Luna hesitates. 'I'm not sure. Maybe five hundred?'

'Is that enough? It's usually four weeks' rent?'

'I can manage the rest. Thank you.'

'I've been leaving messages on your phone. Have you been getting them?' I ask.

'I lost my phone. I've got a new number,' she says, pulling out a no-frills model. 'What's your number? I'll send you the link.'

She sends a message to my mobile and I log the number with her name. It's good to be in contact again.

'Oh, I've been meaning to tell you. I tracked down the detective who led the investigation in Robert's trial. I'm afraid I didn't learn anything about your father.'

'That's okay. I'm not looking for him anymore.'

Since Joe Wasserman had told me the opposite, I hide my surprise.

'If he even exists,' she continues. 'Who needs a father anyway?'

'You made it sound important when we met.'

'Yeah, well, that was then. And this is now. I decided I need to move on.'

'Is that why you left your job?'

'I had to leave. My boss is a creep. And he wasn't paying me properly.'

'I spoke to your boss when you weren't returning my calls. He seemed like a nice guy to me.'

'Everyone says that. He's a sleaze.'

'Yeah, well, appearances can be deceiving.'

It's hard to tell if Luna's search for her father has finally become too painful or if there are other issues in her life. Her problems seem to be everyone else's fault: her employer's, her landlord's, the airline's. Blaming others is always a worrying sign. And money seems to be an issue as well, which isn't surprising, since she no longer had a job.

'Can we go to the ATM?' she asks. 'There's one in the village.'

We drive up the road and Luna waits while I withdraw the cash, sucking on her third cigarette. I offer to drop her home, but she says she needs to do some shopping. She promises to phone me when the lease is settled and give me her new address. I wonder why she couldn't have told me there and then, but I don't want to mother her more than I have or let her think I'm worried about the money.

'Don't be a stranger,' I say. 'I've missed you.'

'Me too,' she says as if she means it and maybe she does. I know it's true for me.

Did I see in Luna parallels with myself? Had an eight-year-old Luna been so different from a twelve-year-old Jane? Luna's losses had been more traumatic and more extreme, but if I am still grappling with my 'bogey word' at this stage in my life, how much further does Luna have to go to deal with hers? My post-traumatic amnesia is starting to lift and my clinical skills are returning. Whether or not I would solve the injustices of Robert's trial remained to be seen, but right now Luna's situation seems to be more pressing.

I phone Joe Wasserman and am disturbed to hear Luna had been asking him for money as well.

'Five hundred. Cash. To help with the bond on a new lease.'

It has a familiar ring. 'How did you find her?'

'A bit strung out. Moving's always a nightmare. Any benefit from her holiday didn't last.'

'She never went to Tasmania. Blamed the airline for getting her dates wrong.'

'That's strange. I booked her ticket.'

'Maybe she cashed it in. Did she mention she'd resigned from her job?'

Joe knows even less than I do, though he did have her new address. I check it out. The building is a former rooming house that has been marked for demolition. Boarded up and ringed with security fences, if it was occupied, it's only by squatters. I hope Joe has made a mistake.

I try the new number Luna gave me but she doesn't pick up. I leave a message which 'would be sent as a text' but have no confidence it will get through.

Tim phones from Sydney. He's been asked to cover for someone in the Jazz at the Lincoln Center Orchestra who had fallen ill on tour. He sounds excited, as if it could lead to other things. I wasn't going to prick his balloon with my concerns about Luna and promise to come up and see a performance. He says he will send me the dates.

Doctor Zhou and Marion confirm appointments and Elizabeth a dinner with Jasmine and Virginia. I phone Zoe in New York and my mother in New Zealand, who both say I am sounding better.

I attend drinks for a friend who has achieved senior counsel status and bump into Peter Debreceny. I don't tell him about the Silver Fox's confession. I don't want him to think I've misused his files in any way.

'Did you find what you were after, Jane?'

'Yes and no. They helped me get my memory back.'

'Then you remember the dinner we had?'

'Sorry. Nothing quite that recent.'

'So, we'll have to do it again?' Peter gives me a knowing grin, except I can't decipher what it's supposed to mean. Is he implying the dinner had been arranged for purposes beyond handing over his files? Is he, however obliquely, suggesting something more than dinner? He knows I'm in a relationship with Tim.

I hadn't only lost part of my recent memory, I had lost my confidence as well. Jane 1.0 would have asked Peter immediately what he meant. Jane 2.0 is too inhibited, too embarrassed to ask a question that might implicate her further, too ashamed of her 'disability' to highlight the gaps that persisted still.

However much I rail against it, my brain injury has redefined my life. However much I push to prove I'm getting better, there's always a moment like this to bring me crashing back to earth.

'That would be nice,' I say. 'Though I've got to fit in a trip to Sydney to see a concert. Maybe something next month?'

Jane 2.0 is her own worst enemy.

Driving back home, I swing past Luna's old address and am pleased to see that the lights are on. But it isn't Luna who's there, but her landlord. He's changing the locks. The rubbish bin and Luna's half-packed boxes still stand in the middle of the lounge room floor.

'Are you her mother?' he asks.

'No. A friend.'

'Pity. I was hoping you'd come to pay the rent.' He explains how the apartment would have to be cleaned and repainted before he could let it again and how hard it is to be a landlord. How the young generation are spoilt and entitled and never honour a lease. How only immigrants like him understand the value of work anymore and how Australia could do with a Donald Trump.

When I ask about Luna's boxes, the subject quickly returns to money. Unless she pays her back rent, he explains, they'd be sent to the tip with the rubbish – and she would be charged for that as well. I agree to pay what he was owed and while he fetches a credit card machine from his car, I do a quick search to see if there was anything else I should take. I collect some cosmetics from the bathroom cabinet along with an alarming array of painkillers including fentanyl tablets and patches, from which an attempt had been made to extract the drug. Our business done, the landlord helps me load the boxes into my car.

I park in my basement carpark and take a quick look to see what I had managed to salvage. There doesn't seem to be anything of value, though what's important to someone else is hard to assess. But one thing does catch my eye: a scrapbook of poems and childish drawings, one of which I had seen before.

Georgie Porgie, picklety pie,
Kissed the girls and made them cry.
When Georgie Porgie comes home to play,
It will be a long and sunny day.
Jack be nimble, Jack be quick,
I give you a stone, you give me a stick.
Keep our secrets alive forever,
And that way we'll be together.

The poem Robert had written during his trial.

33.

Sleep is impossible. The tablets I'd been prescribed aren't working, though I wasn't giving them much of a chance. Sitting up in bed with Luna's scrapbook trying to untangle some recurring thread or hidden code is hardly conducive to slumber.

Two little girls, squashed on toast,
That is the taste we love the most.
Two little boys, squashed on bread,
They taste awful – but at least they're dead.

The poem has the macabre appeal children like – especially little girls concerned about 'boy germs' – but beyond that it is difficult to discern its purpose. Another is in a similar vein, though with a more personal warning at the end.

People are exploding,
You see it all the time.
They try to patch the problem up,
With medicines and twine.
The answer is quite simple,
There are no in-betweens,

You either keep a secret or
Get blown to smithereens.

The need to keep a secret is a recurring theme – though with parents as overpowering as Herman and Skyla, the idea of the children sticking together – or of Robert protecting Luna – is easy to understand.

Jack be nimble, Jack be quick,
I give you a stone, you give me a stick.

Which was clearly a kind of mutual pledge. And:

You're lost without a special friend,
On whom you can rely.

Elsewhere, the bond between Robert and Luna was more magical.

Luna is a silver moon,
She'd come back every night,
For that is where the magic starts,
And fantasies take flight.

But there was a dark side too, beneath the surface rhymes.

Dress me up, dress me down,
Dress me like a crazy clown.
Paint me yellow, paint me blue,
Kill the colours that aren't like you.

'Kill the colours . . .'

'People are exploding . . .'

'At least they're dead.'

Given what had happened, you wouldn't want to run those lines together.

After a sleepless night, I cancel my appointment with Doctor Zhou and leave messages for Luna to let her know I had her boxes. Zoe has a similar tendency to not answer her phone: maybe it's a Millennial thing. So, I go to St Kilda to see if I can find Luna's actual new address, which I figure has to be somewhere near the derelict building. Street and apartment numbers are easy to confuse; I'd start with the apartments that shared the same number as the demolition site.

I park my car opposite the former rooming house and try to get my bearings. There are apartment blocks east and west that look like the sort of accommodation Luna might seek. I decide to sit for a while and maybe do some door-knocking. With her blue hair, Luna is the kind of young person people notice.

A skinny youth in his twenties emerges from the derelict building and squeezes through a gap in the chain-link fencing. He keeps his head down to avoid attention but his jumpiness does the opposite.

'Hi,' I say as sociably as I can manage from behind my screening sunnies. 'I'm looking for someone who lives around here. A young woman called Luna – with bright blue hair.'

'Sorry, can't help you,' he says, determined to continue on his way.

'I was given this as her address.'

'No-one lives here anymore. They're pullin' it down.'

'I can see—'

'Can you spare some change?'

'Sure,' I say, opening my purse and rummaging around for coins. I could have given him a note, but this way I keep him longer. 'You living here yourself?'

'Just till they find me somewhere.' He takes some gold coins and waits for more.

'Anyone else doing the same?'

'They come 'n' go. You can take a look for yourself if you like.'

I hand him a ten dollar note and enter the demolition site the same way he had left, jagging my jacket on the broken wire.

The former rooming house had once been a grand mansion. Built in the 1870s, probably for a prominent Melbourne merchant following the gold rush of the 1850s and '60s, it had been converted into emergency accommodation. It would probably be replaced by a supermarket, the homeless and those at-risk left to fend for themselves.

The building is filled with rancid smoke and smells like a public toilet. Figures, mainly male, hover in unlit rooms in twos and threes, burning discarded furniture and rubbish in the fireplaces that hadn't been removed or boarded up. Some are brewing tea and cooking sausages on sticks, probably given away after their use-by dates had expired. Others are more intent on smoking meth. No-one pays me much attention. To them, I probably look like a social worker.

'I'm looking for a young woman called Luna, with bright blue hair?'

'Sorry. Don't know her. Have you got any cash?'

I can't get out of the place quick enough and am pleased not to find anyone who knows Luna. The address had to be a mistake.

My phone beeps a message. Marion – I've missed my session. Did I want to reschedule? I realise I've cancelled the wrong appointment – the one with Doctor Zhou. It's clear my short-term memory still has a way to go.

As if I need to be reminded.

I have breakfast on St Kilda Pier, check my emails and make a new time with Marion. I phone Joe Wasserman to double-check the address Luna had given him but he isn't sure. It was either 26 or 28, he thinks, or 26/28 or 28/26 – but I had tried all those variations and none of them checked out.

As I walk back along the pier, I think I see a lone figure with blue hair sitting on the beach. It's probably a blue hat. I remove my sunglasses but the glare from the ocean makes things worse. I head along the sand towards the blue beacon, hope exceeding my expectations.

Luna recognises me first. 'Got your message. I was about to send you a text.'

'Hello, Luna. You're a hard one to catch.'

'Yeah, well, I've had a bit on.' She explains how her new accommodation has fallen through. It was just a scam by someone renting an Airbnb and pretending to be the owner. They took the bond, handed over the key – and she was booted out the following day.

'The bad luck continues,' I say.

'Thanks for getting my boxes, though I doubt they were

worth the price. I hope that prick didn't take too much of your money.'

'What are you doing down here? Going for a swim?'

'No, I'm not real good in the water.'

'So where are you staying?' I say, trying not to sound like somebody's mother.

'With friends in Elwood. It'll do till I find something else.'

'I'll drop off your boxes if you like?' I say, hoping to get an address.

'Or dump them. There's nothing of any value.'

'What about your book of poems?'

'I don't need them. I know them by heart. Which one do you want? "*Two little girls, squashed on toast*" . . . ?'

'It's a nice memory to have. Of Robert.'

Luna gives a noncommittal shrug. She looks washed out and tired and on something to keep her awake. Fentanyl, I suspect. I hope it isn't meth.

'So – are you hungry? How are you going for money?'

'I've eaten, but since I was scammed – yes, I could do with a loan. I'll pay you back . . .'

We head to my car and set off for an ATM. I know not to give her cash, but want to keep her with me as long as I can. 'You can stay with me if you like. Until you get yourself sorted.'

'Thanks, but I'm okay with my friends.'

'Whereabouts in Elwood are they?' It's obvious I'm fishing for more.

'By the station.'

We stop at Albert Park and I withdraw a hundred in cash. 'Sorry – I've more in my cheque account – but that would have to be a bank transfer. If you give me your account details.'

'A hungy's cool.'

My anxiety is showing and I can only think of Showbag and the ease with which that old-style cop would have handled this situation. Certainly not by driving a car from which the passenger could so easily escape. We stop at a red light and as it changes to green, Luna opens the door and slips off into the traffic.

'Thanks. I'll catch the train from here. Thanks for the money. See ya.'

It was time to lift my game. The evidence was unequivocal. Resigning from her job and not paying her rent, cashing in her ticket and not going to Tasmania, asking for money, always cash, by peddling the same stories to me and Wasserman. Hard-luck stories, always plausible. Being vague about addresses and 'friends in Elwood', losing her phone and never answering calls; always blaming others. But most of all it was there in her deportment: tired yet always 'up'; unkempt as if she hadn't changed her clothes; a feigned confidence bordering on arrogance; unfailingly polite. The fentanyl was damning; extracting the drug from patches, desperate. To graduate from that to methamphetamine would be an easy step.

My main problem is I have no memory of how Luna was before she approached me to help find her father. No memory of her before the accident, of how and when she first appeared at the hospital. Luna had materialised in my lurid dreams at the big white house. She'd had to 'fill me in' on her quest herself by recounting each one of our meetings. In the beginning, my obsession was all about her brother, his disastrous trial and tragic suicide. I remembered more about Luna at eight years old, when I visited her and her traumatised grandparents, but even that was related to Robert.

My recovery has obscured everything. I have no idea who the real Luna is. Did she take drugs before the accident? Is she a recreational user, like many young people are these days, functioning normally most of the time until stressors of one form or another intervene to capsize the boat? I hope she has friends in Elwood but I'm sure the squat featured somewhere in her routines. Maybe it's where she gets her drugs?

I call by the St Kilda Police Station and engage with a friendly sergeant. She knows about the former rooming house, they keep an eye of the place, know about the squatters – some of them by name. She says the one I had talked to was probably 'Ray'. The loss of the halfway house puts a strain on everyone, the homeless in particular, and there is only so much the police can do. If the squatters weren't assaulting or robbing people, they tended to leave them alone. Drug-taking – even low-level dealing – wasn't their priority. Domestic violence, gang warfare and behaviour around some of the night-time venues was far more pressing.

I ask if someone could accompany me to the squat and ask some questions. A police uniform might garner more information than I had managed to get. I stress how worried I am about Luna, how at-risk I think she is. When the sergeant explains they don't really have the resources for that kind of thing, I ask her to phone Senior Sergeant Poulos. I'm not beneath using an inside contact.

The sergeant withdraws to make the call and returns a few minutes later. It hasn't changed her mind. God knows what

Poulos has told her. Probably that I'd suffered a serious accident and had received severe trauma to the brain.

I give the sergeant my phone number and a description of Luna and she says she'll get her patrols to keep an eye out.

'Good luck,' she says, as she no doubt does to everyone with someone they cared about, lost and alone on the streets.

34.

Tim phones from Sydney. His gig with Jazz at the Lincoln Center is going really well. I had talked about coming up for the weekend, but defer for another week. I'd made a new time with Marion, but push that out a week as well. Joe Wasserman phones. He owns a block of apartments in Balaclava and one of them has become available. He thinks it would be perfect for Luna – if only she'd answer her phone. I tell him I think I can find her but fudge about the squat in St Kilda.

Not prepared to risk another jacket, I dress down and arm myself with what I know will give me some cachet: two very large bags of groceries. I park my car and squeeze in through the gap in the chain-link fence. My helpful druggie is in the overgrown garden, playing with a rescue dog.

'Hi Ray. How are you going?'

He gives me a vague meth grin, bemused I know his name.

'I've brought some stuff for you and the others. Not all fresh fruit and veg, you'll be pleased to hear.'

Ray rummages through the bags like a kid on Christmas morning, separating the things he can sell or wants to keep for himself.

'Seen anything of Luna?'

'With the blue hair and nose ring?'

'Yeah, that's the one.'

'She was in here this mornin.' The groceries have lowered Ray's defences.

'Buying drugs?'

'Well, not from me . . .'

'Did she tell you where she was going?'

'Naw. Isn't she staying in Elwood?'

At least that part of her story was confirmed.

'I think she said she was goin' for a swim.'

There are good swimming beaches all along the bay but I figure she won't have gone too far. I park the car near the Palais Theatre and take the walking track south towards Elwood. I feel like a desperate parent, trying to save their child from drugs, pounding the pavement on scant evidence as if my commitment and determination will show them how much I care, how much their behaviour was hurting me and impacting on my welfare, how much I was prepared to sacrifice to turn them around and bring them to their senses. I know better, of course. I had counselled parents in precisely the same position and told them, with compassion, that they were wasting their time. That until the addict was ready to change there was nothing they could do except get on with their own lives and be there for them. To give them love and support and never, ever cash. I should have been heeding my own advice.

I get all the way to Brighton, where I used to live, before I turn around. My car is in a one-hour parking space and no doubt has a ticket by now. Another wasted morning. I should have had my mind on other things. Like making a decision about whether or not I was returning to the university job and giving Nicholas the answer he deserved. I had justified my obsession with Robert by convincing myself that I was using it as a tool to recover my memory. What justification can I claim with this new obsession with Luna?

My brain hurts. Literally. I pop another couple of pills. I hate my dependence on analgesics. I hate that my horizons have shrunk. I hate the blanks in my memory. I hate that I don't feel like a grown-up anymore, let alone a forensic psychiatrist. I hate that I am using a word as stupid as 'hate'.

Come on, Jane. You are doing better. Accept the parking ticket and give yourself a pat on the back. At least you got some serious exercise this morning and made the walk without your stick.

The clouds to the west are darkening. There's a cool change in the air. Then, as I round the Point Ormond Lookout, I see her, sitting on the beach, her blue hair catching what is left of the sun.

'This is becoming a habit,' I say as I approach across the sand.

'Jane. What are you doing here?'

'Joe Wasserman's been trying to reach you. He's got some accommodation—'

'I've kind of taken the room at my friend's. I don't want to let her down.'

Luna seems less animated than usual; more sedate, if not sedated. I worry it might be chemically induced, but she is speaking sensibly if somewhat flatly about her situation and suggesting her friends in Elwood might even exist.

'So – what are your plans?' I ask.

'I don't know. A swim then fish 'n' chips.'

'I have to rescue my car, so why don't you take your dip and I'll get the food and meet you back here?'

'Sounds good.'

'Or if the weather turns, we can eat at the kiosk.'

Only the day before, Luna had slipped from my car and I know she could disappear on me again. But establishing trust is part of the deal and, like the addict's parent I was trying so hard not to be, I had set a test. If it didn't work out, I could only blame myself.

My car doesn't have a parking ticket; it has two. Cursing the zealotry of the City of Port Phillip, I continue on to the local chippery and drive back to Elwood. As I walk down the path to the beach with my over-order of fish and chips (plus calamari rings and tempura prawns), my heart sinks. Luna is nowhere to be seen. The weather has turned, a cold wind blasting in from the west, whipping up white caps across the bay. There's something down on the sand where Luna had been sitting. It looks like her jacket. Maybe she had left a note? But as I draw near, I see it is more than her jacket: it's a neatly stacked pile of all her clothes, down to her underwear and jewellery. My fears didn't need any assistance – they were already galloping ahead on a horse.

Fifty metres out in the water a naked figure with bright blue hair wades deeper and deeper into the waves.

From my years in Brighton, I know a lot about the bay. It's notorious for sudden changes in weather, quick squalls and some very extreme conditions. I remember the summer of 2009 when five people drowned in these waters, a fact I repeatedly hammered into a twelve-year-old Zoe. And Luna had said she wasn't good in the water.

The bay actually isn't a bay at all and behaves more like a shallow lake. Really a drowned estuary. It's not the currents that trick you, but sudden changes in depth and the chop – the waves on top going the same way as the onshore wind while those below them go in the opposite direction. Inexperienced swimmers often get caught in calm water that is suddenly churned up like a washing machine. It can be exciting of course, like unexpectedly finding yourself in the surf. Yet the results can be fatal.

But it isn't accidental death I fear as I fling off my glasses, watch and shoes. It's a much bigger word than that.

Fully clothed, I plunge into the water, knowing that every second could count. Half-wading, half-swimming, the familiar double-wave action making progress difficult. I'm calling at the top of my lungs but my words are lost to the wind. Luna keeps pushing on, successive waves rolling over her head. Each time she takes longer to surface. I'm struggling to keep her in sight. Her hair isn't helping; blue is the worst colour to spot in the sea. Why hadn't she dyed it fluoro green? The salt stings my eyes and my mouth fills with water every time I call. The waves push me back. Swimming into the wind is futile. My toes dig into the sand and silt, the water now over my chest.

Luna has no idea I am behind her. When I grab her, she lets out a terrified scream as if she's being taken by a shark. As she spins around, her elbow connects with my temple and my wearied brain turns itself off for the second time since the accident.

The next thing I know I'm on the beach with Luna close and naked like a lover, breathing into my mouth. She smiles, pale and blue and otherworldly, clouds of seagulls wheeling behind her. The birds have demolished our lunch and squawk for more. The sky is dark and menacing but I am alive. And so is Luna.

As I lie on the sand, shivering in my soaking clothes, Luna puts on hers. We recover my watch, glasses and shoes and set off for my car. Luna is pleased her handiwork has borne results. She had only tried CPR on a dummy at school. Now she had a real-life one to her credit.

We find dry clothes for me at a Salvo's Store and have coffee and a warming meal at a nearby café.

'How did you get me ashore?' I ask.

'I didn't. It was more you dragging me. You didn't pass out till we hit the beach.'

'Were you in trouble out there?'

'No. Almost at peace.'

'Until I came along?'

'Yeah, something like that.'

'Then I guess we saved each other.'

'If you want to be saved.'

Nothing like brutal honesty to stop a conversation in its tracks.

'I'm sorry you've been feeling so sad, Luna. But I'm very glad you're still here.'

Luna looks off into the distance. I'm not sure she's listening. I had to find a key somewhere. Could I remember one of the poems?

'*Two little girls, squashed on toast,*
That is the taste we love the most.
Two little boys, squashed on bread,
They taste awful – but at least they're dead.'

Luna smiles.

'What does it mean?'

'You'd have to ask Robert,' she says. 'But it made me laugh.'

'Why?'

'Dead little boys are better than dead little girls. And I'm sure they don't taste as good.'

'Were you thinking about Robert today?'

'No.'

'Or your parents?'

'No.'

'Then what?'

'How being alone really sucks.'

'Have you had boyfriends, girlfriends . . . ?'

'I've tried both. But they're not as good.'

'As what?'

'As someone who doesn't live in the real world.'

'Like Robert?'

'Maybe.'

'Let's go for a drive.'

'Where?'

'Let's follow our noses. To somewhere where you were happy?'

'You got a time machine?'

'Next best thing. A BMW. Series 8.'

Taking Inkerman Street towards Chadstone, we're on the M1 in twenty-two minutes. Luna doesn't know where we are headed. I'm not even sure myself. It's probably not a smart thing to do following a minor blackout, but I decide exhaustion had caused my collapse on the beach rather than a blow to the head. Sometimes it can be handy when a physician does their own diagnosis. Either handy or foolish.

35.

The further we get away from Melbourne, the less likely it is that Luna would flee the car when we stopped at traffic lights or give way signs. While not technically kidnap, it's probably a version of that.

It's hard to get her to focus so we talk about nothing in particular. Like how daggy I looked in my op-shop clothes and how earrings look best when they match your eyes.

'Big earrings suggest self-confidence, but I usually wear them when I'm feeling low,' I say.

'You don't look like someone who gets depressed,' says Luna.

'Everyone feels sad from time to time. It's part of the human condition.' I cringe at my glibness and feel a wave of nausea. Maybe I had passed out from the blow to my head, in which case I shouldn't be driving. I pull over to the shoulder of the freeway and rummage in my bag for painkillers.

'Can you drive, Luna?' I ask. 'I'm not feeling a hundred per cent.'

'Your precious BMW? I warn you, I'm a bit of a lead foot.'

We change sides and Luna pulls out into the freeway, quickly joining the faster outside lane. My new coupe is even faster than the car it replaced but Luna drives with confidence, enjoying the speed but keeping within the limit.

'So where are we going?' she asks.

'Why don't you show me where the vineyard was? We're headed in that direction.'

From the road to Flinders, Luna turns left in the direction of Western Port Bay. Rolling pastures slope towards Phillip Island, sheltered from the squalls that had hit the city only hours before.

'Down here I think. It's changed so much. I haven't been here for years,' she says.

Looking for the haunts of her past has lifted Luna's spirits, but she seems unprepared for what she sees when we crest the hill at the top of the ridge. Where the family's vineyard once stood, the newly formed roads of a housing development cling to the landscape like an alien lattice, its 'Lifestyle Opportunity' limited in scale and imagination to eighth-of-an-acre blocks. The former homestead is now an art gallery and restaurant, the outbuildings a craft brewery and garden centre. A wooded area, too steep for subdivision and no doubt gifted to council as 'open space', is the developer's only gesture towards the community.

Luna pulls the car to the side of the road. 'I don't care, you know. It belonged to Robert and me. I'm glad it's different now.' Luna tries to make it sound as if her childhood had been safely sealed in the past, the redevelopment forming a time capsule no-one else could open. But there's a wistfulness in her voice.

'It's good you remember the happy times,' I say. 'My family had a farm when I was young. Well, really just a place to keep horses.'

'We had horses too. We had jumps down there by the trees.' Luna gets out of the car and heads down the slope to explore.

I grab my stick and follow. 'Were you happy here, with Herman?'

'That's a funny question to ask.'

'If you thought he wasn't your father?'

'That was Robert's idea. He thought it was better that way.'

'Because Herman was harming you?'

'No, never that. Though he was tough on us sometimes.'

'So why did Robert think it was better?'

'Because we wouldn't be brother and sister.'

'But you had the same mother?'

'That didn't count.'

'Why not?'

'Half-brothers and half-sisters aren't brothers and sisters at all.'

'What? Legally or biologically?'

'Either.'

'I'm not sure that's right.'

'Look. The jumps are still there.' Luna takes off towards the trees.

Three long logs sag between two tripods and, five strides away, a line of forty-four-gallon drums with turf on top provide a high jump. I catch up with her at the drums.

'I can't remember them being this high. What a brave little girl I was,' she says.

'Luna, if you and Robert weren't brother and sister, what were you?'

'Special friends.'

'And that was better?'

'Robert thought it was.'

'And why was that?'

'Because we could do anything we wanted.'

'Like?'

'Ah, look – the treehouse and the lookout!' Luna runs to the dilapidating structure and starts to climb the ladder.

I stand for a while in the shade of the trees, chilled, not from the mustering wind but from what she had said. *Because we could do anything we wanted.* Luna had been understandably traumatised by the loss of her family, but was there something else in her past? A hope, a possibility, that had been kept alive by her belief – by Robert's belief – that Herman wasn't her father? A belief finally disproved by her futile search for someone who never existed. Is that why she had walked away from her pleasant apartment and a job where she was valued? Why she had sought oblivion in methamphetamine, however empty and short-sighted that was?

In psychiatry, we are always vigilant about pronouns, especially where we sense a relationship has been unequal. Like that between a young man of twenty and his little sister, who was only eight. Though Luna was variously described as 'bright' and 'precocious', the twelve-year gap with her brother could not be ignored. And my antennae went up immediately when she mentioned a 'special relationship' between 'special friends'. Allegations of sexual abuse by Herman had not been substantiated, but the accusation remained in the air. Put there by Robert's guilt or otherwise, I couldn't tell, but the pronoun rule had me alerted. When Luna said, 'Because we could do anything we wanted', did she really mean something else? 'Because *he* could do anything *he* wanted?'

As Luna climbs higher and higher up the mutilevelled treehouse only a father who loved to indulge his children would have built, I lay down my stick and begin the climb too. My balance is nearly back to normal, but to my alarm I discover I've developed a fear of heights. 'Don't look down' is the rule, I think. So I keep on climbing and looking up.

I finally make it to the highest level – the lookout. Luna is excitedly looking through the old telescope.

'Pirate ship ahoy!' she says. 'Prepare to repel all boarders. Boil up the oil to drop on the scurvy knaves. No-one will get us up here.'

The view from the lookout is spectacular, though I can't ignore how much the structure has decayed, built as it was from largely untreated timber. Luna is back in her childhood. I am high in a tree on a rotting platform, just hoping we will make it down.

'Did Herman build this?' I ask.

'Yes. He loved to make things. Mum thought it was far too high.'

'I'm with Skyla,' I say. 'And you would play up here with your friends?'

'Only the brave ones.'

'And Robert?'

'Robert was afraid of nothing. As long as we had each other.'

'Your special relationship. With its special secrets.'

Luna refocuses on the telescope.

'And your pledge of secrecy. *I give you a stone, you give me a stick . . .*'

Still Luna doesn't answer.

'*You either keep a secret or get blown to smithereens.*'

Luna turns her head to me. Her face betrays no emotion. It's an attempt to put up a wall, and also a warning: proceed no further. But I know I'm close.

'You mustn't blame yourself, Luna. You were a child. You were only eight.'

'I don't know what you're talking about.'

'It wasn't easy with parents like yours. Famous, larger than life. Not like anyone else's parents, with their relationships outside the marriage, and their free and permissive ways. I can understand why you and Robert became so close and formed a safe place away from their turmoil.'

'He saved my life.'

'Did he, Luna? Is that what he did? Or did he use you to his advantage? To exploit your special relationship so he could do anything he wanted?'

'No . . .'

'You were only eight but you were extremely smart. So you probably sensed what you were doing was wrong. But if Herman wasn't your father – and you believed Robert when he said you weren't really brother and sister – then somehow that made it okay.'

'He loved me. Robert loved me. More than my parents ever did.'

'I'm sorry, Luna, but whatever it was, it wasn't love. Love wouldn't have left you like this.'

Luna takes hold of the telescope and rips it from its stand. Then, lifting it above her head, throws it down with all the strength she can muster. The telescope crashes through the rotting deck, but it isn't that that does the damage. It's a crossmember below that the heavy object removes as it continues on its way to the ground – a crossmember that supported everything above it. The treehouse starts to collapse from the bottom up.

As insane as it might sound, I'm actually pleased our physical predicament has suddenly become our preoccupation.

My assertions would take time to process. There could be no neat and easy breakthrough in a case like this. It was, at best, a beginning.

Only hours before, Luna and I had helped each other from the sea. Now we had to help each other down from a disintegrating structure, ten metres above the ground. Taking turns to support the one above, we crab our way down the tree, belaying each other with arms instead of ropes, like mountaineers whose mountain was crumbling beneath their feet. As we get to the ground, we run away from the falling timbers and throw ourselves into the long grass by the horse jumps, laughing like children who have escaped from some forbidden adventure with their lives intact. And maybe we had.

Not much is said as I drive back to Melbourne. My headache has passed and I am feeling better, though how Luna is feeling is harder to tell. I hope she senses a beginning, the first glimmerings of a truth that will eventually set her free, however painful the journey might be.

Robert's guilt or innocence in his parents' deaths was suddenly inconsequential. Had they discovered what he and Luna had been doing? Is that what the argument had been about all along? Had Robert shot Skyla and Herman when they'd confronted him with his abuse? Or had Robert shot them both before they discovered a truth too appalling to know? I'm now less convinced that my original assessment had been correct – that Robert had come upon his parents after a murder–suicide and picked up the gun. I'm prepared to admit I'd been wrong, that the first confession had been the right one. Note to self: Always use extreme caution when dealing with a pathological liar.

My search for the truth about what really happened on that terrible day in 2003 has been replaced by something far more pressing: the care and healing of the sole survivor.

When I explain what happened to Marion and Doctor Zhou, they are far from impressed. I still have a distance to go to fully recover my health, and these 'escapades', as the doctor puts it, are not helping that.

I'm grateful when Marion agrees to take on Luna as a client. She and I both know I don't yet have the reserves to see the task through myself. And Marion's patient, step-by-step approach will be the perfect therapy for Luna.

I have demons of my own to conquer, in particular a demon called 'suicide'. So, girding my loins, I book a ticket to New Zealand. It's time for Doctor Halifax to attempt to heal herself.

PART EIGHT

June 2023

I wrote a poem to myself,
Placed above my desk up on a shelf.
To remind me every single day,
That non-believers also pray.
Not to an all-seeing, all-knowing God,
But to the fates, which may seem odd
to Christians. Yet we too have dreams,
And isn't that what praying means?

'Elegy for Robert Millard'
by Jane Halifax

36.

My tension dissipates as the plane lifts up from Sydney Airport bound for Queenstown, a three-hour hop across the Tasman. Given my accident and the interruptions to travel caused by Covid, I haven't visited my mother for three years. Angela is almost eighty and in rude health, still playing eighteen holes of golf twice a week. She was thirty-five when my father died and has shown no interest in another relationship. The odd boyfriend from time to time – inevitably golfers – meets her description of the perfect companion. 'I cook for them when I want to, and when I don't they take me out to a nice restaurant. No washing and cleaning for someone else, no hassle over what to watch on TV, no snoring to interrupt my sleep. You should try it, Jane. And if you're lonely, get a dog.'

She does yoga and pilates to keep her core strong and her posture straight and still walks the golf course. She puts her golf bag on her friend's cart, selecting the two clubs she thinks she'll need for the fairway and inverting them to use like Nordic walking sticks. The only time she rides the cart is on the last leg to the nineteenth hole – and only then to brag about her score or make excuses on the rare occasions she'd lost. An irritating woman, my mother.

Angela and I could not have been more unalike. She'd had no tertiary education and seldom read a book. She had grown up on a farm in West Otago and been sent to Columba College, a good boarding school for girls in Dunedin – not for the education but to meet the right kind of boy. She'd taken up painting to annoy one of her friends and show her she could do better. She has a certain naive talent, but showing off only takes one so far. Apart from golf, Angela works well below her potential. Had she been fifty years younger, she may have been a professional golfer and possibly a very good one. But she had married the man she'd selected, had a child to prove she could and returned to New Zealand the instant I left home for university.

'Hello, Mum,' I say as we hug each other to feel if there is anything there. I doubt we are looking for the same thing.

'You're looking better than you did on Zoom,' she says, as close to a compliment as she can manage. 'For a moment we thought we had lost you there,' she adds without explaining who she means by 'we'. She certainly isn't referring to Zoe – she had told me while she sort of understood step-parenting, stepgrand-mothering was a bridge too far. 'Cup of tea?'

While Angela puts on the kettle, I go outside. Her house is on the shores of Lake Hawea, a deep blue lake surrounded by mountains, those to the north still holding snow into November. An alpine area, it was hot and dry in summer and clear and snowy in winter with cloudless nights and a million stars to nourish the soul. In a place like this, forensic psychiatry and fighting crime seemed pointless endeavours; golf and part-time male companions a perfect work–life balance. Is my mother smarter than me?

Angela's mother – who I called Grandma – had done a better job of bringing me up. A staunch Scottish Presbyterian whom I accompanied to church every Sunday while my godless parents stayed at home, was full of wise advice. 'Don't walk with your head down, Jane, looking for the pennies others have dropped in the gutter. Gaze as far ahead as you can and hold your head high. There's money bid for ye.' The puzzle was she had produced a daughter like my mother.

Angela brings out mugs of tea and we sit on the bench to gaze at the view.

'Do you know how lucky you are to live here, Mum?'

'Every day.'

'What are your plans for your birthday?'

'Well, I am not admitting I'm eighty.'

'Don't people already know?'

'I'm not leaving my seventies until I'm good and ready. Eighty's the beginning of the end.'

'I'd like to visit Grandma's grave,' I say.

'You can do what you like.' There are kinder responses, like 'What a lovely idea, Jane. We can go there together,' but she isn't going to surprise me now.

That night I take her to one of the restaurants in Wanaka her boyfriends frequented, where she flirts with the waiter. She hides her age very well, although he could have counted the rings on her fingers; that much jewellery tells you something. Grit and denial. She was more Halifax than me.

Before bed, Angela makes us Milo, a habit she'd followed all her life. She didn't ask if I wanted one. In her house you did what she did.

'How long have you come for?' she asks.

'I'm not sure. Is that a problem?'

'You didn't book a return?' she says, as if inconvenienced by my lack of planning.

'No. I thought I'd play it by ear.'

'Well, I play golf Mondays and Thursdays.'

'I've been keeping a journal. I can work on that when you're not here.'

'Whatever for? You don't have any children.'

'To keep track of my recovery . . .'

'You should have had five.'

'What?'

'Five children. You would have taken it in your stride.'

Good old Mum, bringing up subjects she knows will get under my skin, half accusation, half regret for me having failed to provide her with grandchildren to indulge. Apparently step-grandparenting was one thing, real grandparenting quite another.

We love each other – up to a point. And know each other not at all.

I can't wait for her to go to bed.

As a child, I envied large families. They seemed to hold more laughter. Grandma always said that children should outnumber the adults, that it was the only way to even things up. Parental authority versus adolescent rebellion. She came from a family of seven children and it had certainly worked for her.

I go outside and wonder at the lake, silver with the magic of the moon.

During breakfast the following morning, my mother does something she has never done before: she apologises.

'When your father died, I'm sorry for the way I handled it. Just blurting it out and letting you run away.'

'That's okay, Mum. You were in shock.'

'When I found the body, I was too angry to approach him to see if he needed assistance. So I phoned the police who came with an ambulance. But it was far too late by then. I should have talked to you about it, but I never did.'

'That's all right. Grandma talked to me about it all the time.'

'A wonderful woman, my mother. Held everything together. Arranged for the sale of the farm to pay for your education.'

'I didn't have to go to a private school.'

'Of course you did, Jane. How else would you meet anyone suitable? Not that you ever did. Mind you, I should never have married your father.'

'Why not?'

'I knew he was a womaniser. Thought I could change him. Our period of exclusivity lasted less than two years.'

'How did you know he was straying?'

'Usual signs. Working back late. Accusing *me* of cheating. Always buying new underpants and asking me how he looked in them.'

Even now I can see that the memories are painful.

'Then he started to miss weekends at the farm. We had to go because of the horses, but more and more he stayed back for work. In the early days he'd bring his files along with him, so I knew he was telling fibs.'

'Why didn't you leave?'

'Because you adored him so much. I was jealous of that as well.'

'Why do you think he killed himself?'

'He got his PA pregnant. Of course, I didn't know at the time. She told me several years later. Wanted me to know they loved each other, which I said was nice. Wouldn't want to think they were only doing it for the sex.'

'Did she have the child?'

'No. She miscarried. Probably from the shock. I don't know why he just didn't leave. Would have been better for everyone. You'd still have a father. And maybe a half-brother or -sister. And we'd still have the farm, which you and your grandma loved. And I wouldn't have needed to give up golf and get a job. As far as cheating goes, that was the worst of it. Cheating us out of that.'

'Did you hate him?'

'No. I don't do the big emotions. But I buried him with his underpants collection. There was some satisfaction in that.'

'I hated him for years for leaving the way he did.'

'You put him up on a pedestal, Jane. So high you couldn't get him down.'

'My therapist said something like that.'

'Therapist. What nonsense. It's just common sense. You should have been a lawyer like your father wanted.'

'You don't like what I do?'

'Jane, I don't understand it. Forensic psychiatry? I don't even know what that is.'

After Angela had left for golf, I look around the house for any remnants of my childhood. There is my grandmother's award from the Pioneer Women's Association and my mother's golf trophies dating from when I was two. In an old album, there are photos of Grandma's beach shack – or 'crib' as they call it down south – at Shag Point where we went for holidays before we came to Australia. Had my father used it for shagging? There is an unsettling photo of me aged five standing on a dead whale that had been beached near Warrington. I look like a Spanish conquistador – a pose no doubt inspired by my father, who took the shot. There are photos of me and my mother and grandmother – but very few of my father. Is that because he took the photos or because my mother had removed him from her life?

There are lots of golfing magazines around the house but very few novels. There are some large format books on painters – Gauguin, Van Gogh and the Impressionists – reflecting Angela's interest in art. And tucked among them, something I had almost forgotten: the catalogue of the photographic exhibition I had been part of in 2020 – *Portraits in Black and White.* My section stood up well among the others, many of them professional photographers. The portraits of Zoe and Ben are there; the originals used to hang in the house at Brighton. Zoe took hers with her to New York, but I can't remember what had happened to Ben's. Had I edited him out of my life like my mother had cancelled my father? But it's the final portraits I had totally forgotten – a number of nude studies of Tim. Beautifully lit and, if I say so myself, beautifully photographed – though how can you go wrong with a body like that?

When Angela returns from golf, I'm making dinner. I had left the catalogue out on the table. She picks it up.

'I've been looking for this. Where did you find it?'

'In among your art books.'

She flips through to my photos of Tim. 'I was going to ask you – who's this?'

'That's Tim. He's a jazz musician and cello player. He was a very close friend of Ben's.'

'Is he gay?'

'No. Why do you say that?'

'He's too beautiful to be straight. Will you look at that penis.'

'Yes, he is a very beautiful man.'

I omit to tell her we are living together, that we'd been in a relationship for almost two years. I knew one thing would lead to another and that I would end up discussing our 'problems'. Or am I cancelling Tim as well?

'Are you still doing photography, Jane?'

'No, I got too busy. I'll get back to it one day.'

'You really should. You've got quite an eye. I wouldn't waste a talent like that.'

It had been a strange day. It had begun with an apology and ended with a compliment – maybe the first time my mother had ever said anything positive to me in her life. I give her a hug, which she endures before escaping to open the wine. As Angela said herself, she doesn't do the big emotions.

37.

By the time I return to Melbourne, six glorious weeks have slipped by at the lake and my journal records that my memory had almost totally returned. Doctor Zhou has recommended rest from the start, but I had been too obsessed with Robert and Luna. After many delays and adjournments, Bathgate's trial is about to begin. Will I be up to the mark in the witness stand defending my expert opinion?

Marion is seeing Luna twice a week and is pleased with the progress they are making. Joe Wasserman has created a job for her at his office, redesigning their logo and the way they present his business. After that, his wife wants Luna to join her electoral team. She is in very good hands.

And so am I. My apartment is filled with candles and lilies and there's a Christmas tree in the corner. 'Christmas in July' is an unexpected surprise. There are piles of presents wrapped and waiting to be opened, colourful lights illuminate the balcony, and Tim has fashioned a somewhat irreverent Nativity scene from papier mâché. He's gone to a lot of trouble.

His time with Jazz at the Lincoln Center had been a huge success and there is talk of him going on their European tour.

He's also moved all his cellos and guitars from his apartment to mine and set up the third bedroom as his studio.

'So how was New Zealand?' he asks that first night back.

'Wonderful, as always. There's something about the landscapes of your youth that never leaves you.'

Tim serves dinner with a selection of wines, a Moët et Chandon Imperial Brut, the glorious Torbreck The Struie and a Grand Rutherglen muscat. There's nothing unusual about that; he likes to pamper me and it clearly gives him pleasure. What a beautiful, lovely man.

'You've never met my mother, have you? She's in admiration of your . . . body. She keeps the catalogue of the photography exhibition among her art books. I had forgotten about that as well.'

'But you think your memory's back?'

'Apart from the days before and after the accident.'

'So, I'm not so much of a stranger anymore?'

'No, Tim, you're like an old sock.' A joke is as close to an answer as I can give. I am still unable to tell him the truth, that I still couldn't remember precisely when it was we got together – when we graduated from regular companion to something more intimate, of the nights he'd spent at my place and the nights I'd spent at his. There's still something blocking that.

I pace myself with the wine selection, but Tim goes for broke and falls asleep on the couch. It is almost a relief. One more night without that pressure, one more night when we would keep to our sides of the bed, one more night to prepare myself before the resumption of hostilities. Had my sex life been reduced to that? Taking what is left of the Struie, I go out to the balcony to enjoy the city lights, sparkling with the promise of a mid-winter Christmas and good cheer for all.

Do I aspire to being my mother's daughter? Had she discovered a better work–life balance than me? To occupy her house on her terms with a some-time boyfriend – when she needed one; to keep the big emotions in check? I run through my boyfriends and my failures to commit. Should I have settled on Eric Ringer way back then? Or would he have left me as well? Am I attracted to men like my father, who liked women too much? Too many women. Do I seek impermanence because my hero – my father – had left me or because I am congenitally addicted to risk? Am I only happy when distracted by a major crime or major moment when life and death are in the balance?

I finish my wine, make myself a Milo, cover Tim with a light blanket and sneak off to bed gloriously alone. I open my journal to write the day's entry. The previous one is illuminating. I had written it the night before I left Lake Hawea.

> *My mother is a survivor. As wounded as we all are by life's setbacks and catastrophes, she has found a way to operate that suits her and keeps her on an even keel. I am sure she learnt resilience from her mother. Surely she was told, as I was, that there was 'money bid for ye'?*

If I look at the worst of my parents, I am a combination of commitment-phobe and sexual utilitarian. But if I look at their most admirable traits, I am smart and effective, someone strong who does good in the world (like my father did) and someone who is happy and indestructible (like my mother). Halifax is only half my inheritance. The Gregories and, in particular, my grandma deserve some credit too.

Encouraged by my mother's compliment at the lake, I had renewed my interest in photography. Fixing myself a cup of tea, I head back down to my dark room in the basement where I've been printing some of the shots Tim had taken at Ben's memorial. They're disappointing. The fixer is starting to go off in its tray and I'm surprised there hasn't been a complaint about the strong, stale vinegar odour. Donning my gloves, I empty the tray into a storage tub but can't find the lid. I will have to find a way of sealing it and make a mental note to get a lid from one of the boxes in my study. I replenish the tray with fresh fixer and set up to print some photos I had taken of Zoe at one of her early gigs.

I am vaguely aware of someone outside the door and assume it's the caretaker doing his rounds, so am unprepared for the person who suddenly enters, closing the door behind him. He turns to face me in the half-light, the red glow of the lamp accentuating his leer: it's Paul Bathgate. My shock stifles any reaction.

'Doctor Halifax.'

'Paul. How did you get in here?'

'That was the easy bit,' he says, placing a pass key on the bench.

'Or should I say, *why* are you here – knowing the consequences?'

'That's the least of my worries right now, Doctor. I'm running out of options.' His breath is heavy with alcohol, his eyes devoid of life.

'You know we can't be talking?'

'But how can you make a proper assessment if we're not allowed to meet?'

'Paul, you're making things worse.'

'You need to understand one thing,' he says, slowing his voice for emphasis. '*I am never going to go to jail.*'

'Well, this isn't going to help you. You're prejudicing your case before it starts.'

'No, you did that. With your lazy assessment, based on what? A single meeting? I'm sorry, Doctor, but not even you are that good.'

'Paul, I need you to leave.' As I reach for my phone, his right hand grips my wrist like a vice.

'Do you know what you're dealing with here? Do you know the consequences? You owe it to the court. And you owe it to me.'

'My assessment is one opinion, which I'm sure your lawyers will challenge.'

'Do you want my blood on your hands? Do you?'

His voice is quiet, his height and bulk filling the room.

'*I am not going to prison, ever*. I can promise you that. I'll end it all before that happens.'-

He takes the phone from my hand and drops it into the developer tray. As it bubbles to the bottom, he releases my wrist, smiling to relieve the tension. It had the opposite effect.

'Can we talk somewhere else?' I say, stalling for time.

'No, this is fine, with its soft mood lighting. You could almost call it intimate. I'm sorry it's come to this, but you can't say I haven't tried to reach you through proper channels.'

Bathgate is blocking my route to the door, the benches on either side limiting any escape. Without telegraphing what I am thinking, I use my peripheral vision to survey my defensive options: broom, developing tongs, various drums of chemicals, a screwdriver, a paring knife. Defensive weapons in my hands: offensive ones in his.

'I blame myself,' he continues. 'I squandered the time we spent together and that was wrong. Instead of being nice and explaining my mental condition, I came across as a prick. But I was under pressure and you know how bipolar goes. Up one moment, down the next, irrationally aggressive . . .'

I know engaging in debate is futile, but as long as we keep talking, I have some kind of control. What I need is a change of subject.

'How did you get that?'

Bathgate is confused.

'The pass key?'

'Oh, that little stroke of good fortune,' he says as he takes up the pass key from the bench. 'Candy. Candy Lane. She used to live on one of the upper floors. Probably before your time. A renter I think, living beyond her ex-husband's means as Candy always did. All about show, was Candy. We got on really well until she started to share her lollies behind my back. So, she lent me her spare key to prove her faithfulness. Said I could turn up any time to see she wasn't cheating. But I dropped her anyway. She couldn't be trusted. And I almost threw this away.' He rotates the pass key through his fingers. 'What a coincidence it was when I discovered you lived here, too.'

'If you leave now, I'm prepared to keep this between us.'

'Bullshit.'

'If I changed my assessment, it would be under duress. You are better off taking your chances in court.'

'Bullshit.'

'Do you really believe my report's so crucial?'

'Don't you?'

'It's a factor in a range of things. I'd be more concerned about other people's evidence if I were you.'

'Well, *she's* not going to change her mind, the lying little bitch.'

Bathgate sneers his contempt for Laura Semple. It is impossible to gauge his next move. Or mine, for that matter. Like Bathgate, I am running out of options.

'Was that you in the stairwell, the day I fell?'

Bathgate doesn't answer.

'Not that I think you pushed me or anything like that. The fall was entirely my fault. But if you've been trying to meet me . . .'

'Don't try and pin that on me.'

He wasn't admitting anything. Nor denying he was there.

His eyes fall on the paring knife only seconds before I was thinking of picking it up. Had my anxiety betrayed my intentions? He picks up the knife and tests its sharpness with his thumb. I knew if I was going to act, I would have to do it soon.

'Self-harm's a characteristic of bipolar, isn't it, Doctor? Come on, you're the expert. What if I cut my wrists in front of you – right here and now? What would you tell the court? Would you tell the truth? That it was the last act of a desperate man whose condition you had misdiagnosed? That you'd made a terrible mistake and expected the court to grant you its forgiveness? That it was all because of your arrogance and inflated sense of importance that you'd denied a mentally afflicted man a second chance?'

He pushes up his sleeves and adjusts the knife in his hand.

'You have no idea how often I've thought about this. But never with a witness. Maybe it makes it easier. Gives me the courage I haven't had.'

He holds the knife in his left hand then puts it back in his right.

'Let's go up to my apartment,' I say. 'These chemicals are making me sick.'

As if feeling faint, I take off my headscarf and slump to one side, steadying myself by gripping the sides of the fixing tray. I know my advantage, if any, will be fleeting, a second or less: a single heartbeat. Channelling fear into strength, I raise up the tray and throw the contents as forcefully as I can in Bathgate's face.

It is amazing what the mind will do, the effect that context plays. The solution was weak and diluted, but in a dark room reeking with stale fixer, the brain plays tricks. Chemicals you imagine, toxic chemicals, eating the skin and burning the eyes. It was all the advantage I needed. As Bathgate reels away, the solution momentarily stinging his eyes, I scramble outside, turning the bolt with the keys I had thankfully left in the lock.

A good old-fashioned lock and key. Has there been a better invention? His stolen pass key is no use to him now.

I wait for my heart to move back inside my chest.

Bathgate wails and pounds on the door. I tell him to flood his eyes with water until the ambulance arrives. I tell him to do it now, that every second counts. I hear him cross to the sink and turn on the tap.

In the foyer, I get the concierge to dial Triple Zero and hand me the phone. With a calmness that surprises me, I describe the situation and ask for an ambulance and the police. Without my phone and its speed dial listings, I would phone Poulos and Abbas later when I found their cards and thank them for their foresight.

I was not yet able to appreciate how close I had come to things going terribly wrong. But I would.

38.

I think Nicholas knew before I did what I was going to say, that I was not coming back to the department.

'It's not that I haven't been happy here, but I'm not a natural academic. I think I only applied to please Ben.'

'You know the students adore you?' he says with a fond smile.

'I know I can teach, I know I can hold an audience . . .'

'But?'

'Deep down, I'm a detective. I need to confront the criminal mind in action, to grapple with its machinations in real time. Studying what happened after the event and analysing trends and warnings – well, there are others who do that better. The other day, I went to see a mate who I worked with on the last case. He's lost his wife and broken his back but it hadn't dampened his spirits. He thought we should open a detective agency called Showbag and Campbells.'

'Pardon?'

'Just a silly idea based on our nicknames. It would never work. He's an unreconstructed misogynist. But we understand each other. I think I was a cop in a former life. I think I'm a cop in this one.'

'Would you do the odd lecture? And work with the doctoral candidates?'

'No. As you said yourself, I'm either in or out. I'm sure you'll find someone else.'

We go to Amiconi's for lunch and tease Michael Cardamone over why he still has rabbit traps hanging on the walls.

'Don't people complain about such a brutal implement?' asks Nicholas.

'Only when we tell them we don't serve rabbit,' says Michael with a grin.

We share garlic mushrooms and a Caesar salad and have *mussels alla pescatore* and, seated beneath the flags of Firenze, Calabria, Pisa, Sardinia, Venezia and Sicily, swap stories about our time in that wonderful country. Nicholas had been on exchange with the University of Padua; Ben and I had house-swapped for a month in Tuscany.

'I think that reveals the real academic right there,' I say with a smile.

'How have you adjusted to life since Ben?' Nicholas asks with his usual compassion.

'Oh, up and down.'

'Have you found another relationship?'

'Yes. Haven't you met Tim?'

'No. Is he a secret?'

'Obviously.' But had I really kept him to myself? Elizabeth had accused me of the same thing. 'Did you find me secretive when I worked at the university?' I ask.

'If it was about an investigation, you were always discreet, but you can't really talk about that.'

'But in personal matters?'

'No. In fact when it came to Ben and Zoe, I would probably call you the opposite.'

'A blabbermouth?'

'Let's say you weren't backwards in discussing problems at home. It was your way of workshopping solutions.'

'Yet I never once mentioned Tim?'

'Not to me.'

I had been on leave from the university since Ben's death but had made a point of staying in touch with Nicholas – and he with me – so it seemed remarkable that Tim's name had not come up.

As I walk home through the city, I feel relieved. I had made my decision and Nicholas had taken it well, but the Tim issue really played on my mind. My behaviour after the accident could be easily explained as could the slow recovery of my memory. But being overly discreet before that – if not deliberately obscure – was not the Jane Halifax I knew. I was prepared to accept that my personality had been affected by the accident: that I was both more cautious and more cavalier, not unlike someone who had experienced a near-death incident and had resigned themselves to providence. But why had I kept the exquisite Tim to myself?

To complete my housekeeping chores, I load the car with Peter Debreceny's files and head over to his house in the evening. He opens a bottle of chianti and we sit out on his terrace. Peter had never married though he had been with a number of spectacular women – usually barristers – one of whom I knew had broken his heart. I had remembered that we once shared the same group of friends and I find myself enjoying his company.

'So, were my files any help?' he asks.

'Yes, they were. Though given what had happened to them I'm surprised you lent them to me again. Wasn't that risky?'

'No more so than the first time.'

'So why did you do it?'

'To get on your good side, I suppose.'

I stifle a laugh. 'So you weren't just being nice when you made me dinner that night?'

'Are you joking?'

'And knowing my boyfriend was away—'

'What boyfriend? You never mentioned him. I didn't know he existed until he brought you here when we tried to restage that night.'

'Peter, are you telling me that dinner was a date?'

'It was for me. God knows what you were thinking. Do you think I would risk lending you prosecution files and go to all that trouble with a meal if I didn't have expectations?'

'And I never told you about Tim?'

'If that's his name. Anyway, isn't he gay?'

God, not Peter as well. Aren't male heterosexuals allowed to be beautiful?

'When I was in hospital, I had this dream that you had given me a date-rape drug and that's what caused the accident.'

'My desperation does have its limits,' he says, only mildly offended.

'I'm sorry, Peter. I am usually more attuned to what's going on.'

'You were on a mission.'

'Apparently, so were you.'

We laugh about that and I say I'm flattered, though not really on the market. That I enjoy his company, that I hope we can still be friends, that I really admire his intellect.

'I'm sorry, Jane. I'm at that stage where none of that's enough. I am actively looking for someone to spend the rest of my life with and I'd be lying if I said we could just be friends. I'd be wanting a whole lot more than that.'

I feel uncomfortable. Had I been leading him on? Had I been oblivious to his feelings for years?

I know I can get obsessive when a case is on. Tunnel vision is both the investigator's curse and their principal asset. But I'm supposed to be an expert in human behaviour. And why had I failed to mention Tim?

On the way home, I stop on Yarra Boulevard where the accident had taken place. Even in Melbourne, a city of five million people, it is, at this time of night, a lonely and seldom-used road. I had been fortunate a Samaritan had come my way.

I get out of the car and walk to the broken guttering where my car had left the road. The tree that had saved me from the river is still bruised and barked at its base. It's chilling to think how close I'd come to death, but for some reason I am calm and don't feel alone.

Hoping it might provoke some kind of memory, I walk back to the centre of the curve where I imagine the collision had taken place. The silence of the night surrounds me, the hum of the distant motorway the only sound. I listen to my breathing, meditating to clear my mind.

A car veers into view, its high-beam blinding, its speed aggressive and out of character with the tranquil setting. Like a startled rabbit, I find myself immobilised in its path, exposed and vulnerable.

The car speeds past, horn screaming its displeasure, as if I am standing there tempting fate or worse – hoping to die.

As the SUV nudges my right-rear fender, the BMW spins out of control, rolling over and over at a hundred kilometres an hour in an explosion of glass and metal and air bags and blood that ends with the car caught in a tangle of vegetation not ten metres from a river in which I would certainly have drowned.

The car alarm wails at the moon. I am unable to move, the taste of blood metallic in my mouth. I can hear the Telluride stop. I can hear running feet and frightened voices, the one arguing to flee, the other to see if the driver was still alive. I look up and try to call out, but my voice makes no sound. Two frayed youths in their early twenties look down at me, one small and scared, the other bigger and desperate to make his escape.

'He's dead. Let's get outta here.'

'It's not a he – it's a she. We gotta get help.'

'I am not goin' to fuckin' jail again.'

'If she dies, it'll be worse than stealin' a fuckin' car.'

'We'll torch the thing. They'll never know.'

'You had to bloody ram her, didn't yer, yer stupid fat prick.'

'You stay if you like. I'm fuckin' outta here.'

And still arguing, they hurry away.

It feels such a silly way to die, discarded like rubbish on the side of the road after a career that had started with so much promise. All those victories and accolades, all those big cases against the best the Victoria Bar could offer, all those major police operations run to conclusions through meticulous forensic psychiatry. I am at the height of my powers, in my prime and in demand. This is not the exit I had imagined.

The car lights look up into the sky and seem to suggest a path, a way towards the light and peace and the absence of fear, where the pain that is beginning to build as blood fills my brain would be eradicated like a blessing's kiss.

'Hang in there, Jane. This is no time to go. You'll regret it in the morning.'

'Are you my Samaritan?'

'Yes, if you want. I'm here to tell you to embrace the pain and resist the light. Death will come soon enough, when it's ready. You don't have to meet it halfway. And never give up, like I did, Jane. Fight and hang on to your precious gift – as if the whole world depends upon it.'

My father holds my hand and my focus changes, leading me away from the light and into the pain, though I am afraid I will not be able to endure it.

My head hurts. My brain feels defeated. I am shivering violently and as cold as death. But I'm not alone. And he doesn't let go of my hand.

39.

If anyone required their faith in the criminal justice system to be restored, they simply needed to be present in court when Magistrate Miriam Levy found Paul Bathgate guilty of the multiple charges against him. It was unusual for someone in her position to make what amounted to a political statement, but Levy's praise of the new coercive control laws was so balanced and non-partisan that it was never going to provide any grounds for appeal.

I had not been called upon to present my testimony and was pleased that my profession had not offered up an expert to claim that the accused was bipolar II. I was reassured that Bathgate's lawyers at least had the decency to drop that part of their defence and focus instead on his alcoholism and need for treatment. As the magistrate delivered her decision, the court was jam-packed with reporters eager to spread the good news. This was a red-letter day for women everywhere – though the law's passage had been too late for many.

Outside the court, I chatted with Poulos and Abbas. They were awaiting extradition of the car thieves, who had been tracked down in Queensland. I told them of the memory I'd had of them arguing after the accident and said I'd be surprised if they turned out to be more than joyriders. The detectives had pretty well come to the same conclusion. I thanked them again for all they had done to find the persons involved, though they seemed disappointed there had not been more to uncover. Even the minor cases demand the same amount of shoe leather.

After a Devonshire tea at Fairfield Park, we hired a rowboat, Luna and I each taking an oar while Marion sat bemused in the stern, three generations of women united by circumstance and a genuine concern for each other.

I knew the toll Luna's therapy would have taken on Marion, the unending patience required to negotiate predictable setbacks: Luna's anger; her denial; her instinct to run. Marion's need to listen and resist making any suggestion. The damage done in the name of 'recovered memory' is well documented, with various techniques like hypnosis, journalling, past-life-regression and guided imagery (without even mentioning the use of drugs and religion) having constructed too many fictional pasts – usually for little more than the self-gratification of the so-called therapist.

Luna had come to admit her sexual abuse at her brother's hands and, while it hadn't included penetration, the damage his need for sexual gratification had wrought on her life had been immense. Her sexuality was confused, her ability to relate to others extremely compromised and her experiences had been abusive, both as victim and perpetrator.

It was predictable that Luna would feel guilty, as if she was as much to blame as Robert – or even more so. It's the technique the abuser uses to protect himself: the lies and secrets and codes of silence – in Robert's case, his poems – the exclusive fantasy world the abuser creates to 'protect' his victim from life's harsh realities. Unfortunately, Robert was without peer in this area – and Marion's task was to enable Luna to see the truth about her brother while keeping the good parts of his character intact. It is unhelpful for an abuser to be seen as a monster or evil incarnate, for that is to accord them too much power at the victim's expense. The focus instead must remain on the client (yes, a better word than patient in this context) and to give them the techniques they will need to build a normal life, a life that they have never had.

As we turned the boat to head downriver, Luna missed her stroke but caught enough water with her oar to splash Marion. Laughing, Marion responded with a scoop of her hand and then, in case I felt I was missing out, they turned their attention on me. By the time we returned to the boathouse, we were cold and wet and full of laughter, our friendship baptised by the muddy waters of an upside-down river that suddenly felt sacred.

If only my life had been making the same progress as Luna's.

Doctor Zhou reported that my brain was back to functioning normally. The gaps in my memory that remained were, to him, entirely expected. He laughed when I told him I still couldn't recall the beginning of my relationship with Tim. He was grateful his wife wasn't asking him similar questions.

'I have no memory of our first date, let alone what she was wearing. And I certainly can't remember who it was who asked the other out – though in our culture it's a fair assumption to think it was me. But isn't a large part of what we call "memory" reconstructed? Part truth, part wishful thinking, part making it up to fill the gaps?'

'I think you should stick to dicing and slicing,' I replied with a grin, 'and leave the mumbo jumbo to me.'

When Tim returned from Sydney after the conclusion of his season, I knew he would be disappointed that I hadn't made it up to the Opera House. But as soon as he'd mentioned a series of concerts at the Lincoln Center – and a trip to New York with the chance to catch up with Zoe as well – I had immediately, in my head at least, reallocated my resources to that. My mistake had been in not making this clear to Tim.

'When you cancelled your flights the second time, I knew you weren't going to make it.'

'I'm sorry, Tim. As soon as you mentioned New York—'

'There's no rule that says you couldn't have done both.' The fragile pride of the artist. 'I was hoping to show you off.'

That sentiment was a little less admirable, though I suppose I could have taken it as a compliment. Instead, I stayed silent, recalling that Ben would never have said such a thing; that there was something needy in Tim I generally found unattractive in a partner. How many warning signs did I need?

As usual, when Tim felt slighted, he retreated to the bottle, no doubt trying to show me that alcohol at least carried no expectations, that he could find approval there in his solipsistic bubble, immune from the disappointment of others. I didn't like that either – though when he finally fell asleep on the couch from one scotch too many, I can't say I was unhappy. And despite my tiredness and my empty bed beckoning like some sublime sanctuary, I didn't take that option either. Jane Halifax 2.0 was in heightened detective mode.

Leaving Tim on the couch, I grabbed my keys and headed to Collingwood. It was after one am and the streets were empty, the converted warehouse in which Tim had his apartment quiet and asleep. I worried the noisy elevator might wake the building but no-one called out to complain. A solitary cat met me on the top floor landing before fleeing down the stairs.

I opened the door to Tim's apartment and turned on the lights. Apart from his cellos and guitars, which he had moved to my apartment along with the bulk of his clothes, everything was as I remembered it. Utilitarian, male and lacking in style – right down to his appalling rug. There were clothes of mine in the bedroom, simple changes of clothes – essentially casual – as one might wear to breakfast in Gertrude Street. Tim had said I had put them there in the same way as he had placed some of his clothes at my place. It made sense if I spent the night at his apartment after we had attended something on that side of town. Other things seemed less thought through, like a favourite dress I had almost forgotten and a rather eclectic collection of shoes. But it is what I found in 'my' underwear drawer that chilled my heart and made me want to cry.

40.

Tim awoke with the first rays of the eastern sun. I was sitting across the room at the dining table with my journal, laptop and a page of scribbled notes. I had been up all night but was too adrenalised to sleep. It was like the feeling I got at the end of a long and challenging case: sleep and food and a rewarding shower could wait.

'Shit!' said Tim, disoriented. 'What's the time?'

'Twenty past six,' I said.

Tim pushed himself up onto an elbow. 'What happened last night?' he asked.

'You finished what was left of that whisky and fell asleep.' The rising sun glinted on the empty bottle as if to highlight Exhibit A.

'Have you been there all night?'

'No. I went to your apartment at one am.'

'Why would you want to do that?'

'To have a look around.'

'My head hurts.'

'That's Panadol on the coffee table beside the glass of water. I figured you might need them.'

'Very thoughtful.' He swallowed a couple of tabs. 'I'm sorry.'

'For what?'

'For passing out on you.'

'Not at all. You did me a favour. Gave me time to think and check some stuff. And do a little detection.'

'I need a shower.'

'We both need a shower, Tim. But before that, we need to talk.'

'Am I in the doghouse?'

'Should you be?'

'I know you don't like it when I drink too much. I've been under a lot of pressure.'

I had to laugh at that. '*You've* been under pressure?'

'Well, not as much as you but . . .'

I gave him the space to finish his sentence, knowing very well he couldn't. 'Let's talk about Perth. Specifically, Sunday the twenty-first.'

'Pardon?'

'The night we supposedly "got together". Was that before or after I had dinner with Professor Brown?'

'What—'

'It was Sunday, so you had an early concert and I had the closing session of the conference.'

'Do we have to do this now?'

'I've been sitting here all night, Tim. You're lucky I didn't wake you up.'

Tim finished the water as I checked my laptop.

'Afterwards, I had dinner with Warwick Brown. Which finished rather late, according to my Mastercard receipt. I paid my half of the tab at 12:45 am on Monday morning. I remember they were closing the bar. So, what happened then? Did I knock on your door or you knock on mine?'

'Would you get to the point?' Tim was still confused about my purpose but he couldn't misinterpret my investigatory tone.

'Okay. Let's try something else. Your birthday weekend at Daylesford. As I recall, you paid for that wonderful dinner for everyone at the Boathouse and I paid for the accommodation.'

'Whatever you say.'

'"The honeymoon suite", you called it a few weeks ago when I struggled to remember the weekend. You used such colour and detail you had me convinced.'

Tim said nothing as I looked for the statement on my computer.

'Funny really. They charged me for two double rooms. Though I only paid the minibar tab for one – you must have looked after your own.'

'Is this leading somewhere?'

'Separate rooms? For a couple who had been together for more than a year? Was that your idea or mine, that we couldn't make things public even then? My friends have called me secretive when it comes to my work. Were you being even more underhand with your friends?'

'I need some more water.' Tim got up and went to the kitchen to refill his glass from the filter. When he returned, he opened the slider to the balcony and stood in the breeze.

'Tim, we've been friends, very good friends, for as long as I can remember. You knew Ben before I did and I think you miss him as much as me. And, united in our loss, it was normal that our friendship would continue, that we would inevitably be the other's plus one when needed. But you abused that closeness when I was at my most vulnerable, when I couldn't even recognise myself in the mirror.'

Tim was silent.

'I never placed any of my clothes at your place. You did – when I was sick.'

Tim turned to face me. 'That's not true—'

'Oh, yes it is. Do you really think I would take the underwear from my bottom drawer and put it at your place? All the old, worn-out stuff that would be thrown out at the next cull? Don't you think if I was leaving underwear at your place it might be something recent, even sexy, something I wouldn't mind you seeing me in? You placed my clothes in your apartment to perpetuate a lie.'

'You're wrong – it wasn't me,' he said.

'But forget about the underwear. It got me thinking about other things. Two incidents affecting me and Ben that nearly broke us. The first was when you refused to lie for Ben one night when he asked you for an alibi. You had to take the high moral ground and tell me that Ben had asked you to lie. It led to the worst argument we ever had. Ben refused to tell me where he was or who he was with. I knew he had no-go areas he simply refused to discuss, but I don't think I ever fully trusted him after that. And all because his supposed best friend refused to do him a favour.'

'Are you saying I was wrong to tell the truth?'

'Yes, I think I am. In retrospect I think we both know he was probably with Zoe's mother, trying to come to an arrangement where she would agree to go away. Mandy was making his life – and by extension, mine and Zoe's – unbearable. Was it so terrible to ask a mate to give him cover?'

Tim didn't respond.

'The second incident was worse. Do you remember confiding in me one day to tell me you knew why Ben dealt in cash so much, which I worried might be linked to drugs? But you assured me you knew it wasn't that – because you knew what his real problem was: compulsive gambling.'

'Which was true.'

'No, Tim. That was another lie. Ben was being blackmailed by Mandy. We know that from her trial. Gamblers have random patterns of spending; Ben's cash transactions were as regular as clockwork, desperate as he was to settle things once and for all with Mandy so she would go back to her life on the other side of the world. But Mandy couldn't ween herself off the golden goose. And when he finally said no she had him killed.'

'He wasn't good enough for you, Jane. Ben was cheating on you behind your back with his fucking ex for Christ's sake!'

'Not good enough for me, Tim? As opposed to whom?'

'I love you, Jane. I have loved you for years.'

'Don't even use the word. You have no concept of what it means.'

His eyes began to moisten. 'If you loved me, you might understand.'

'I understand the word perfectly well. It's what I feel for Zoe. And my mother. And still feel for Ben. And my grandmother and my father. In fact, I think a part of me still loves Eric Ringer. And Showbag. Even Peter Debreceny might be a contender. Nothing's set in stone. Except my anger at you, at your betrayal, that you would prostitute our friendship like you have.'

'But we're perfect together.'

'Are we? How? Aesthetically? A man whose beauty makes people gasp and whose music is a form of transcendence? And a moderately attractive woman with a steel-trap mind and a resilience that surprises even me?'

'If you let yourself love me—'

'Oh, if love were only that simple. A public commitment, a declaration of intent. Who wants a world like that?'

'I've always loved you and you've never noticed.' Now fury was replacing his tears.

'Don't blame it on me. I'm a pretty good judge of human behaviour. It's what I'm trained to do. But I'll say this in your defence: you kept your obsession gloriously hidden.'

'After all I've done for you – this is what I get?'

'Don't think I'm not grateful for the care you've shown. And your patience. And Elizabeth's and everyone else's. I am sure I have been appalling at times—'

'Don't patronise me, Jane. And you can lie to yourself – and your very selective memory – all you like. But if you want to break things off, this is not the way to do it.'

'We're not breaking up, Tim. We were never together in the first place.' My voice was calm, my perception clear, my position unequivocal. 'You took advantage of me at the most vulnerable time of my life to construct a relationship – for your own advantage – that never existed. And I thought I was the one with the problem because I couldn't remember a thing.'

'You selfish, ungrateful, cold-hearted—'

Humiliated by his exposure, Tim sprang across the room and pushed me as hard as he could. I cannoned off the wall and slid to the floor, shocked and fearful of what might come next, but largely unharmed.

'I love you,' he implored, standing over me. 'Look what you've made me do.'

Waving away his attempt to help, I got to my feet, my absence of emotion my only protection, an unbreachable wall between us.

'If you gave me a chance you'd love me, I know you would. We're made for each other, Jane.'

'You are a beautiful man in so many ways, but beauty doesn't guarantee anything. Real beauty's inside, where you can't always see it. And you will know love when you find it, Tim. You won't have to construct a thing.'

'What would you like me to do?'

'Have a shower, get changed. Take your cellos and guitars and anything else that belongs to you and leave. No, on second thoughts, just go. You can shower at your place.'

Tim withdrew to get his keys and wallet and I went out onto the balcony. He came back into the lounge, paused behind me to say, 'Happy Christmas', and left.

For the first time in a very long while, I felt like myself again.

After staying up all night, I was desperate for sleep, but I needed to savour my freedom, the peace of being alone – and most of all, the glory of a functioning memory. I sat down to make the final entry in my journal.

> *I am Jane Halifax, scientist, truth seeker, semi-professional sleuth, sometime photographer, a physician and specialist in the transgressive mind. A former teacher, a humanist, a widow, a childless stepmother, a lover, a friend, a believer, a sceptic, an environmentalist, an anti-capitalist rusted-on-Laborite trending Teal.*
>
> *Single, but not alone. As they say in sports, I am on the bench. Monogamist in waiting, patient but anxious, staring down the barrel of the big six-o, terrified and fearful of becoming my mother, but grateful for her genes.*
>
> *Still in mourning for the love of my life, the irreplaceable, imperfect, infuriating Ben Sailor. And my father – the most imperfect male of them all. The most like me. Incomplete, striving for higher things, a spiritual non-believer, respected*

and respectful, irrepressibly hopeful in love. To his cost. And everyone else's.

A woman whose heroes are cops because I know what they do: the calling, the sacrifice, the cost. The addiction to the adrenaline you get from chasing crooks, making the world safer, solving the mysteries of the mind.

I'd like to be a writer one day – but who's got time for that? Note to self: aren't you writing now? But isn't this a journal? Maybe – but it's a start. And remember, your mother's surprise that you didn't have five kids and thinks you would have been a better mother than she, so you don't even know your limits. One of her rare moments of insight, though we know your mother often flaps her lips without engaging her brain, with no quality control over what comes out. A half-decent painter and a golfing whizz? Three holes in one? Really. Did anyone see them, Mum? So, surprise her. Write a book. But not to show your mother you can do it. Do it for yourself – not her.

So, what will it be? Non-fiction? A text on forensic psychiatry? Or a novel maybe, a murder mystery which starts with a rhyme . . .

Two little girls, squashed on toast,
That is the taste we love the most . . .

Now you're raving like Angela. The genes are kicking in. So, take your meds and go to bed. You're overdoing it again and your brain is starting to hurt. Who's surprised?

But everything will be all right. You'll wake up to a new day and new adventures and something diabolical to solve. How can you not? You're an f.p. after all.

ACKNOWLEDGEMENTS

The future is a fantasy; the present, a mirage that vanishes as it appears. The only thing that holds any truth is the past. Lose that – and we lose who we are.

I have many people to thank for helping me navigate Jane's journey in this book. Neurosurgeon Dr Michael Biggs has been my anchor, but others with an intimate knowledge of the mysterious world of memory have also helped me enormously with insights and personal experience. In particular, I would like to thank Beatrix Loomes, Rosalind Wells and Dr Christoph Lenzer.

Once again, my publisher Cassandra Di Bello and my two editors, Lauren Finger and Kylie Mason, have humbled me with their insight, commitment and care. There is nothing singular about being a writer when you have a team like that in your corner.

Thanks also to Dan Ruffino, Michelle Swainson, Ben Ball and Gabrielle Oberman of Simon & Schuster. And Dave Gray for his technical advice.

To my loyal agent Mel Berger and his colleagues at WME in New York – thank you.

And to my tennis mates, El Presidente, Bad-Hand, Unforced Error, Sir Les, Reply-All, The Wall and Ugly Dave – and the original crew – Tom, Peter, Graeme and 'Dead Howard' – thank you for keeping me sane and semi-fit.

ABOUT THE AUTHOR

Roger Simpson practised law in Auckland for three years before heading to Sydney to chance his arm as a professional writer.

After writing cop shows for Crawford Productions (*Homicide, Division 4*) and adaptations for the ABC (*Power Without Glory, I Can Jump Puddles*) his break-through came with the feature film, *Squizzy Taylor*, which led to the creation of Simpson Le Mesurier Films with his producing partner, Roger Le Mesurier.

Roger has since become one of Australia's leading writers and producers and has created twenty series for television including *Halifax Retribution, Satisfaction, Something In The Air, Stingers, Silver Sun, Good Guys Bad Guys, Halifax f.p., Snowy, Skirts, Darlings Of The Gods, Nancy Wake, Sword of Honour, Players To The Gallery, The Trial Of Ned Kelly, Children Of Fire Mountain* and *Hunter's Gold.*

Roger is the winner of twelve awards for writing including nine Australian Writers Guild AWGIE Awards as well as numerous awards as a producer including two Logies, four AFIs and an Astra.

Resurrection is his second book. It follows *Transgression* (2022), with the third book in the series to be published in 2024.

SNEAK PEEK AT BOOK THREE IN THE JANE HALIFAX SERIES

UNBLESSED

Silicon Valley, Wall Street and the American Dream on steroids as Jane takes a case with celebrity lawyers on the world's most public stage.

New York hadn't lost its allure. It still felt like a city where important things happened, in arts and ideas and commerce; a meeting place, a trading hall, a centre that recognised accomplishment and nurtured anything new, a town where the rich and powerful lived in co-dependence with the less well-heeled to keep the cogs in motion, a place of hard, unyielding pavements and towering buildings that somehow retained a human scale, a city of hope and hustle and bountiful reward with a song for every mood: 'Park Avenue', '42nd Street', 'Chelsea Morning', 'New York I Love You, But You're Bringing Me Down'.

It had been ten years since Jane last passed through the city on her way to Quantico to speak at an FBI conference and joust with Tom Saracen. How unexpected it had been to work with him in 2020 to defeat the Melbourne Shooter. Tom had been lured back to Victoria on the promise he'd become Chief Commissioner, forgetting the unspoken power of the police union to veto any appointment. No-one likes a Minister for

Police who selects a 'blow-in' – even if Tom was once 'a good cop from Brisbane who had made it big in the States'. There were others who had stayed at home and worked their way up that the union thought more deserving.

Jane had found a way to work with Tom as she had with Eric Ringer in 2022 on those appalling Torture Murders. Cops and cases had defined Jane's life – well apart from 2023 – her 'lost year' following the car accident and her struggle to regain her memory.

But it was good to be on holidays at last and listen to Zoe make music in a Soho club. Zoe had worked hard to get her album out and was on the cusp of something big. Or so her agent, manager and publicist believed and her 'deferred contingency' lawyer. America hadn't lost its ability to magnify everything. No-one talked about a million dollars anymore. The new normal was five of those and if your enterprise aimed below that, then how could it support everyone else? Deduct 20% for the agent, 7% for management, 5% for publicity and a healthy split for legal – not to mention studio costs and the record company nut – then aiming at sales less than 'an even five' didn't cut the mustard.

Jane worried about Zoe, of course she did, but Zoe was having the time of her life and her voice had never sounded better. Jane had come to New York to make up for lost time and replenish their relationship. She hadn't come to pop her twenty-seven-year-old step-daughter's balloon on the brink of a brilliant career.

After Zoe's set, the entourage retired to a local restaurant. Jane felt it strange Zoe's fleek young lawyer, Jake Arnold, came along as well and more so when he insisted on being seated beside her.

'You're a forensic psychiatrist,' he began. 'Of some note, according to Google.'

New Yorkers. They're so direct.

Jane was about to ask Jake about his legal career to take the focus away from herself, but Jake was on a mission.

'There is someone who's eager to meet you. Sam Karkar. You've probably heard of him.

'Not that I can recall,' said Jane trying to select a cocktail. 'Is he a film star?'

'No. He's a lawyer. One of the country's most prominent defenders.'

'Jake, I'm on holiday. I'm here to see Zoe. I don't have much time for anything else.'

'I need to make a confession, Jane. When Zoe told me about you, I kind of promised. Sam's in town at the moment and he's hoping to see you tomorrow. He's got one of those celebrity cases where he is struggling to find someone who is independent enough to assess his client, someone who can come to his case without having been prejudiced by all the b.s. that's been in the press.'

'I don't want to seem impolite, but my time in New York is limited and right now, I'm here to have dinner with Zoe . . .'

'An hour of your time. It's all Sam wants. If only to get your advice.'

'Are you a lawyer, Jake, or a high-pressure salesman?'

'His client is Sarah Noble.'

Sarah Noble! Jane might not have heard of Sam Karkar, but everyone had heard about the infamous Ms Noble. Even the Melbourne *Age* had followed the story as had every major newspaper around the globe. Sarah's case was one of the most reported scandals anywhere. A thirty-two-year-old Silicon Valley billionaire who had been charged with conspiracy to murder, finding someone to assess Sarah Noble who didn't already know of her existence was a legal impossibility. It was like asking someone who had never heard of Prince Andrew or Ghislaine Maxwell to pretend they'd been living on Mars.

'Jake, I'm sorry . . .'

'My problem is, Jane, Sam is actually expecting you. At eleven a.m. An hour, that's all. You can name your price.'

'It isn't the money . . .'

'Please?'

Jane knew the young lawyer had been working for Zoe on a deferral basis, that he would never be paid unless Zoe landed a major record deal, that he had probably invested many hours of his time and his firm's in her musical career. And here was Jane, quibbling about sixty minutes?

The waiter took the drinks order and Jane tried to get Jake to focus on the menu. 'I'm having the fish. What about you?' She wasn't saying yes and she wasn't saying no, but Jake knew as well as Jane did that she was already on the hook.